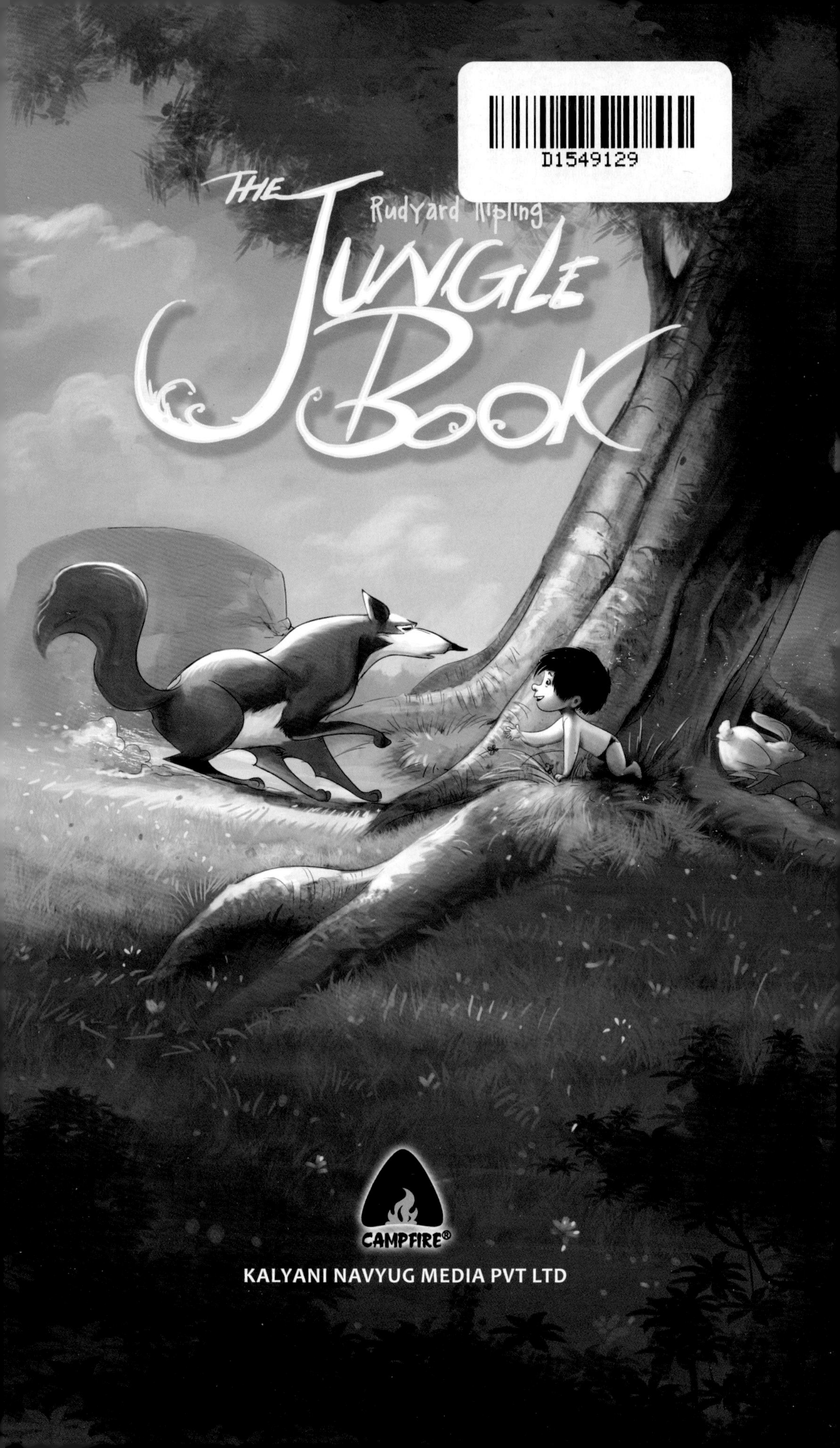
D1549129
THE
Rudyard Kipling
JUNGLE
BOOK
CAMPFIRE®
KALYANI NAVYUG MEDIA PVT LTD

THE Rudyard Kipling JUNGLE BOOK

WORDSMITH **DAN JOHNSON**
ILLUSTRATOR **AMIT TAYAL**
COLORIST **ANIL C. K.**
LETTERER **BHAVNATH CHAUDHARY**
EDITOR **ADITI RAY**

COVER ART **AMIT TAYAL & ANIL C. K.**
DESIGNER **AJO KURIAN & MUKESH RAWAT**

CAMPFIRE®
www.campfire.co.in

Mission Statement

To entertain and educate young minds by creating unique illustrated books that recount stories of human values, arouse curiosity in the world around us, and inspire with tales of great deeds of unforgettable people.

Published by Kalyani Navyug Media Pvt. Ltd.
101 C, Shiv House, Hari Nagar Ashram, New Delhi 110014, India

ISBN: 978-81-907515-4-4

Printed in India

About the author
RUDYARD KIPLING

Rudyard Kipling was born on December 30,1865 in Bombay, India, to Alice and John Lockwood Kipling. Kipling's father was a sculptor and professor of architectural sculpture at the Sir Jamsetjee Jeejeebhoy School of Art and Industry in Bombay, where he also served as Principal.

When Kipling was six, he and his three-year-old sister, Trix, went to live in Portsmouth, England, while his parents stayed in India. Kipling eventually traveled to many countries, including South Africa, Australia, New Zealand, America, and Japan, but he always thought of himself as an Anglo-Indian—a British citizen who lived in India.

Kipling started his career in 1882 as assistant editor of the *Civil & Military Gazette*. Besides writing articles, he was enlisted to write short stories for the newspaper. Among his other works are such classic novels as *Captains Courageous* and *Kim*, the short stories that make up *The Jungle Book* and *The Second Jungle Book*, including the Mowgli stories, 'Rikki-Tikki-Tavi', and 'The White Seal', and poems like 'Mandalay' and 'Gunga Din'. He was the first English language recipient of the Nobel Prize for Literature in 1907.

Rudyard Kipling died on January 18, 1936 of a perforated duodenal ulcer. He was cremated, and his ashes buried in Poets' Corner in Westminster Abbey.

About the artist
AMIT TAYAL

A self-taught artist from Faridabad, India, Amit has a diploma in computer graphics and 2D animation. Starting his career as a 2D animator and children's book illustrator, Amit expanded his art into the graphic novel medium, which he feels stimulates his creative instinct. He has worked on *The Swiss Family Robinson*, *The Three Musketeers*, *Conquering Everest*, and *Ali Baba and the Forty Thieves: Reloaded*—all bestselling titles from Campfire.

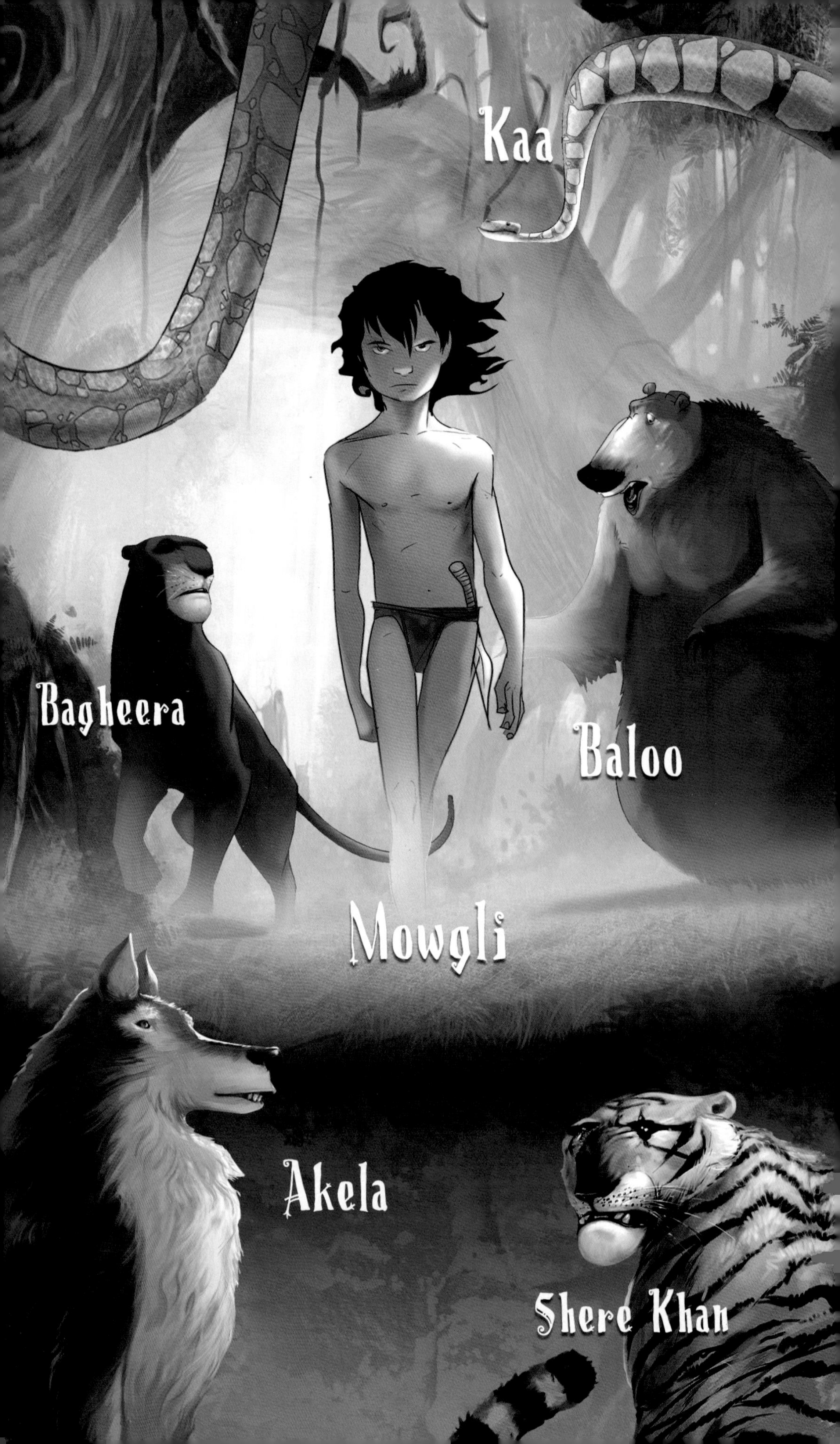
Kaa
Bagheera
Baloo
Mowgli
Akela
Shere Khan

Now Chil the Kite brings home the night
That Mang the Bat sets free –
The herds are shut in byre and hut
For loosed till dawn are we.
This is the hour of pride and power,
Talon and tush and claw.
Oh, hear the call! – Good hunting all
That keep the Jungle Law!

Aurgh! It is time to hunt again.

It was seven o'clock of a very warm evening in the Seeonee Hills when Father Wolf woke up from his day's rest.

He spread out his paws to get rid of the sleepy feeling in their tips. Mother Wolf lay with her big gray nose dropped across her four tumbling, squealing cubs.

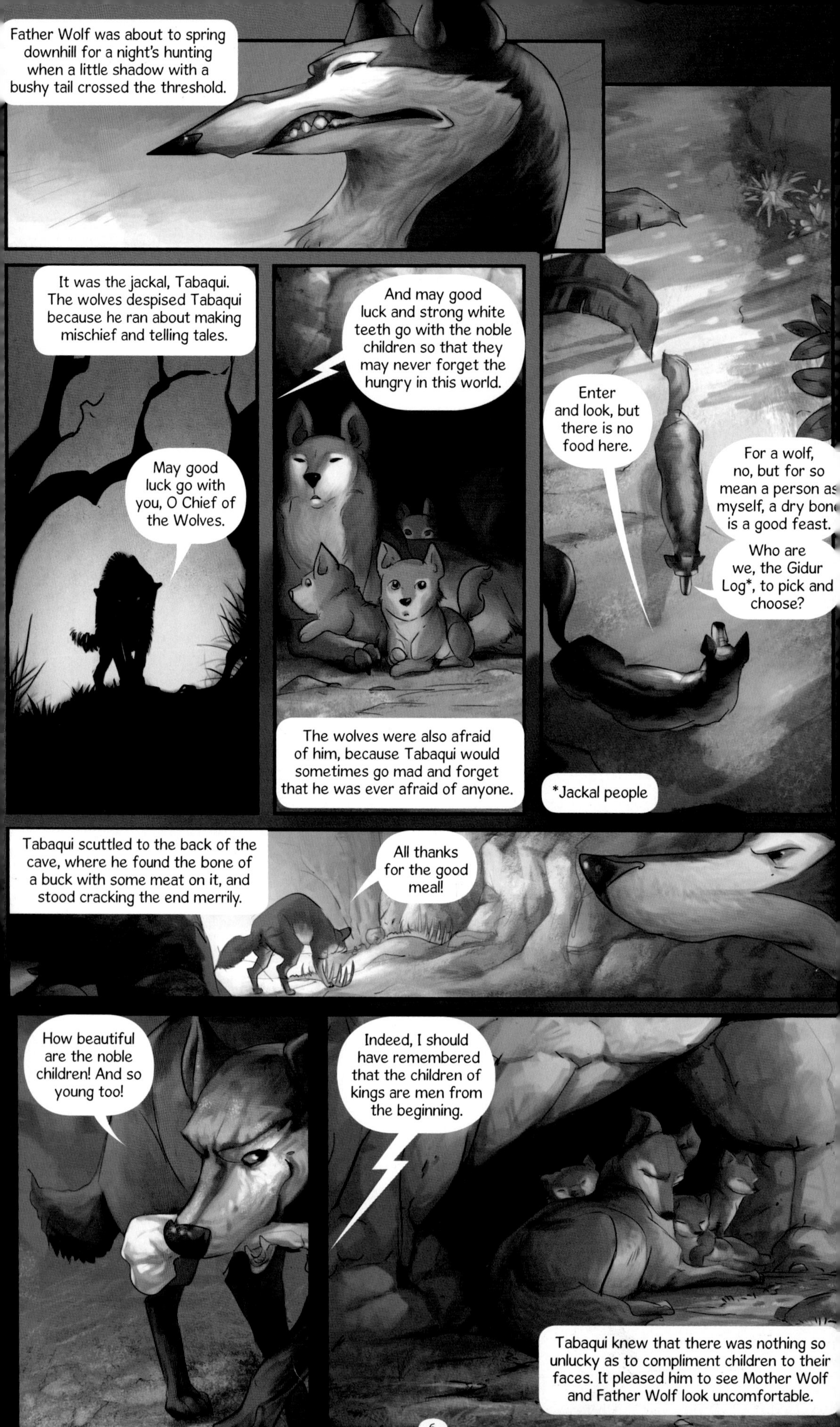

Father Wolf was about to spring downhill for a night's hunting when a little shadow with a bushy tail crossed the threshold.
It was the jackal, Tabaqui. The wolves despised Tabaqui because he ran about making mischief and telling tales.
May good luck go with you, O Chief of the Wolves.
And may good luck and strong white teeth go with the noble children so that they may never forget the hungry in this world.
The wolves were also afraid of him, because Tabaqui would sometimes go mad and forget that he was ever afraid of anyone.
Enter and look, but there is no food here.
For a wolf, no, but for so mean a person as myself, a dry bone is a good feast.
Who are we, the Gidur Log*, to pick and choose?
*Jackal people
Tabaqui scuttled to the back of the cave, where he found the bone of a buck with some meat on it, and stood cracking the end merrily.
All thanks for the good meal!
How beautiful are the noble children! And so young too!
Indeed, I should have remembered that the children of kings are men from the beginning.
Tabaqui knew that there was nothing so unlucky as to compliment children to their faces. It pleased him to see Mother Wolf and Father Wolf look uncomfortable.

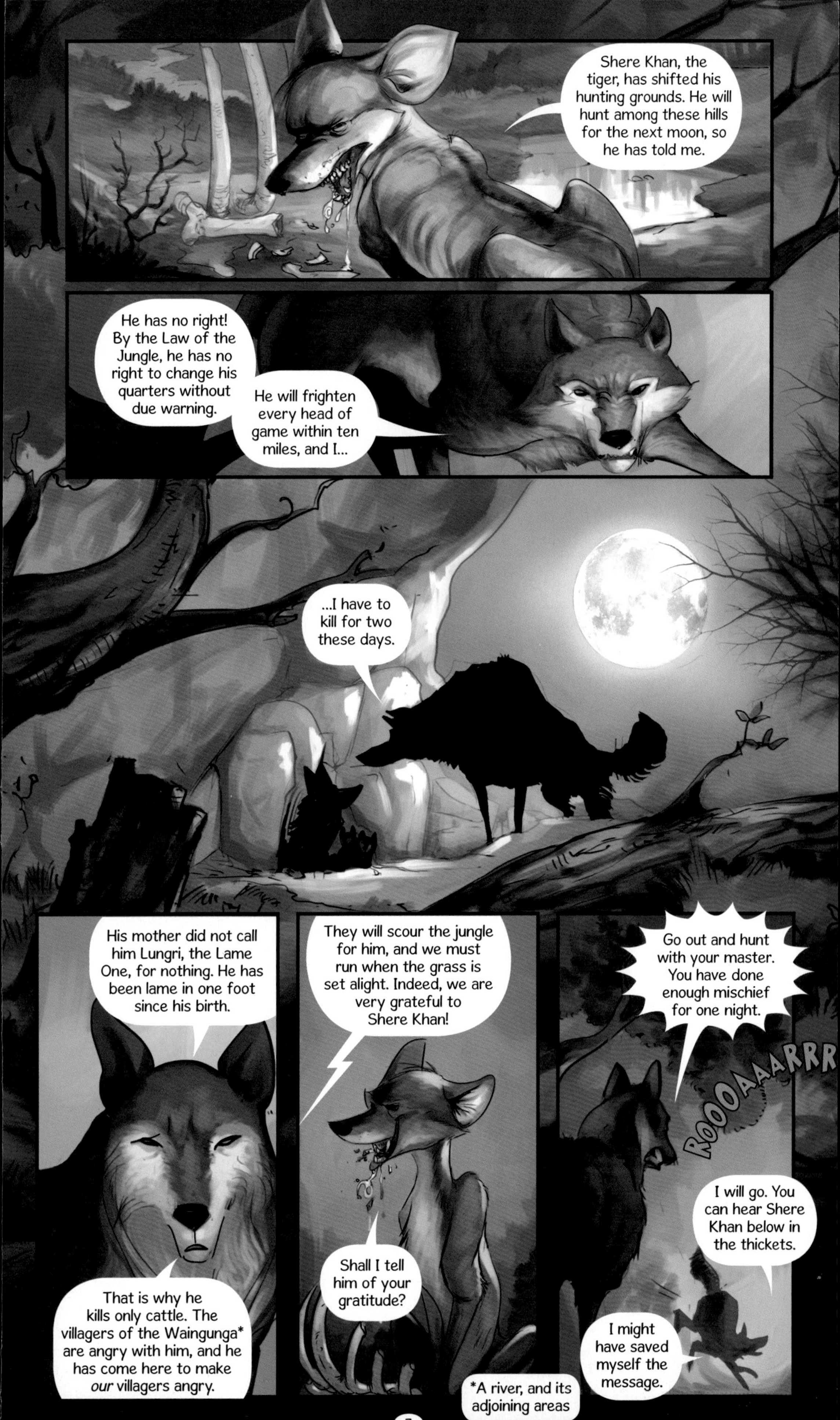

Shere Khan, the tiger, has shifted his hunting grounds. He will hunt among these hills for the next moon, so he has told me.
He has no right! By the Law of the Jungle, he has no right to change his quarters without due warning.
He will frighten every head of game within ten miles, and I...
...I have to kill for two these days.
His mother did not call him Lungri, the Lame One, for nothing. He has been lame in one foot since his birth.
That is why he kills only cattle. The villagers of the Waingunga* are angry with him, and he has come here to make *our* villagers angry.
They will scour the jungle for him, and we must run when the grass is set alight. Indeed, we are very grateful to Shere Khan!
Shall I tell him of your gratitude?
Go out and hunt with your master. You have done enough mischief for one night.
ROOOAAARRR
I will go. You can hear Shere Khan below in the thickets.
I might have saved myself the message.
*A river, and its adjoining areas

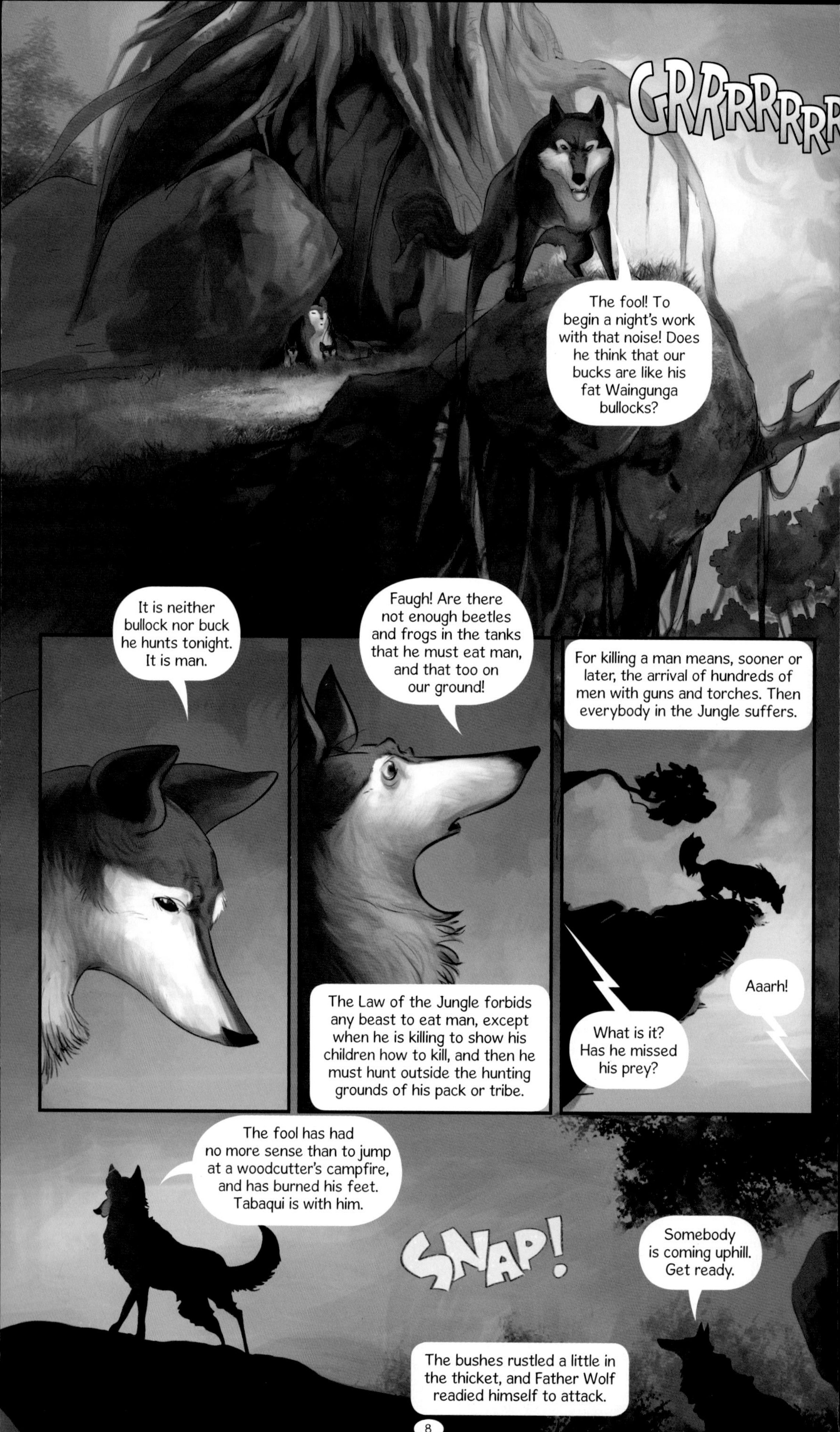
GRRRRRRR
The fool! To begin a night's work with that noise! Does he think that our bucks are like his fat Waingunga bullocks?
It is neither bullock nor buck he hunts tonight. It is man.
Faugh! Are there not enough beetles and frogs in the tanks that he must eat man, and that too on our ground!
The Law of the Jungle forbids any beast to eat man, except when he is killing to show his children how to kill, and then he must hunt outside the hunting grounds of his pack or tribe.
For killing a man means, sooner or later, the arrival of hundreds of men with guns and torches. Then everybody in the Jungle suffers.
Aaarh!
What is it? Has he missed his prey?
The fool has had no more sense than to jump at a woodcutter's campfire, and has burned his feet. Tabaqui is with him.
SNAP!
Somebody is coming uphill. Get ready.
The bushes rustled a little in the thicket, and Father Wolf readied himself to attack.

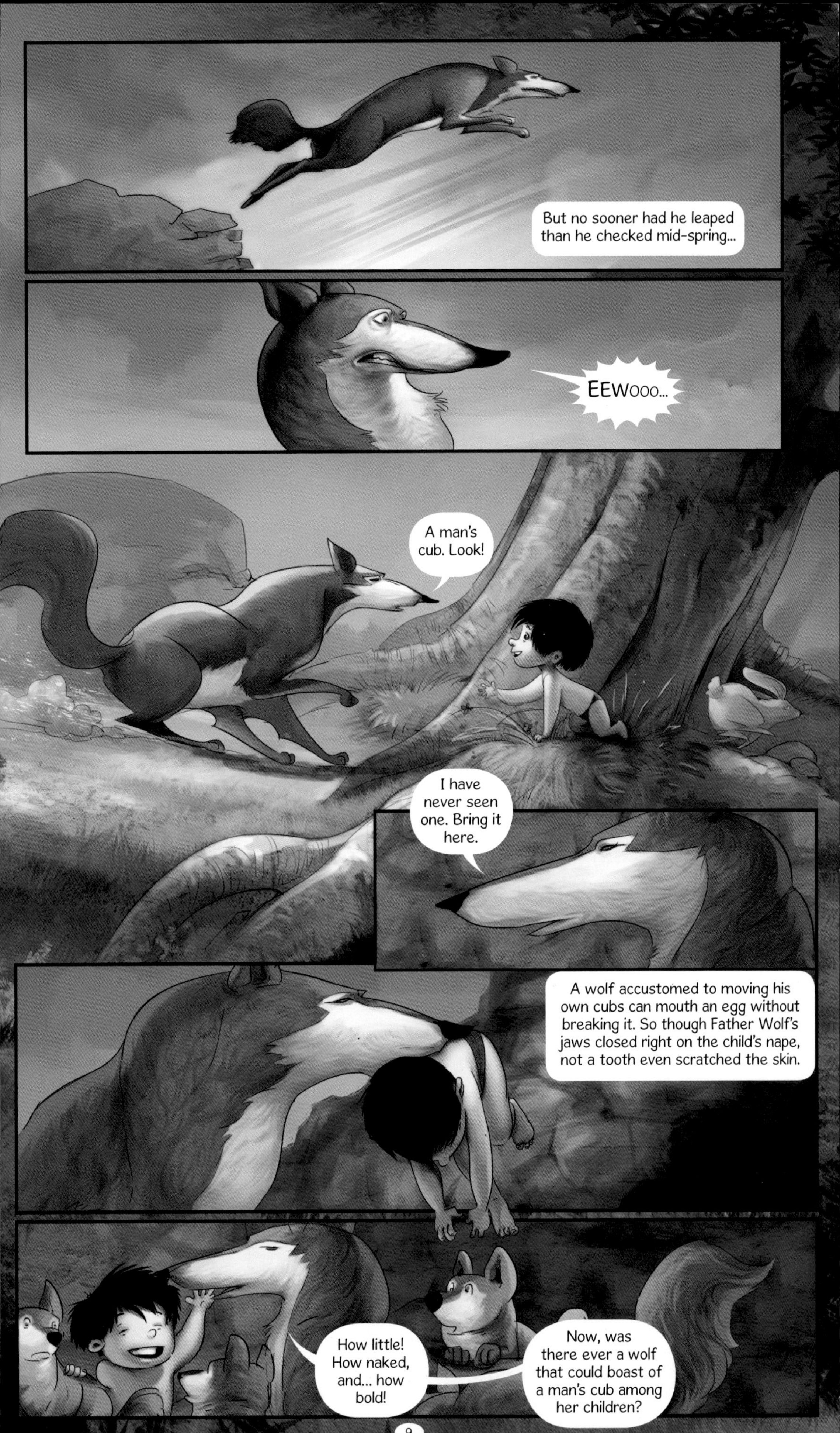
But no sooner had he leaped than he checked mid-spring...
EEWooo...
A man's cub. Look!
I have never seen one. Bring it here.
A wolf accustomed to moving his own cubs can mouth an egg without breaking it. So though Father Wolf's jaws closed right on the child's nape, not a tooth even scratched the skin.
How little! How naked, and... how bold!
Now, was there ever a wolf that could boast of a man's cub among her children?

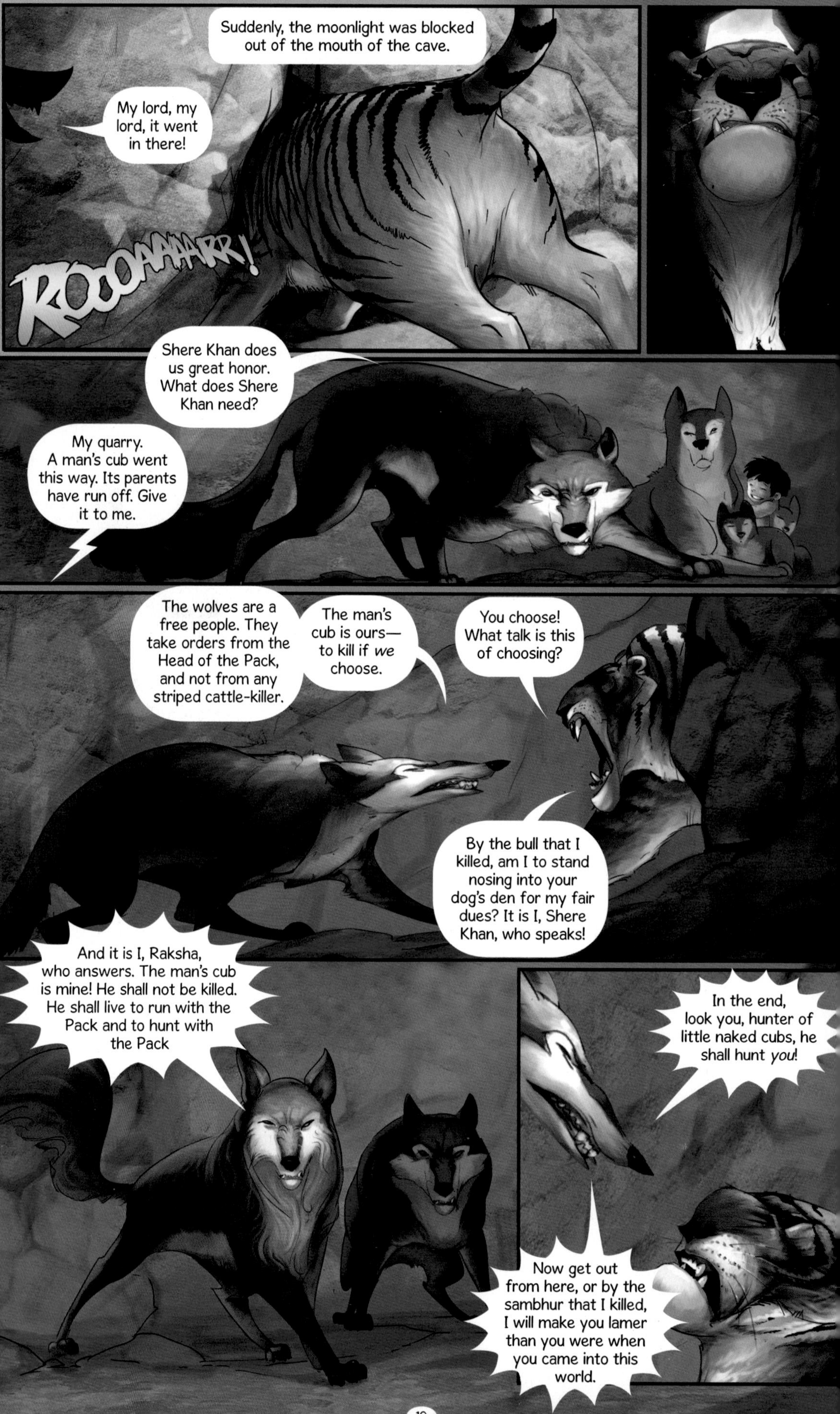
My lord, my lord, it went in there!
Suddenly, the moonlight was blocked out of the mouth of the cave.
ROOOAAAARR!
Shere Khan does us great honor. What does Shere Khan need?
My quarry. A man's cub went this way. Its parents have run off. Give it to me.
The wolves are a free people. They take orders from the Head of the Pack, and not from any striped cattle-killer.
The man's cub is ours— to kill if *we* choose.
You choose! What talk is this of choosing?
By the bull that I killed, am I to stand nosing into your dog's den for my fair dues? It is I, Shere Khan, who speaks!
And it is I, Raksha, who answers. The man's cub is mine! He shall not be killed. He shall live to run with the Pack and to hunt with the Pack
In the end, look you, hunter of little naked cubs, he shall hunt *you*!
Now get out from here, or by the sambhur that I killed, I will make you lamer than you were when you came into this world.

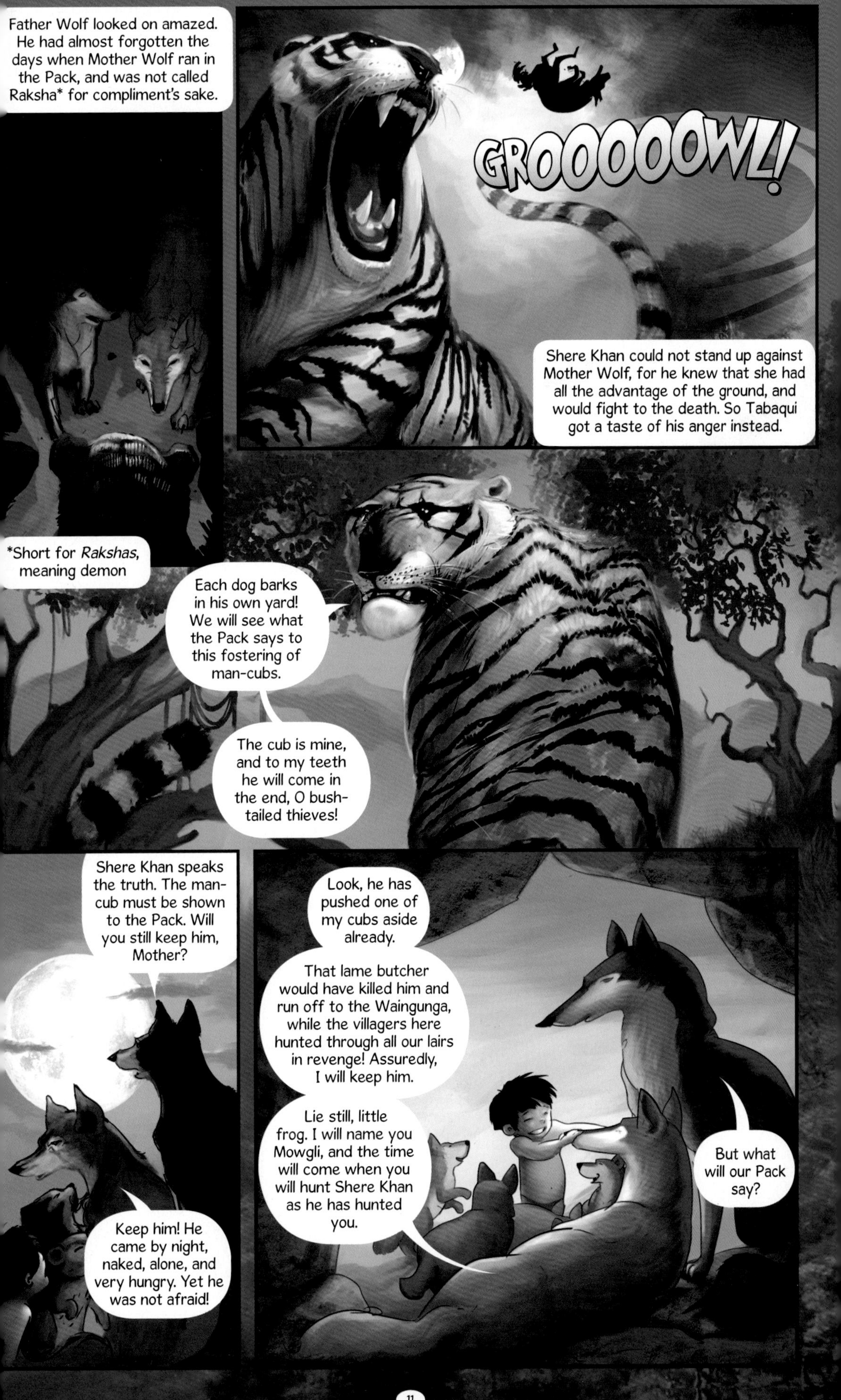

Father Wolf looked on amazed. He had almost forgotten the days when Mother Wolf ran in the Pack, and was not called Raksha* for compliment's sake.
*Short for *Rakshas*, meaning demon
GROOOOOOWL!
Shere Khan could not stand up against Mother Wolf, for he knew that she had all the advantage of the ground, and would fight to the death. So Tabaqui got a taste of his anger instead.
Each dog barks in his own yard! We will see what the Pack says to this fostering of man-cubs.
The cub is mine, and to my teeth he will come in the end, O bush-tailed thieves!
Shere Khan speaks the truth. The man-cub must be shown to the Pack. Will you still keep him, Mother?
Keep him! He came by night, naked, alone, and very hungry. Yet he was not afraid!
Look, he has pushed one of my cubs aside already.
That lame butcher would have killed him and run off to the Waingunga, while the villagers here hunted through all our lairs in revenge! Assuredly, I will keep him.
Lie still, little frog. I will name you Mowgli, and the time will come when you will hunt Shere Khan as he has hunted you.
But what will our Pack say?

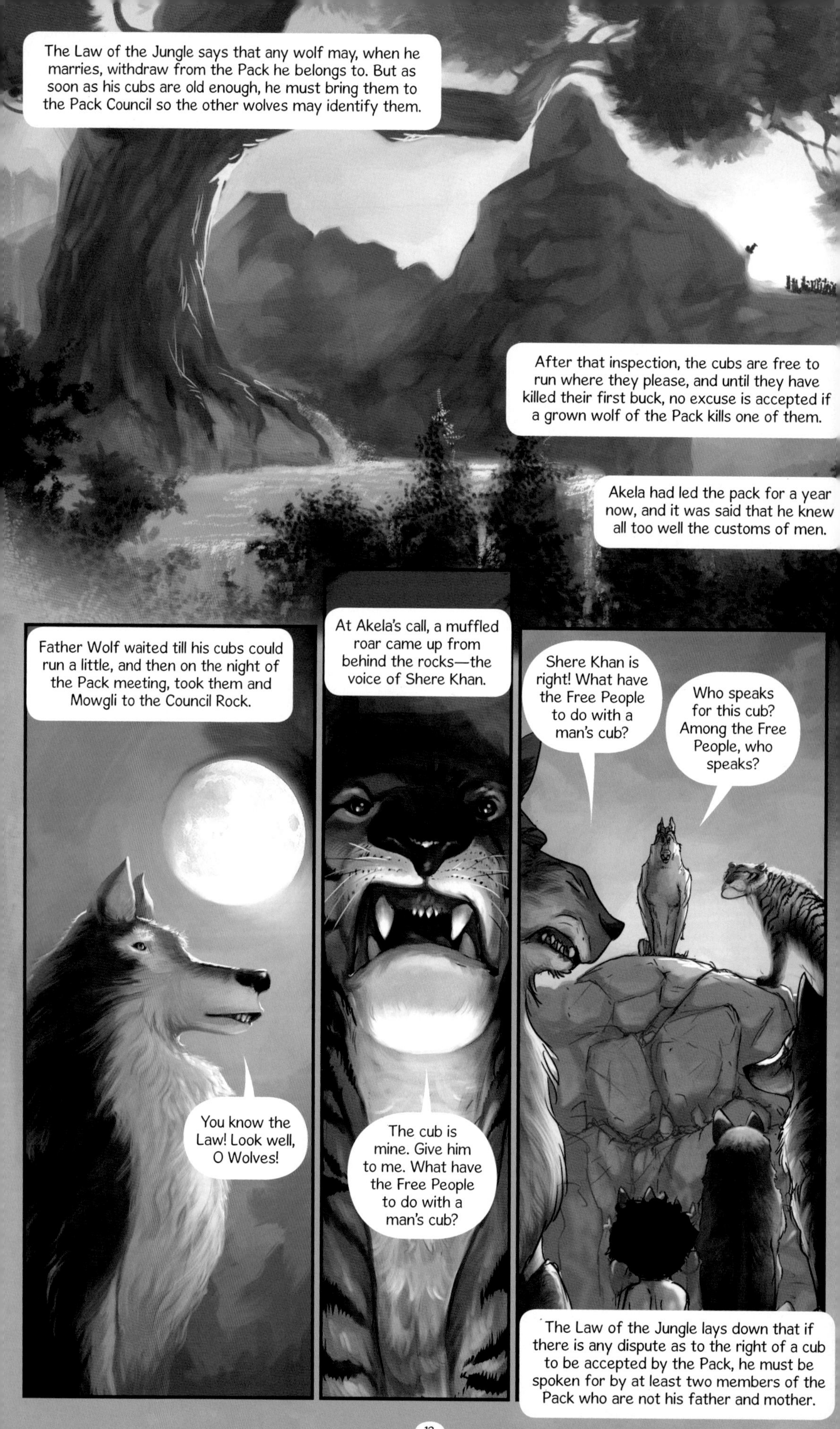
The Law of the Jungle says that any wolf may, when he marries, withdraw from the Pack he belongs to. But as soon as his cubs are old enough, he must bring them to the Pack Council so the other wolves may identify them.
After that inspection, the cubs are free to run where they please, and until they have killed their first buck, no excuse is accepted if a grown wolf of the Pack kills one of them.
Akela had led the pack for a year now, and it was said that he knew all too well the customs of men.
Father Wolf waited till his cubs could run a little, and then on the night of the Pack meeting, took them and Mowgli to the Council Rock.
You know the Law! Look well, O Wolves!
At Akela's call, a muffled roar came up from behind the rocks—the voice of Shere Khan.
The cub is mine. Give him to me. What have the Free People to do with a man's cub?
Shere Khan is right! What have the Free People to do with a man's cub?
Who speaks for this cub? Among the Free People, who speaks?
The Law of the Jungle lays down that if there is any dispute as to the right of a cub to be accepted by the Pack, he must be spoken for by at least two members of the Pack who are not his father and mother.

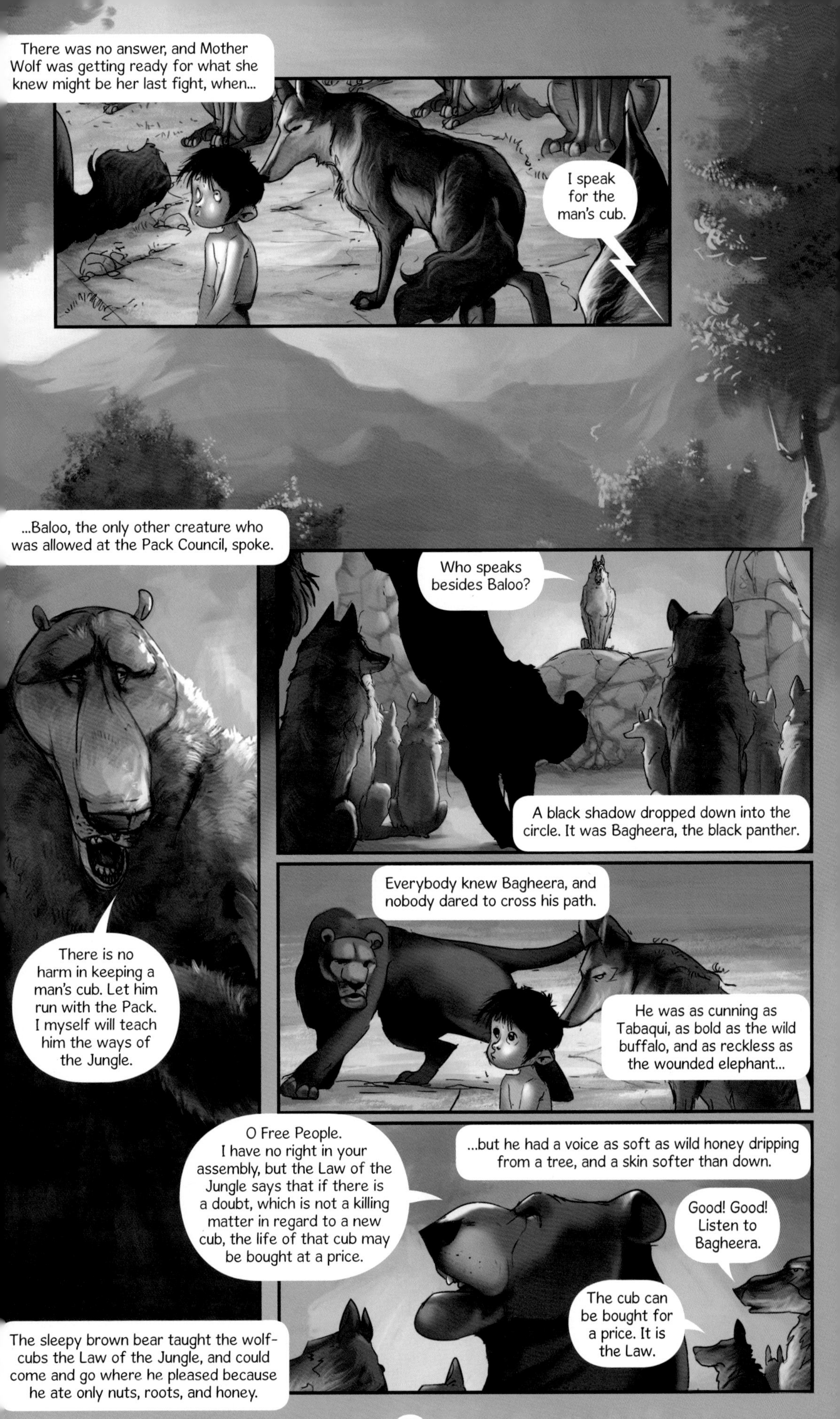
There was no answer, and Mother Wolf was getting ready for what she knew might be her last fight, when...
I speak for the man's cub.
...Baloo, the only other creature who was allowed at the Pack Council, spoke.
There is no harm in keeping a man's cub. Let him run with the Pack. I myself will teach him the ways of the Jungle.
The sleepy brown bear taught the wolf-cubs the Law of the Jungle, and could come and go where he pleased because he ate only nuts, roots, and honey.
Who speaks besides Baloo?
A black shadow dropped down into the circle. It was Bagheera, the black panther.
Everybody knew Bagheera, and nobody dared to cross his path.
He was as cunning as Tabaqui, as bold as the wild buffalo, and as reckless as the wounded elephant...
O Free People. I have no right in your assembly, but the Law of the Jungle says that if there is a doubt, which is not a killing matter in regard to a new cub, the life of that cub may be bought at a price.
...but he had a voice as soft as wild honey dripping from a tree, and a skin softer than down.
Good! Good! Listen to Bagheera.
The cub can be bought for a price. It is the Law.

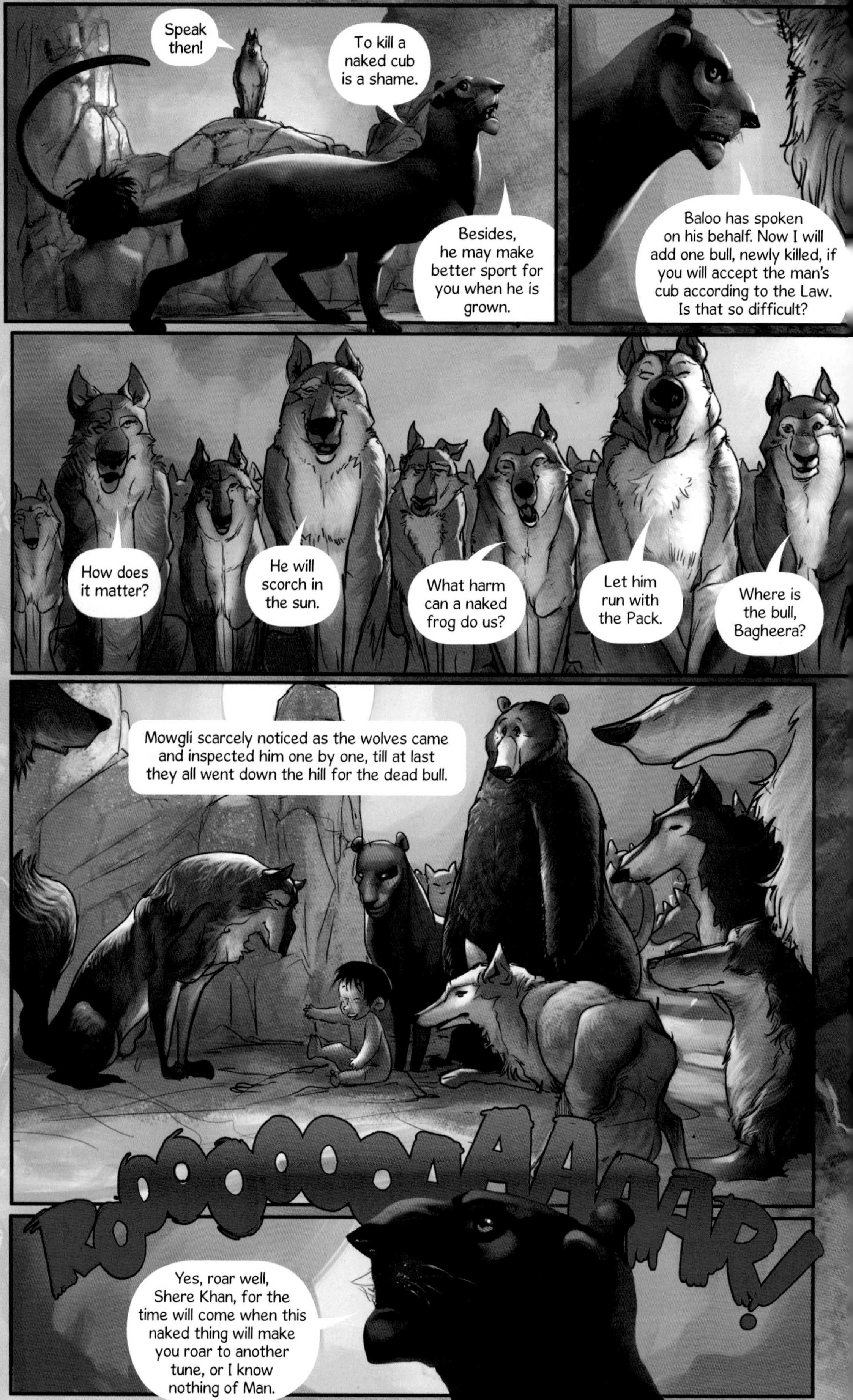
Speak then!
To kill a naked cub is a shame.
Besides, he may make better sport for you when he is grown.
Baloo has spoken on his behalf. Now I will add one bull, newly killed, if you will accept the man's cub according to the Law. Is that so difficult?
How does it matter?
He will scorch in the sun.
What harm can a naked frog do us?
Let him run with the Pack.
Where is the bull, Bagheera?
Mowgli scarcely noticed as the wolves came and inspected him one by one, till at last they all went down the hill for the dead bull.
ROOOOOOOAAAAAR!
Yes, roar well, Shere Khan, for the time will come when this naked thing will make you roar to another tune, or I know nothing of Man.

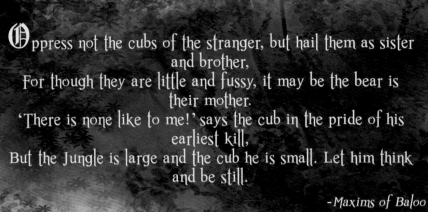

Oppress not the cubs of the stranger, but hail them as sister and brother,
For though they are little and fussy, it may be the bear is their mother.
'There is none like to me!' says the cub in the pride of his earliest kill,
But the Jungle is large and the cub he is small. Let him think and be still.

-Maxims of Baloo

Despite what some in the Pack thought, Mowgli not only survived in the Jungle, but thrived. When he was seven, Baloo set out to teach him the Law of the Jungle.

Baloo was delighted to have so quick a pupil, for young wolves will only learn as much of the Law of the Jungle as applies to their own pack and tribe, and then run away.

Mowgli had to learn a great deal more than that. Baloo schooled the boy on the Wood and Water Laws, but sometimes the boy grew very tired of saying the same thing over a hundred times.

I have had it!

When this happened, Mowgli would test Baloo's patience, and the large bear would have to punish him.

Sometimes Bagheera would come lounging through the Jungle to see how his pet was getting on...

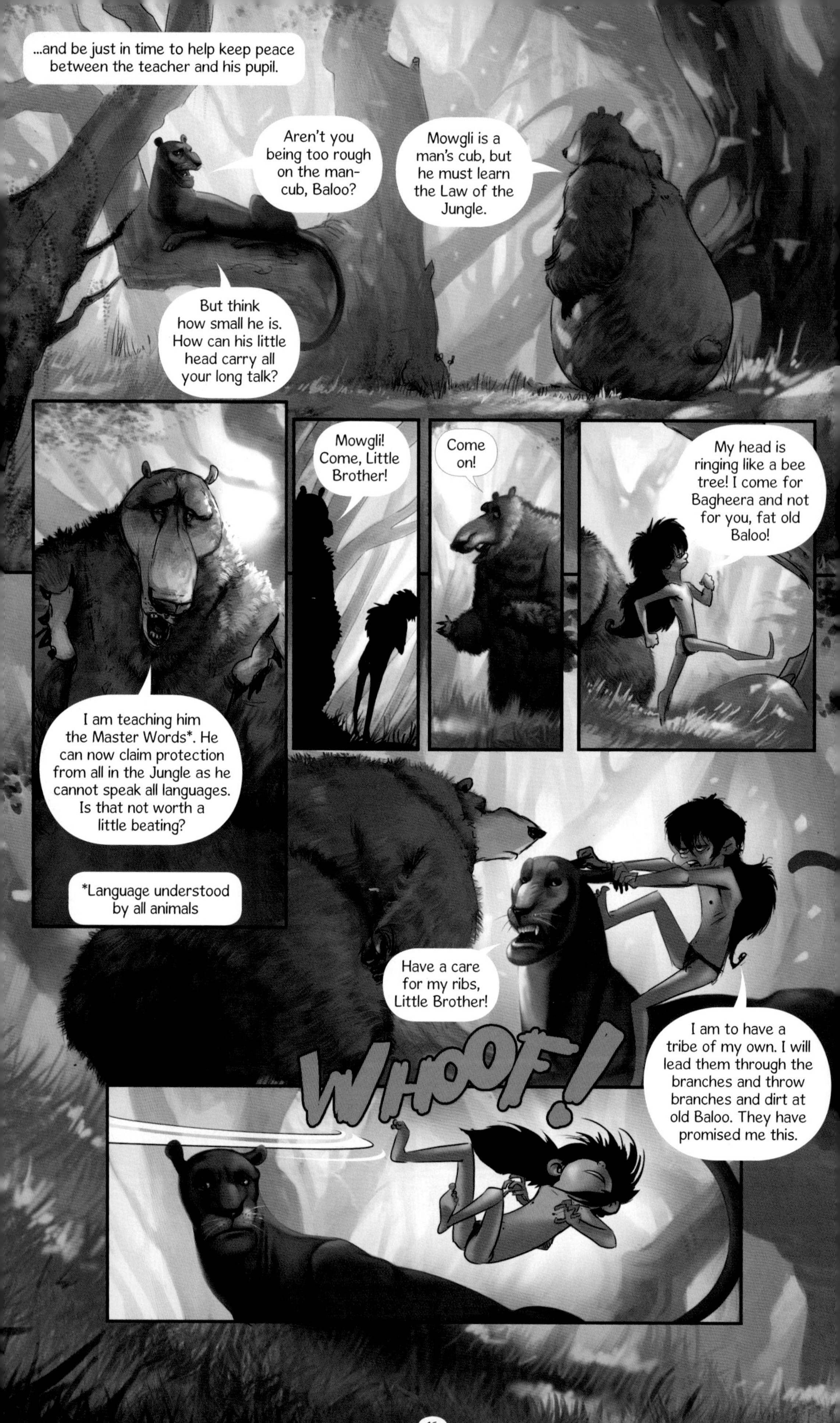

...and be just in time to help keep peace between the teacher and his pupil.
Aren't you being too rough on the man-cub, Baloo?
Mowgli is a man's cub, but he must learn the Law of the Jungle.
But think how small he is. How can his little head carry all your long talk?
I am teaching him the Master Words*. He can now claim protection from all in the Jungle as he cannot speak all languages. Is that not worth a little beating?
*Language understood by all animals
Mowgli! Come, Little Brother!
Come on!
My head is ringing like a bee tree! I come for Bagheera and not for you, fat old Baloo!
Have a care for my ribs, Little Brother!
I am to have a tribe of my own. I will lead them through the branches and throw branches and dirt at old Baloo. They have promised me this.
WHOOF!

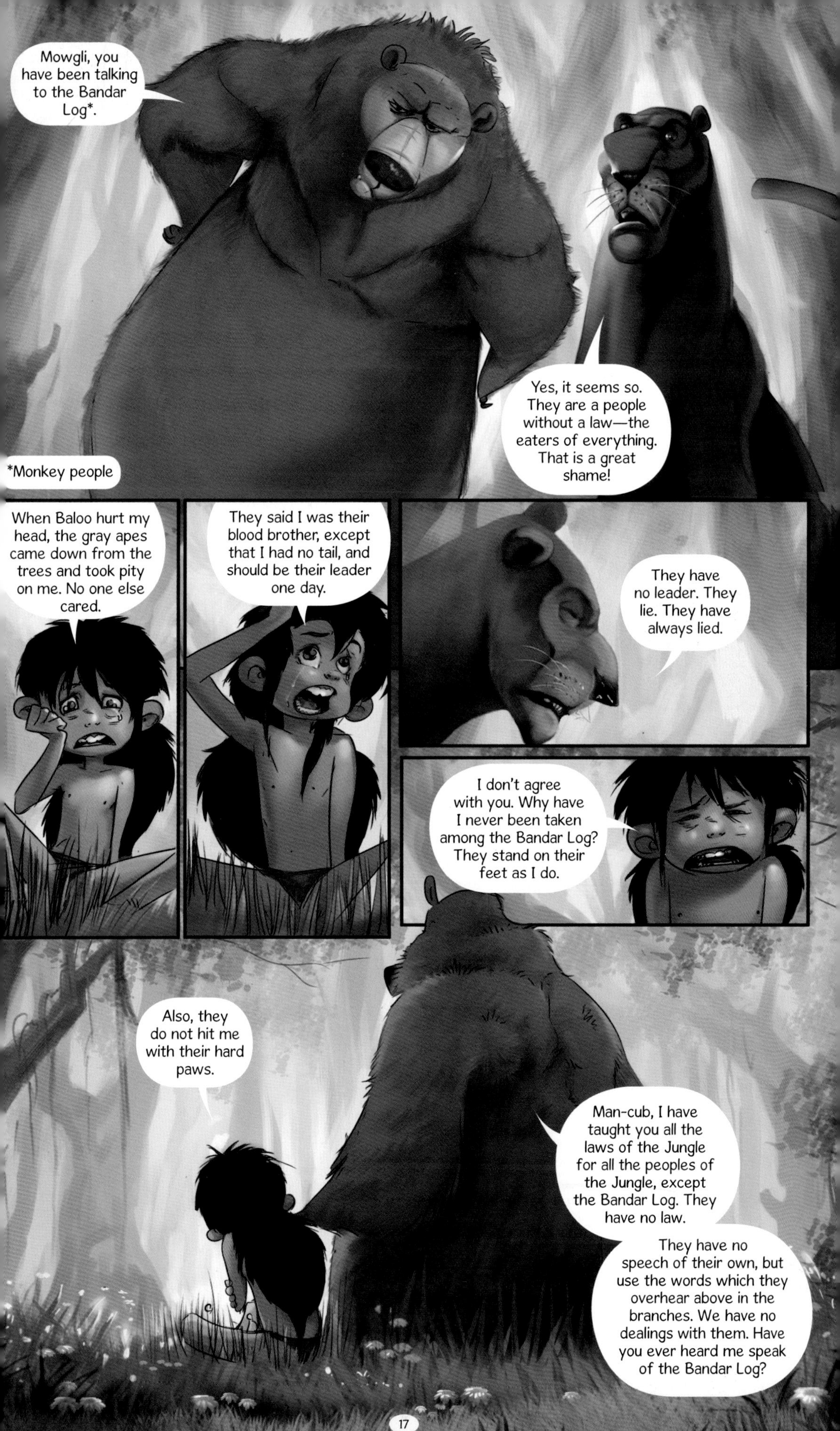
Mowgli, you have been talking to the Bandar Log*.
Yes, it seems so. They are a people without a law—the eaters of everything. That is a great shame!
*Monkey people
When Baloo hurt my head, the gray apes came down from the trees and took pity on me. No one else cared.
They said I was their blood brother, except that I had no tail, and should be their leader one day.
They have no leader. They lie. They have always lied.
I don't agree with you. Why have I never been taken among the Bandar Log? They stand on their feet as I do.
Also, they do not hit me with their hard paws.
Man-cub, I have taught you all the laws of the Jungle for all the peoples of the Jungle, except the Bandar Log. They have no law.
They have no speech of their own, but use the words which they overhear above in the branches. We have no dealings with them. Have you ever heard me speak of the Bandar Log?

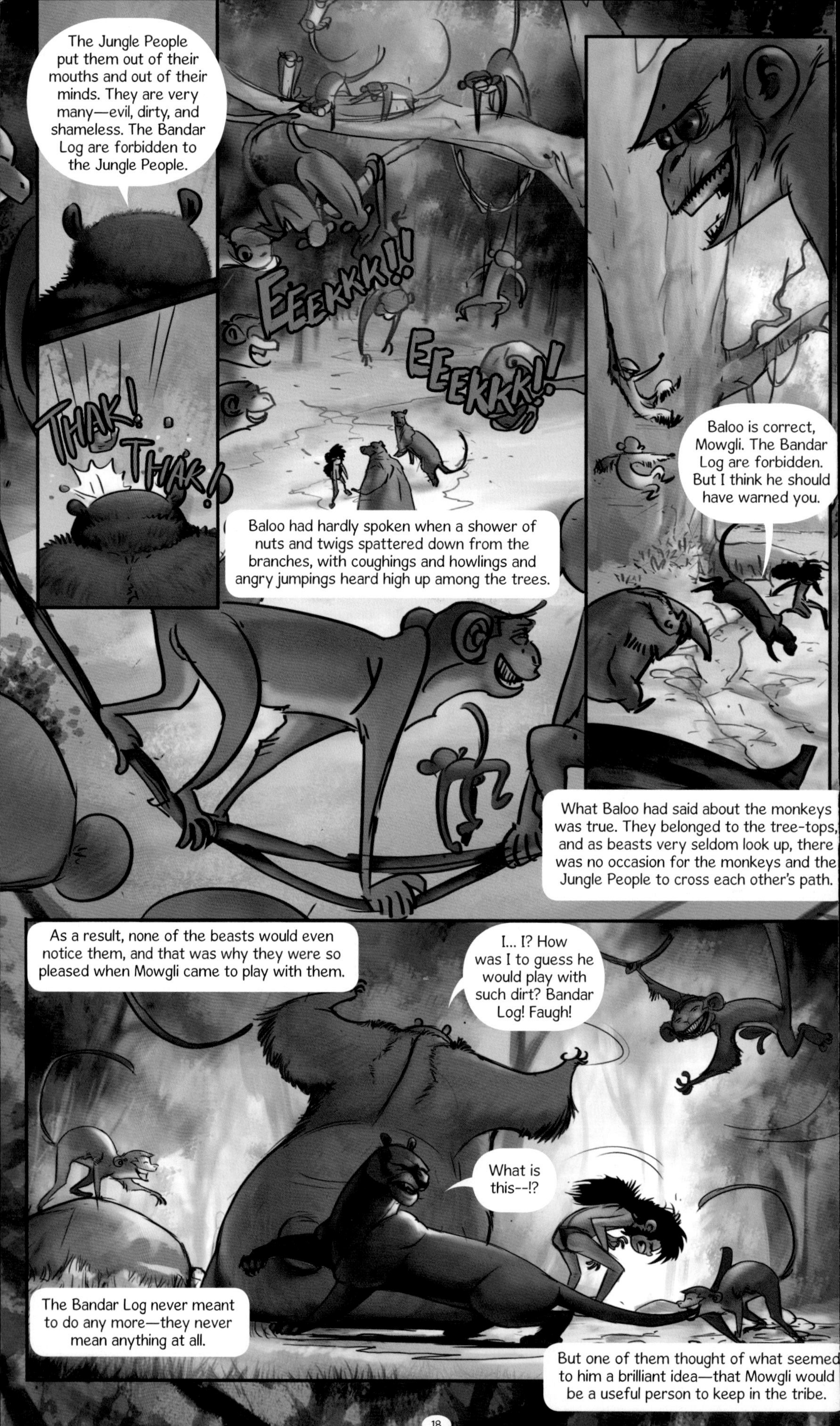
The Jungle People put them out of their mouths and out of their minds. They are very many—evil, dirty, and shameless. The Bandar Log are forbidden to the Jungle People.
THAK!
THAK!
EEEKKK!!
EEEKKK!
Baloo had hardly spoken when a shower of nuts and twigs spattered down from the branches, with coughings and howlings and angry jumpings heard high up among the trees.
Baloo is correct, Mowgli. The Bandar Log are forbidden. But I think he should have warned you.
What Baloo had said about the monkeys was true. They belonged to the tree-tops, and as beasts very seldom look up, there was no occasion for the monkeys and the Jungle People to cross each other's path.
As a result, none of the beasts would even notice them, and that was why they were so pleased when Mowgli came to play with them.
I... I? How was I to guess he would play with such dirt? Bandar Log! Faugh!
What is this--!?
The Bandar Log never meant to do any more—they never mean anything at all.
But one of them thought of what seemed to him a brilliant idea—that Mowgli would be a useful person to keep in the tribe.

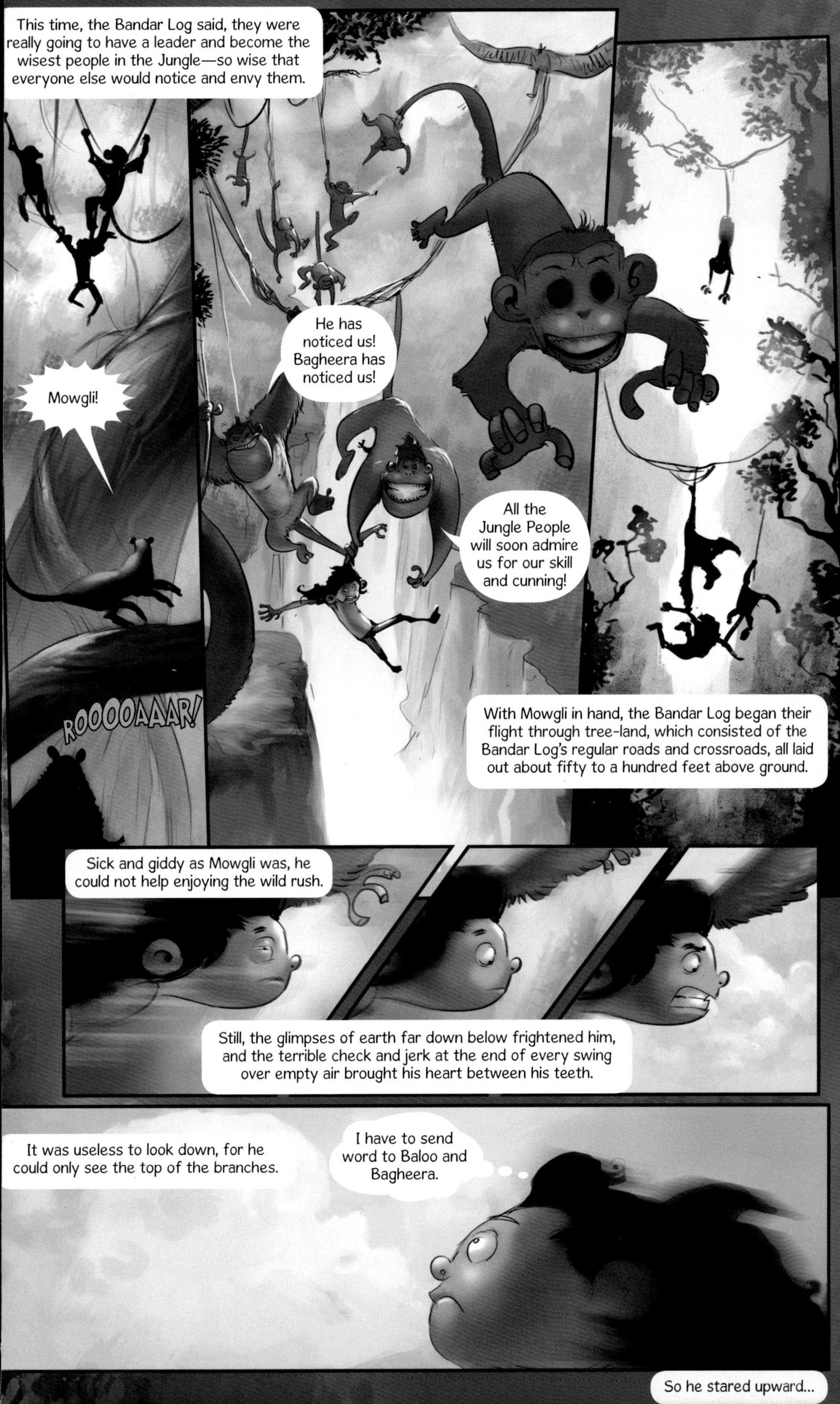
This time, the Bandar Log said, they were really going to have a leader and become the wisest people in the Jungle—so wise that everyone else would notice and envy them.
Mowgli!
ROOOOAAAR!
He has noticed us! Bagheera has noticed us!
All the Jungle People will soon admire us for our skill and cunning!
With Mowgli in hand, the Bandar Log began their flight through tree-land, which consisted of the Bandar Log's regular roads and crossroads, all laid out about fifty to a hundred feet above ground.
Sick and giddy as Mowgli was, he could not help enjoying the wild rush.
Still, the glimpses of earth far down below frightened him, and the terrible check and jerk at the end of every swing over empty air brought his heart between his teeth.
It was useless to look down, for he could only see the top of the branches.
I have to send word to Baloo and Bagheera.
So he stared upward...

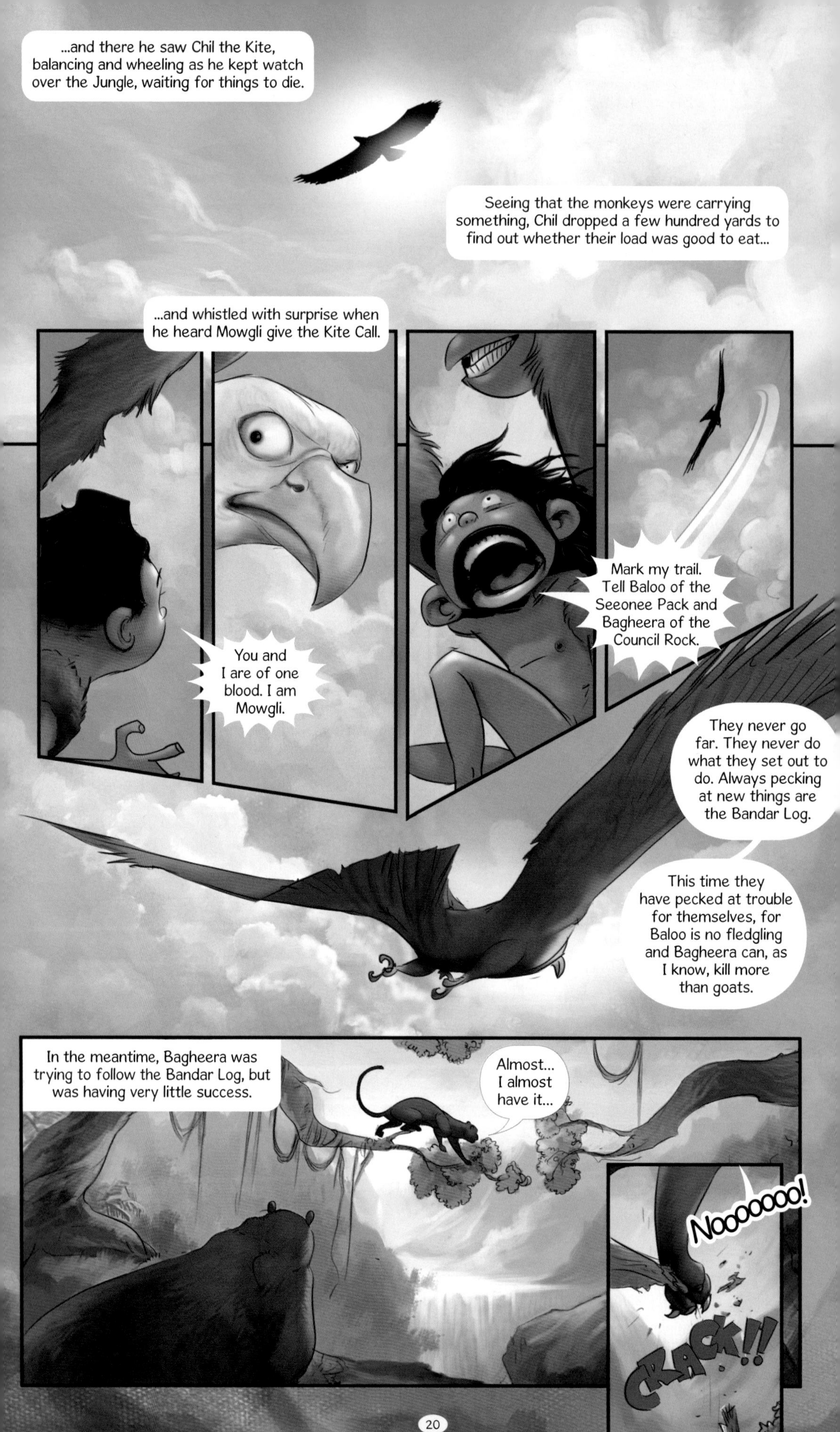

...and there he saw Chil the Kite, balancing and wheeling as he kept watch over the Jungle, waiting for things to die.
Seeing that the monkeys were carrying something, Chil dropped a few hundred yards to find out whether their load was good to eat...
...and whistled with surprise when he heard Mowgli give the Kite Call.
You and I are of one blood. I am Mowgli.
Mark my trail. Tell Baloo of the Seeonee Pack and Bagheera of the Council Rock.
They never go far. They never do what they set out to do. Always pecking at new things are the Bandar Log.
This time they have pecked at trouble for themselves, for Baloo is no fledgling and Bagheera can, as I know, kill more than goats.
In the meantime, Bagheera was trying to follow the Bandar Log, but was having very little success.
Almost... I almost have it...
Noooooo!
CRACK!!

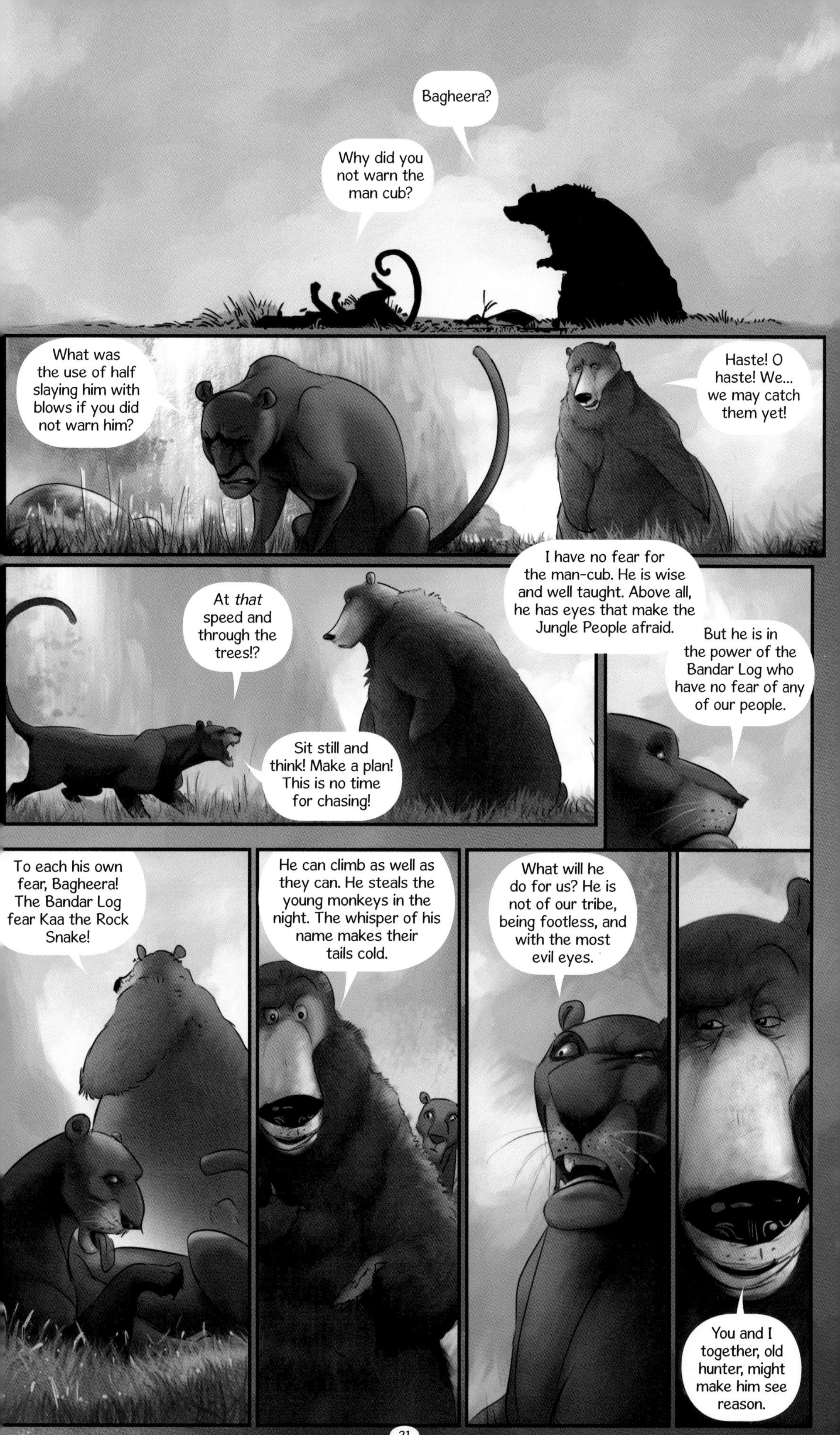
Bagheera?
Why did you not warn the man cub?
What was the use of half slaying him with blows if you did not warn him?
Haste! O haste! We... we may catch them yet!
At *that* speed and through the trees!?
Sit still and think! Make a plan! This is no time for chasing!
I have no fear for the man-cub. He is wise and well taught. Above all, he has eyes that make the Jungle People afraid.
But he is in the power of the Bandar Log who have no fear of any of our people.
To each his own fear, Bagheera! The Bandar Log fear Kaa the Rock Snake!
He can climb as well as they can. He steals the young monkeys in the night. The whisper of his name makes their tails cold.
What will he do for us? He is not of our tribe, being footless, and with the most evil eyes.
You and I together, old hunter, might make him see reason.

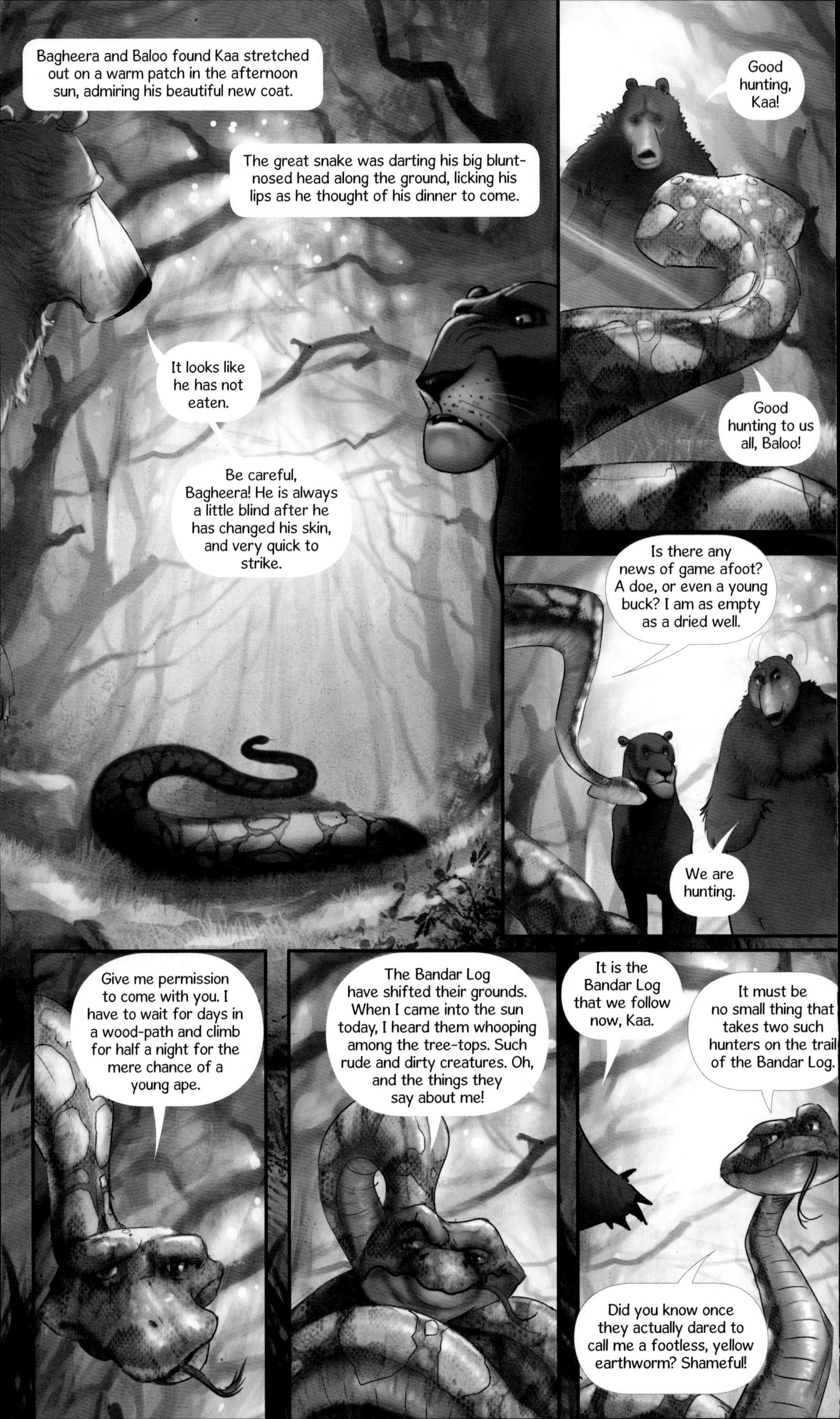
Bagheera and Baloo found Kaa stretched out on a warm patch in the afternoon sun, admiring his beautiful new coat.
The great snake was darting his big blunt-nosed head along the ground, licking his lips as he thought of his dinner to come.
It looks like he has not eaten.
Be careful, Bagheera! He is always a little blind after he has changed his skin, and very quick to strike.
Good hunting, Kaa!
Good hunting to us all, Baloo!
Is there any news of game afoot? A doe, or even a young buck? I am as empty as a dried well.
We are hunting.
Give me permission to come with you. I have to wait for days in a wood-path and climb for half a night for the mere chance of a young ape.
The Bandar Log have shifted their grounds. When I came into the sun today, I heard them whooping among the tree-tops. Such rude and dirty creatures. Oh, and the things they say about me!
It is the Bandar Log that we follow now, Kaa.
It must be no small thing that takes two such hunters on the trail of the Bandar Log.
Did you know once they actually dared to call me a footless, yellow earthworm? Shameful!

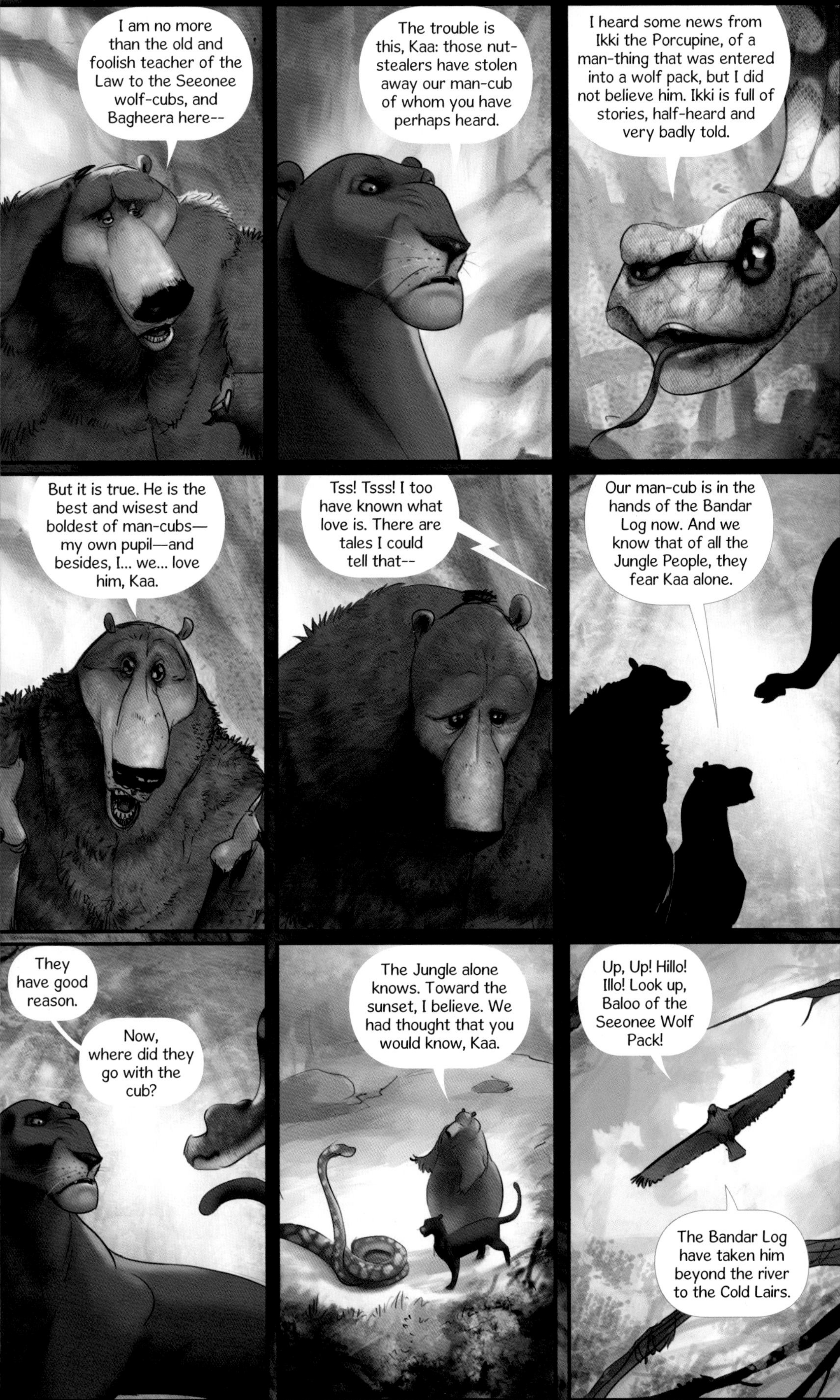
I am no more than the old and foolish teacher of the Law to the Seeonee wolf-cubs, and Bagheera here--
The trouble is this, Kaa: those nut-stealers have stolen away our man-cub of whom you have perhaps heard.
I heard some news from Ikki the Porcupine, of a man-thing that was entered into a wolf pack, but I did not believe him. Ikki is full of stories, half-heard and very badly told.
But it is true. He is the best and wisest and boldest of man-cubs—my own pupil—and besides, I... we... love him, Kaa.
Tss! Tsss! I too have known what love is. There are tales I could tell that--
Our man-cub is in the hands of the Bandar Log now. And we know that of all the Jungle People, they fear Kaa alone.
They have good reason.
Now, where did they go with the cub?
The Jungle alone knows. Toward the sunset, I believe. We had thought that you would know, Kaa.
Up, Up! Hillo! Illo! Look up, Baloo of the Seeonee Wolf Pack!
The Bandar Log have taken him beyond the river to the Cold Lairs.

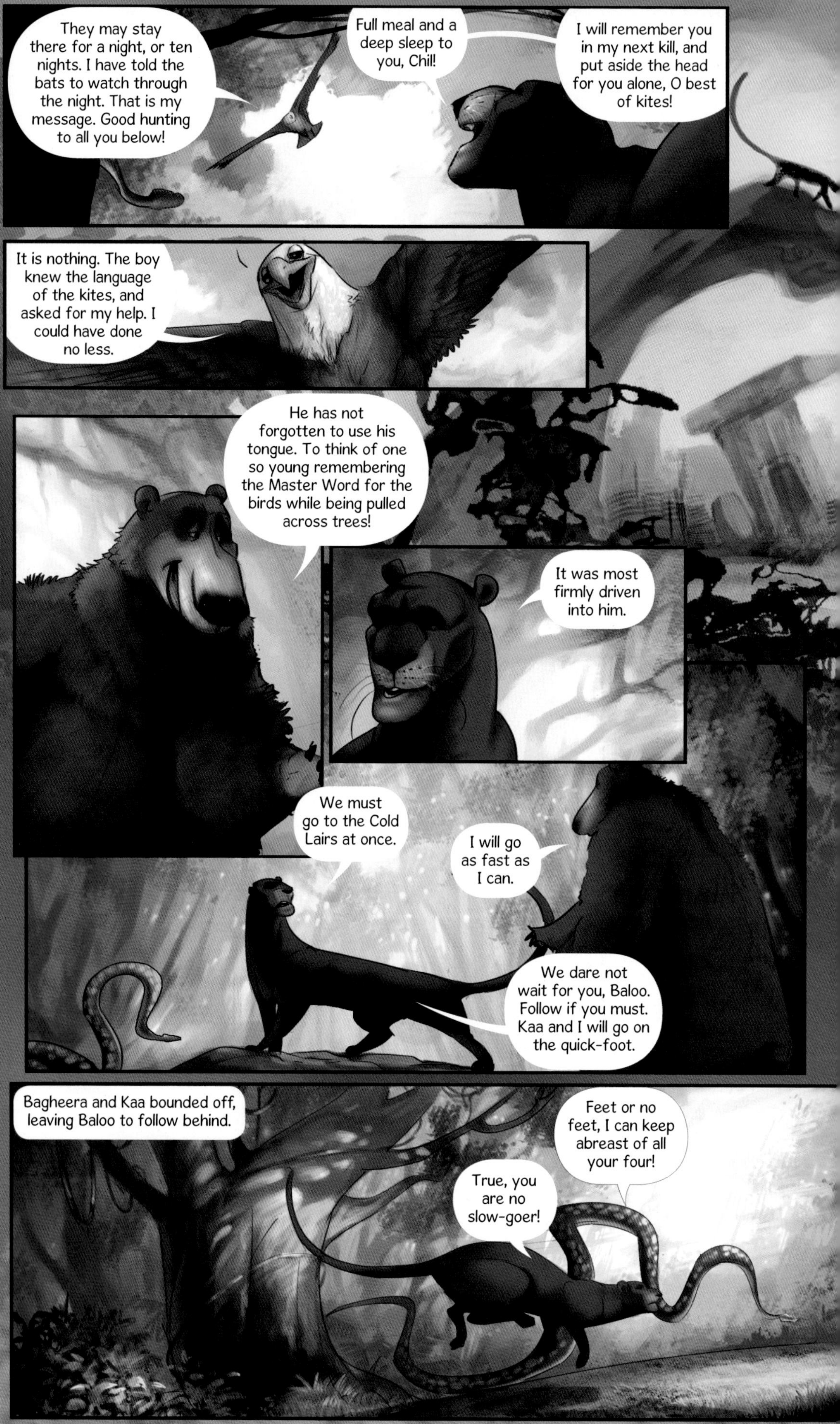
They may stay there for a night, or ten nights. I have told the bats to watch through the night. That is my message. Good hunting to all you below!
Full meal and a deep sleep to you, Chil!
I will remember you in my next kill, and put aside the head for you alone, O best of kites!
It is nothing. The boy knew the language of the kites, and asked for my help. I could have done no less.
He has not forgotten to use his tongue. To think of one so young remembering the Master Word for the birds while being pulled across trees!
It was most firmly driven into him.
We must go to the Cold Lairs at once.
I will go as fast as I can.
We dare not wait for you, Baloo. Follow if you must. Kaa and I will go on the quick-foot.
Bagheera and Kaa bounded off, leaving Baloo to follow behind.
Feet or no feet, I can keep abreast of all your four!
True, you are no slow-goer!

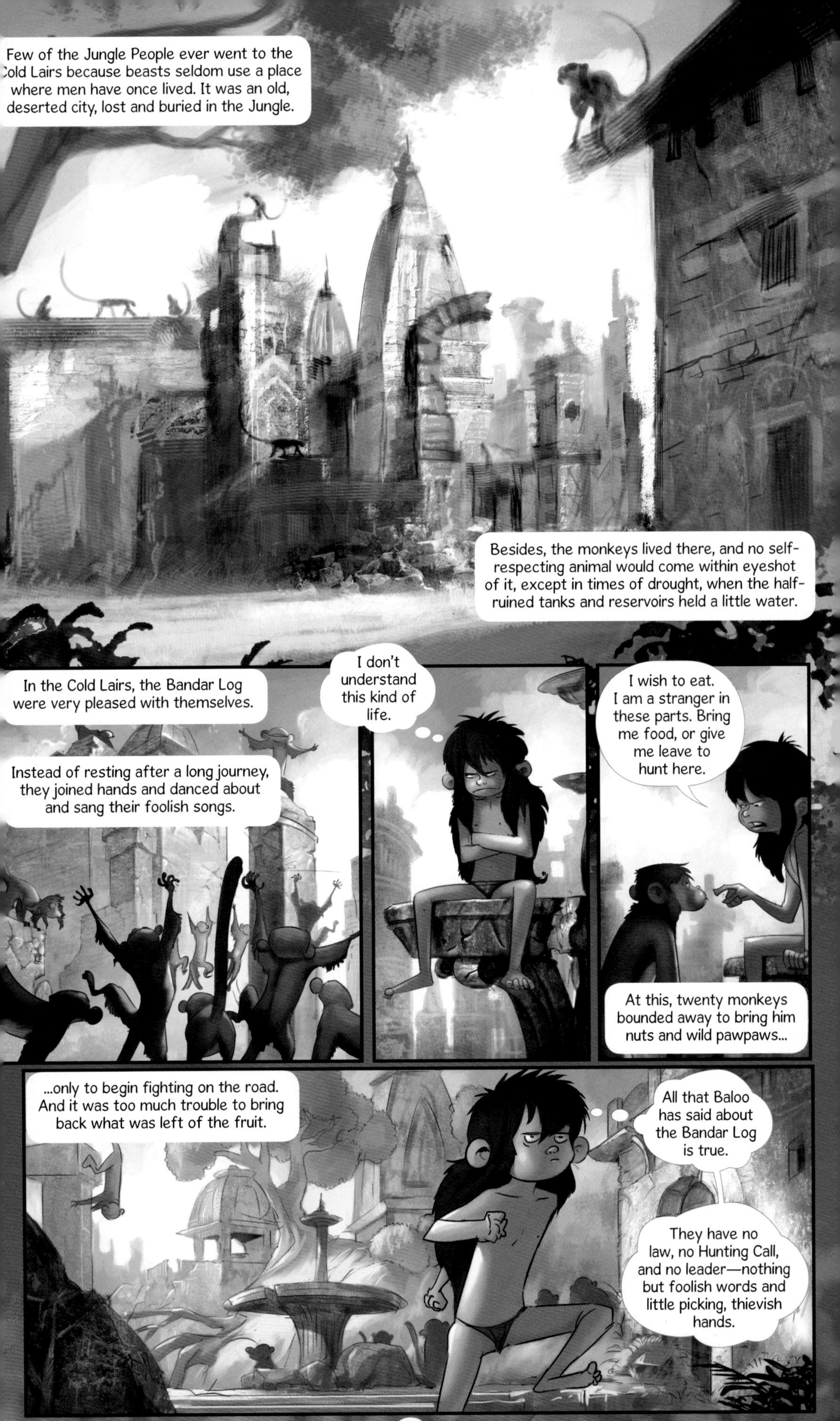
Few of the Jungle People ever went to the Cold Lairs because beasts seldom use a place where men have once lived. It was an old, deserted city, lost and buried in the Jungle.
Besides, the monkeys lived there, and no self-respecting animal would come within eyeshot of it, except in times of drought, when the half-ruined tanks and reservoirs held a little water.
In the Cold Lairs, the Bandar Log were very pleased with themselves.
Instead of resting after a long journey, they joined hands and danced about and sang their foolish songs.
I don't understand this kind of life.
I wish to eat. I am a stranger in these parts. Bring me food, or give me leave to hunt here.
At this, twenty monkeys bounded away to bring him nuts and wild pawpaws...
...only to begin fighting on the road. And it was too much trouble to bring back what was left of the fruit.
All that Baloo has said about the Bandar Log is true.
They have no law, no Hunting Call, and no leader—nothing but foolish words and little picking, thievish hands.

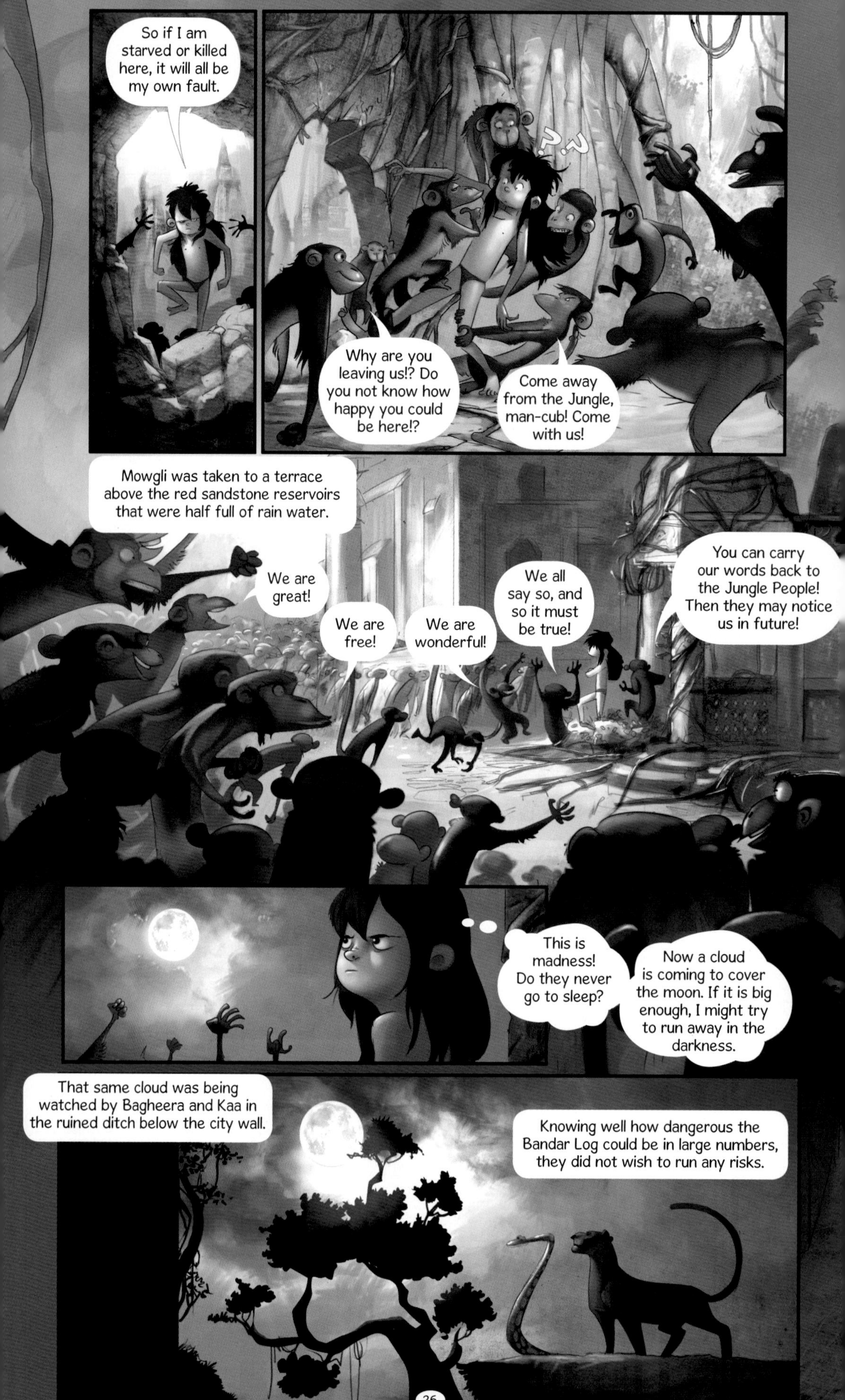
So if I am starved or killed here, it will all be my own fault.
??
Why are you leaving us!? Do you not know how happy you could be here!?
Come away from the Jungle, man-cub! Come with us!
Mowgli was taken to a terrace above the red sandstone reservoirs that were half full of rain water.
We are great!
We are free!
We are wonderful!
We all say so, and so it must be true!
You can carry our words back to the Jungle People! Then they may notice us in future!
This is madness! Do they never go to sleep?
Now a cloud is coming to cover the moon. If it is big enough, I might try to run away in the darkness.
That same cloud was being watched by Bagheera and Kaa in the ruined ditch below the city wall.
Knowing well how dangerous the Bandar Log could be in large numbers, they did not wish to run any risks.

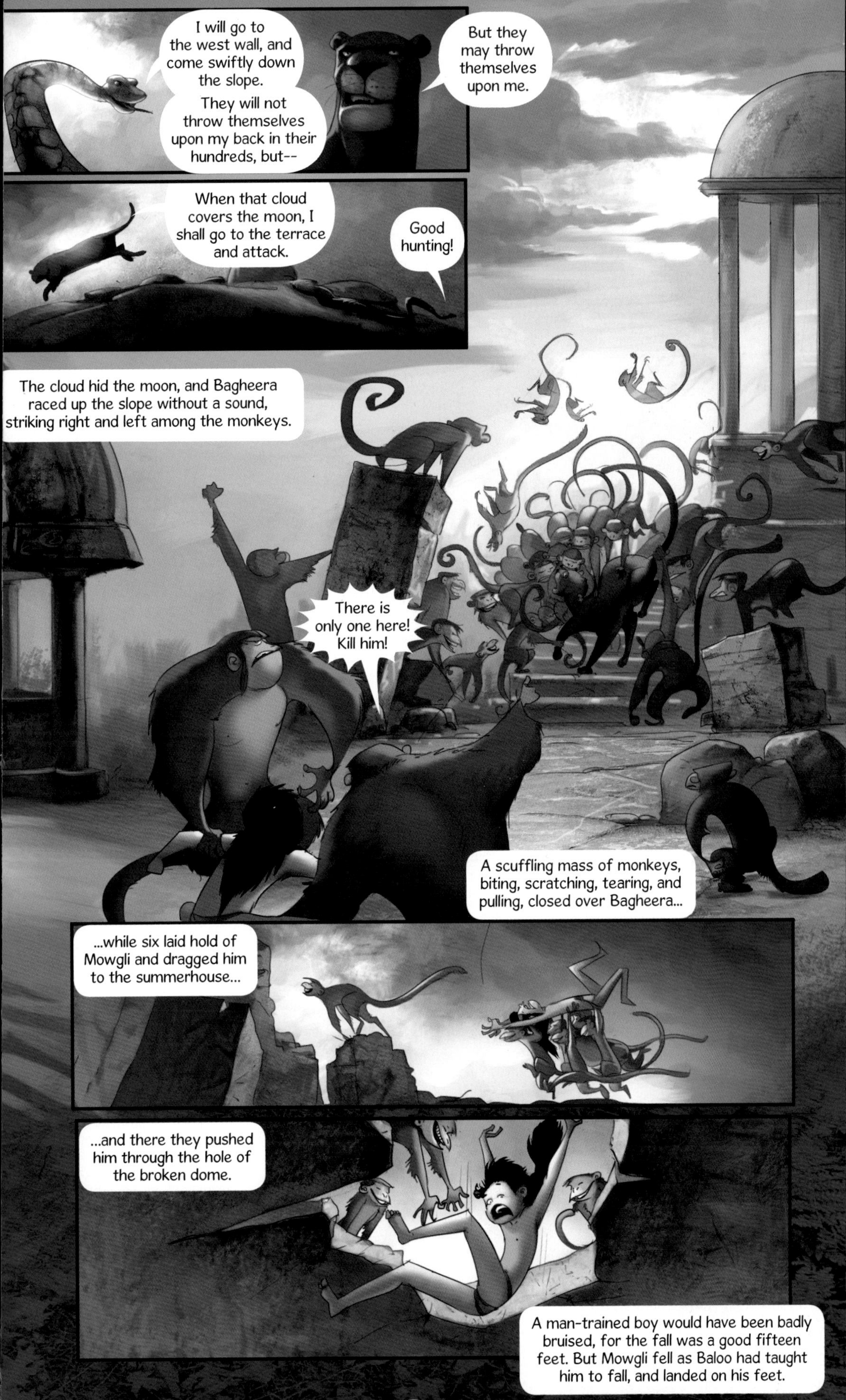
I will go to the west wall, and come swiftly down the slope.
They will not throw themselves upon my back in their hundreds, but--
But they may throw themselves upon me.
When that cloud covers the moon, I shall go to the terrace and attack.
Good hunting!
The cloud hid the moon, and Bagheera raced up the slope without a sound, striking right and left among the monkeys.
There is only one here! Kill him!
A scuffling mass of monkeys, biting, scratching, tearing, and pulling, closed over Bagheera...
...while six laid hold of Mowgli and dragged him to the summerhouse...
...and there they pushed him through the hole of the broken dome.
A man-trained boy would have been badly bruised, for the fall was a good fifteen feet. But Mowgli fell as Baloo had taught him to fall, and landed on his feet.

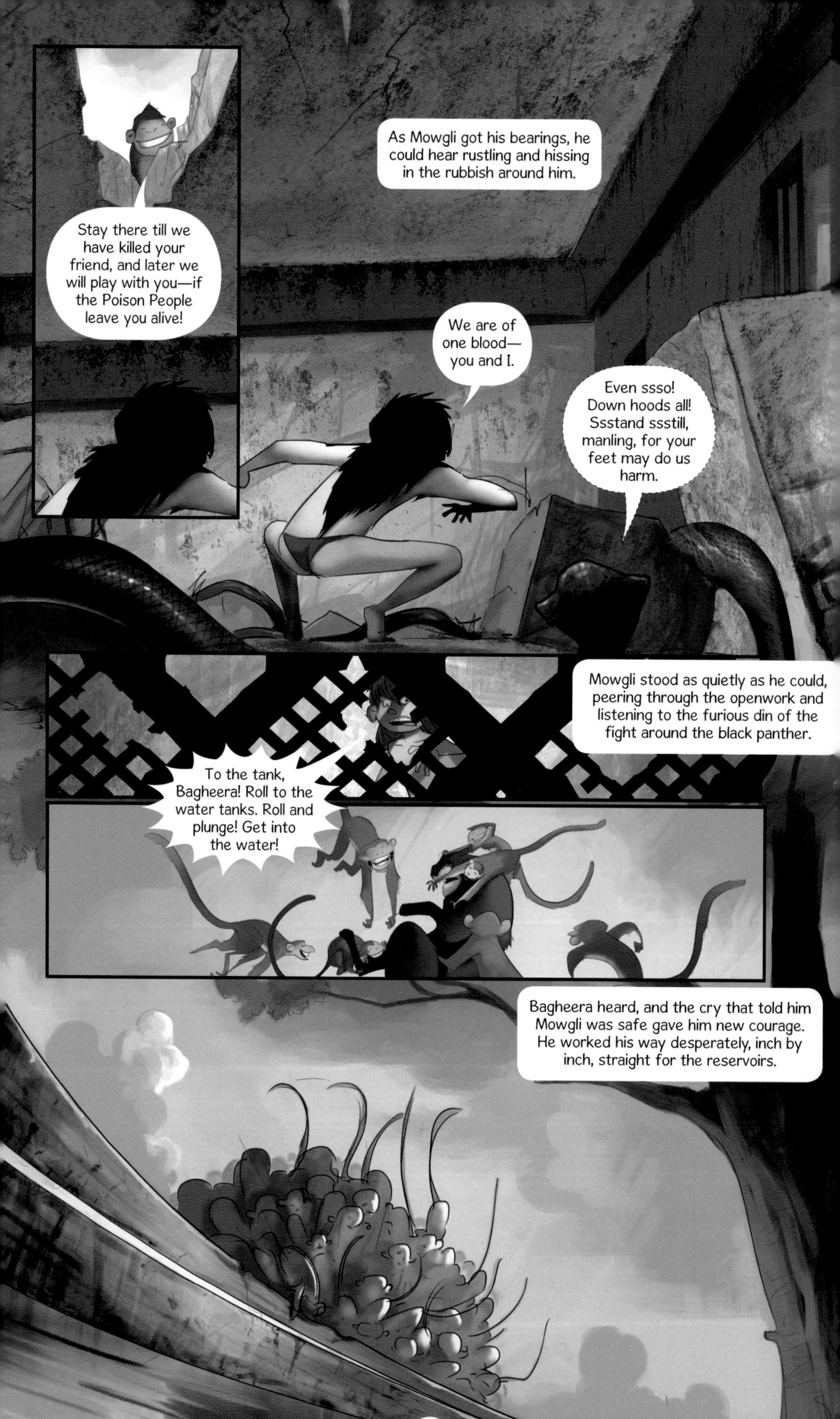
Stay there till we have killed your friend, and later we will play with you—if the Poison People leave you alive!
As Mowgli got his bearings, he could hear rustling and hissing in the rubbish around him.
We are of one blood— you and I.
Even ssso! Down hoods all! Ssstand ssstill, manling, for your feet may do us harm.
Mowgli stood as quietly as he could, peering through the openwork and listening to the furious din of the fight around the black panther.
To the tank, Bagheera! Roll to the water tanks. Roll and plunge! Get into the water!
Bagheera heard, and the cry that told him Mowgli was safe gave him new courage. He worked his way desperately, inch by inch, straight for the reservoirs.

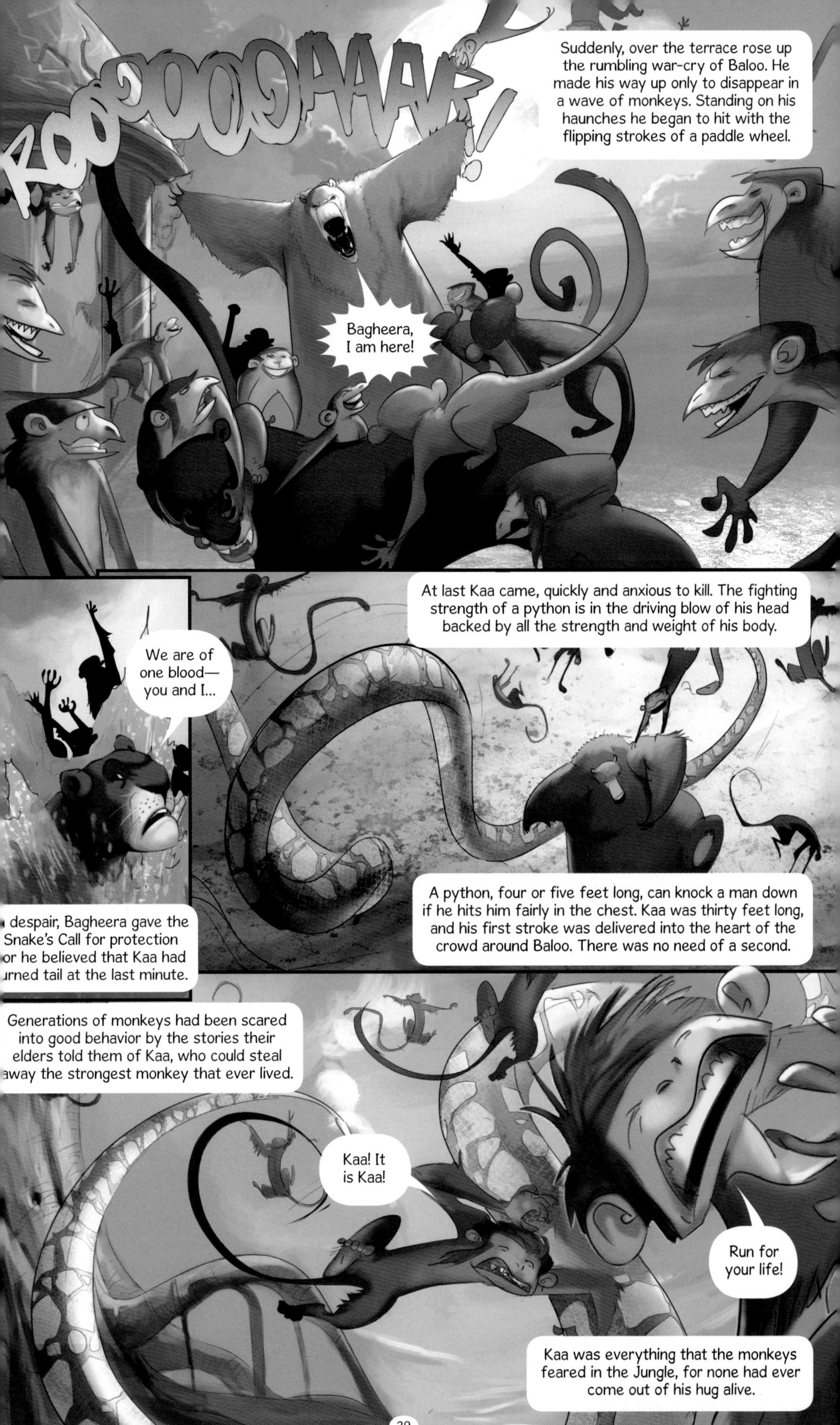
ROOOOOOAAAR!
Suddenly, over the terrace rose up the rumbling war-cry of Baloo. He made his way up only to disappear in a wave of monkeys. Standing on his haunches he began to hit with the flipping strokes of a paddle wheel.
Bagheera, I am here!
We are of one blood— you and I...
despair, Bagheera gave the Snake's Call for protection or he believed that Kaa had urned tail at the last minute.
At last Kaa came, quickly and anxious to kill. The fighting strength of a python is in the driving blow of his head backed by all the strength and weight of his body.
A python, four or five feet long, can knock a man down if he hits him fairly in the chest. Kaa was thirty feet long, and his first stroke was delivered into the heart of the crowd around Baloo. There was no need of a second.
Generations of monkeys had been scared into good behavior by the stories their elders told them of Kaa, who could steal away the strongest monkey that ever lived.
Kaa! It is Kaa!
Run for your life!
Kaa was everything that the monkeys feared in the Jungle, for none had ever come out of his hug alive.

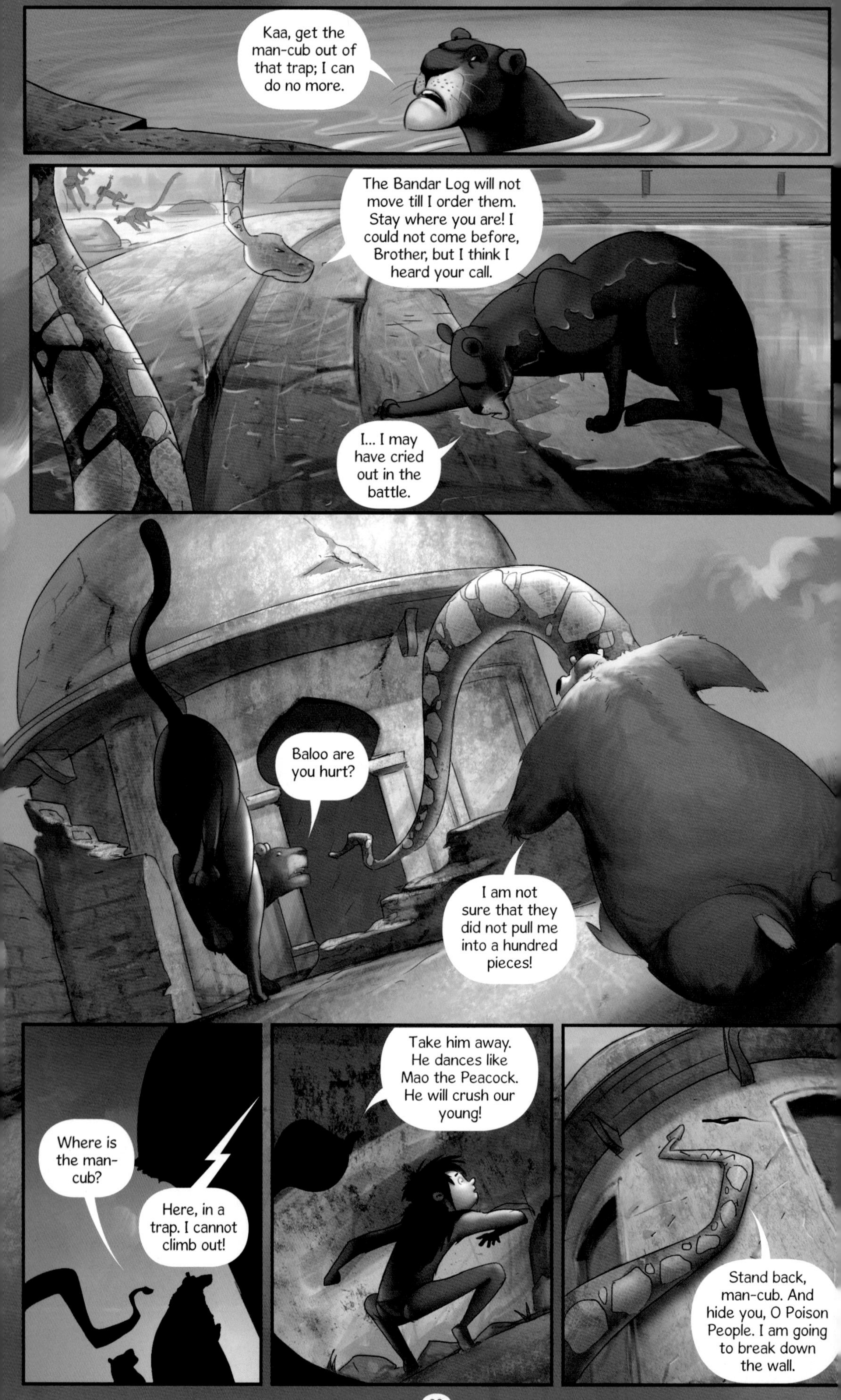
Kaa, get the man-cub out of that trap; I can do no more.
The Bandar Log will not move till I order them. Stay where you are! I could not come before, Brother, but I think I heard your call.
I... I may have cried out in the battle.
Baloo are you hurt?
I am not sure that they did not pull me into a hundred pieces!
Where is the man-cub?
Here, in a trap. I cannot climb out!
Take him away. He dances like Mao the Peacock. He will crush our young!
Stand back, man-cub. And hide you, O Poison People. I am going to break down the wall.

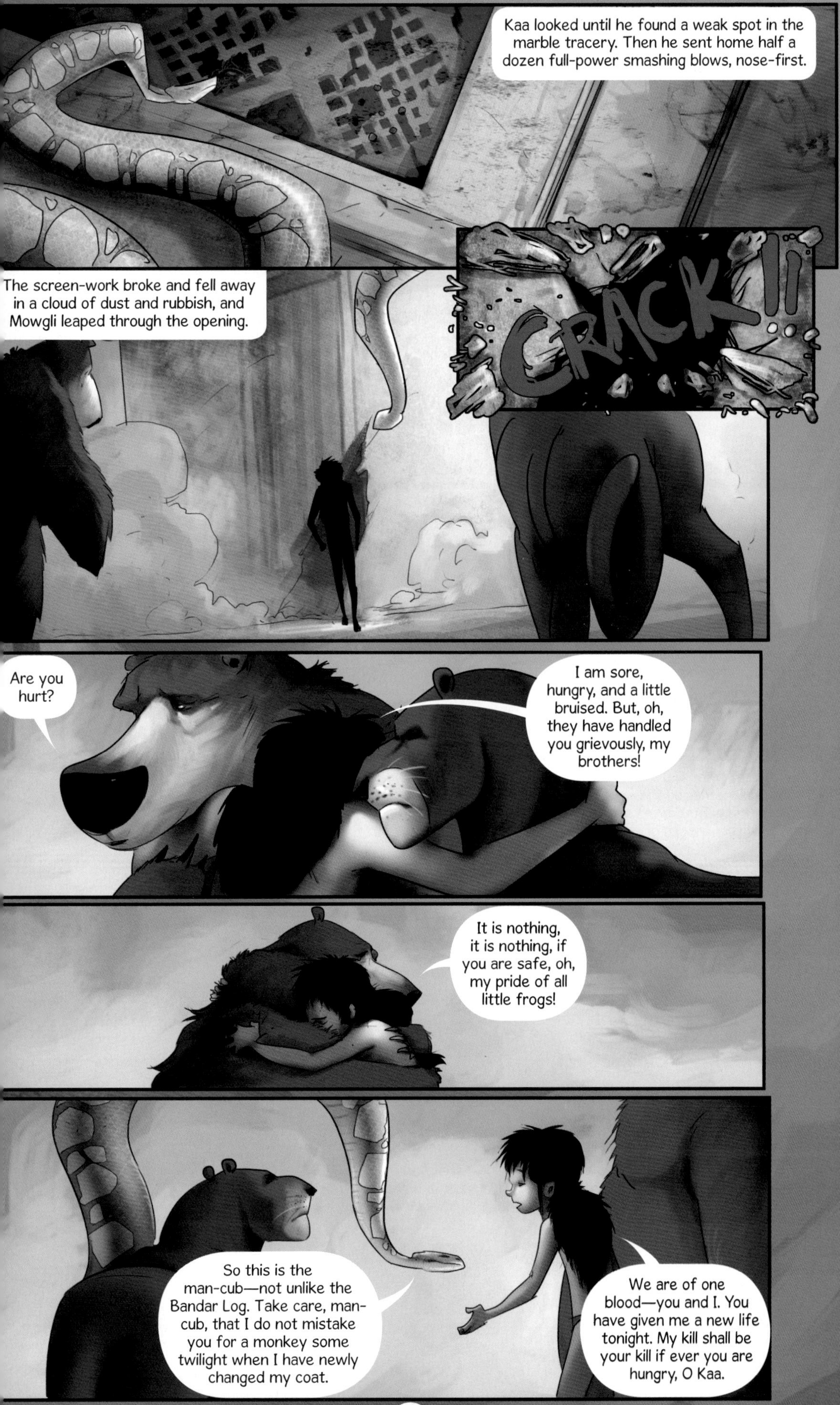
Kaa looked until he found a weak spot in the marble tracery. Then he sent home half a dozen full-power smashing blows, nose-first.
CRACK!!
The screen-work broke and fell away in a cloud of dust and rubbish, and Mowgli leaped through the opening.
Are you hurt?
I am sore, hungry, and a little bruised. But, oh, they have handled you grievously, my brothers!
It is nothing, it is nothing, if you are safe, oh, my pride of all little frogs!
So this is the man-cub—not unlike the Bandar Log. Take care, man-cub, that I do not mistake you for a monkey some twilight when I have newly changed my coat.
We are of one blood—you and I. You have given me a new life tonight. My kill shall be your kill if ever you are hungry, O Kaa.

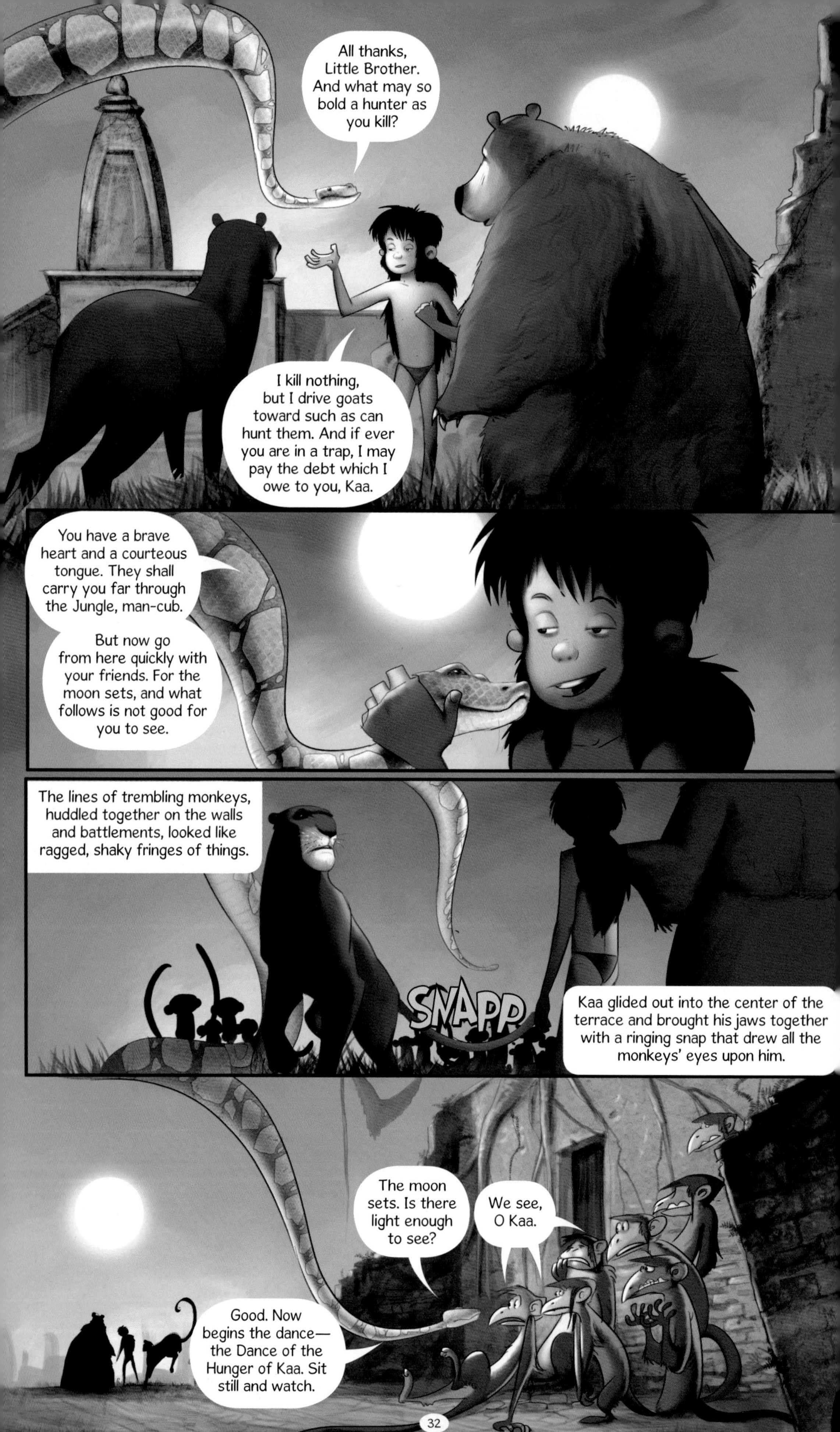
All thanks, Little Brother. And what may so bold a hunter as you kill?
I kill nothing, but I drive goats toward such as can hunt them. And if ever you are in a trap, I may pay the debt which I owe to you, Kaa.
You have a brave heart and a courteous tongue. They shall carry you far through the Jungle, man-cub.
But now go from here quickly with your friends. For the moon sets, and what follows is not good for you to see.
The lines of trembling monkeys, huddled together on the walls and battlements, looked like ragged, shaky fringes of things.
SNAPP
Kaa glided out into the center of the terrace and brought his jaws together with a ringing snap that drew all the monkeys' eyes upon him.
The moon sets. Is there light enough to see?
We see, O Kaa.
Good. Now begins the dance—the Dance of the Hunger of Kaa. Sit still and watch.

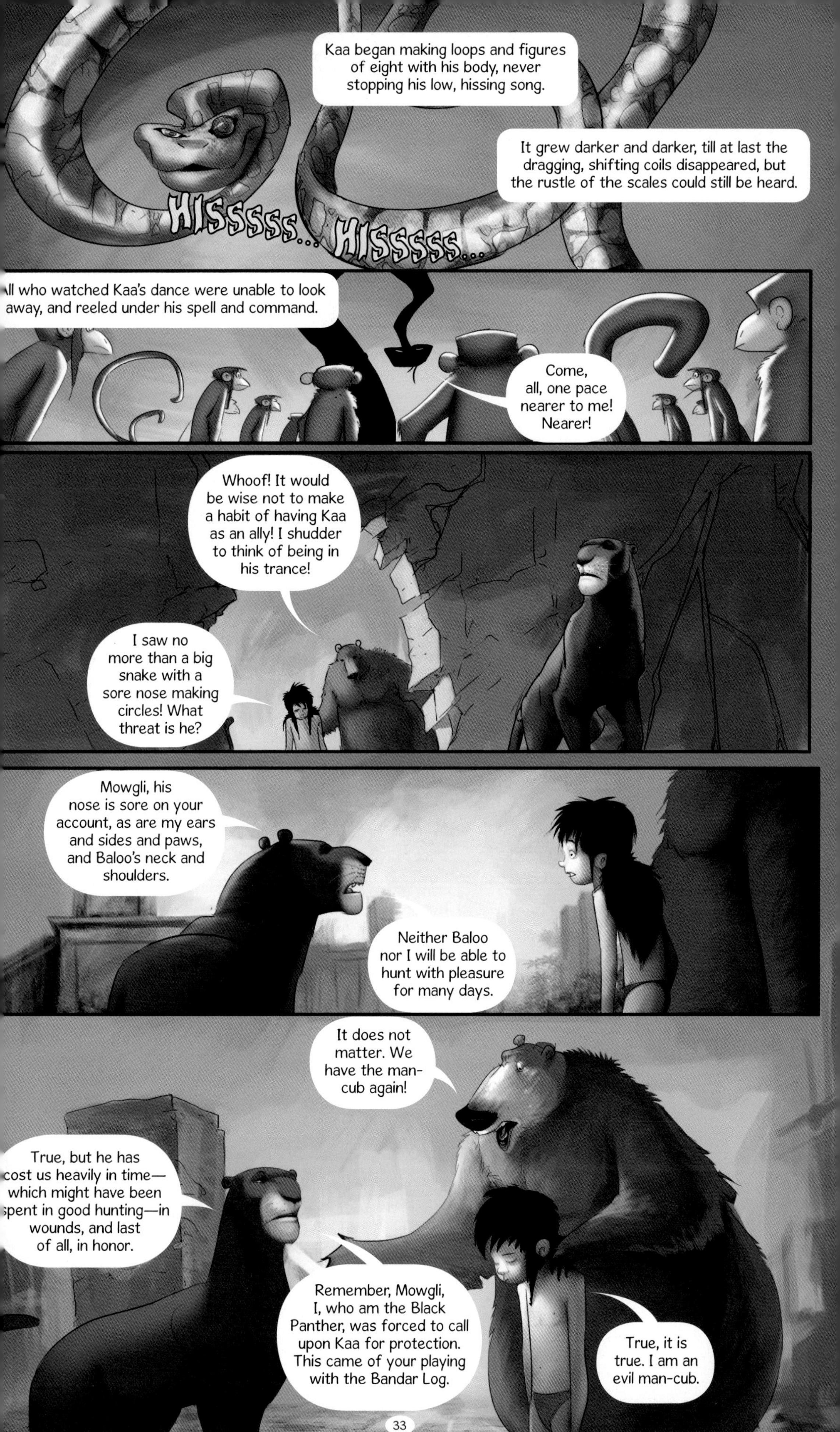
Kaa began making loops and figures of eight with his body, never stopping his low, hissing song.
It grew darker and darker, till at last the dragging, shifting coils disappeared, but the rustle of the scales could still be heard.
HISSSSS... HISSSSS...
ll who watched Kaa's dance were unable to look away, and reeled under his spell and command.
Come, all, one pace nearer to me! Nearer!
Whoof! It would be wise not to make a habit of having Kaa as an ally! I shudder to think of being in his trance!
I saw no more than a big snake with a sore nose making circles! What threat is he?
Mowgli, his nose is sore on your account, as are my ears and sides and paws, and Baloo's neck and shoulders.
Neither Baloo nor I will be able to hunt with pleasure for many days.
It does not matter. We have the man-cub again!
True, but he has cost us heavily in time—which might have been spent in good hunting—in wounds, and last of all, in honor.
Remember, Mowgli, I, who am the Black Panther, was forced to call upon Kaa for protection. This came of your playing with the Bandar Log.
True, it is true. I am an evil man-cub.

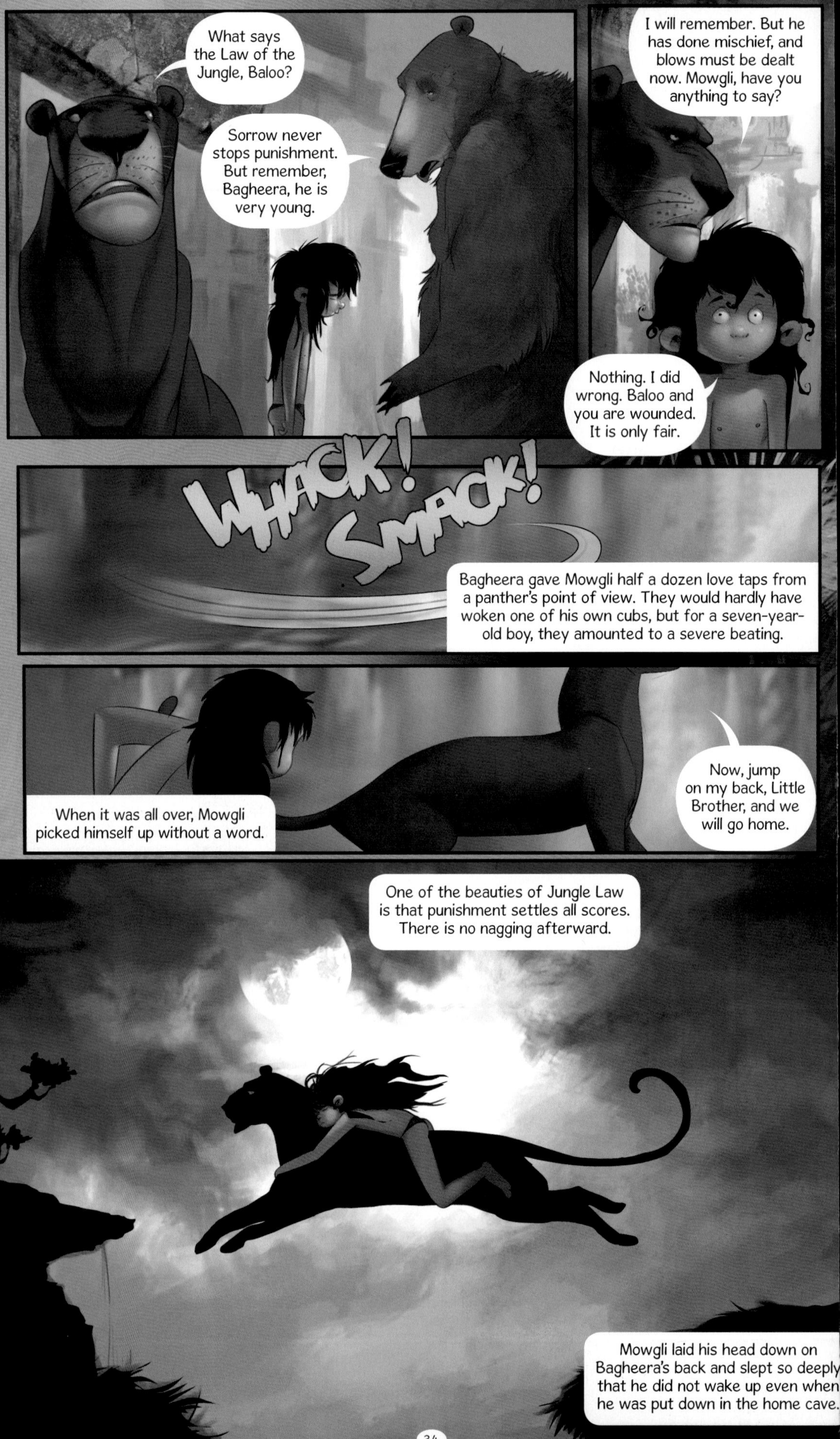
What says the Law of the Jungle, Baloo?
Sorrow never stops punishment. But remember, Bagheera, he is very young.
I will remember. But he has done mischief, and blows must be dealt now. Mowgli, have you anything to say?
Nothing. I did wrong. Baloo and you are wounded. It is only fair.
WHACK!
SMACK!
Bagheera gave Mowgli half a dozen love taps from a panther's point of view. They would hardly have woken one of his own cubs, but for a seven-year-old boy, they amounted to a severe beating.
When it was all over, Mowgli picked himself up without a word.
Now, jump on my back, Little Brother, and we will go home.
One of the beauties of Jungle Law is that punishment settles all scores. There is no nagging afterward.
Mowgli laid his head down on Bagheera's back and slept so deeply that he did not wake up even when he was put down in the home cave.

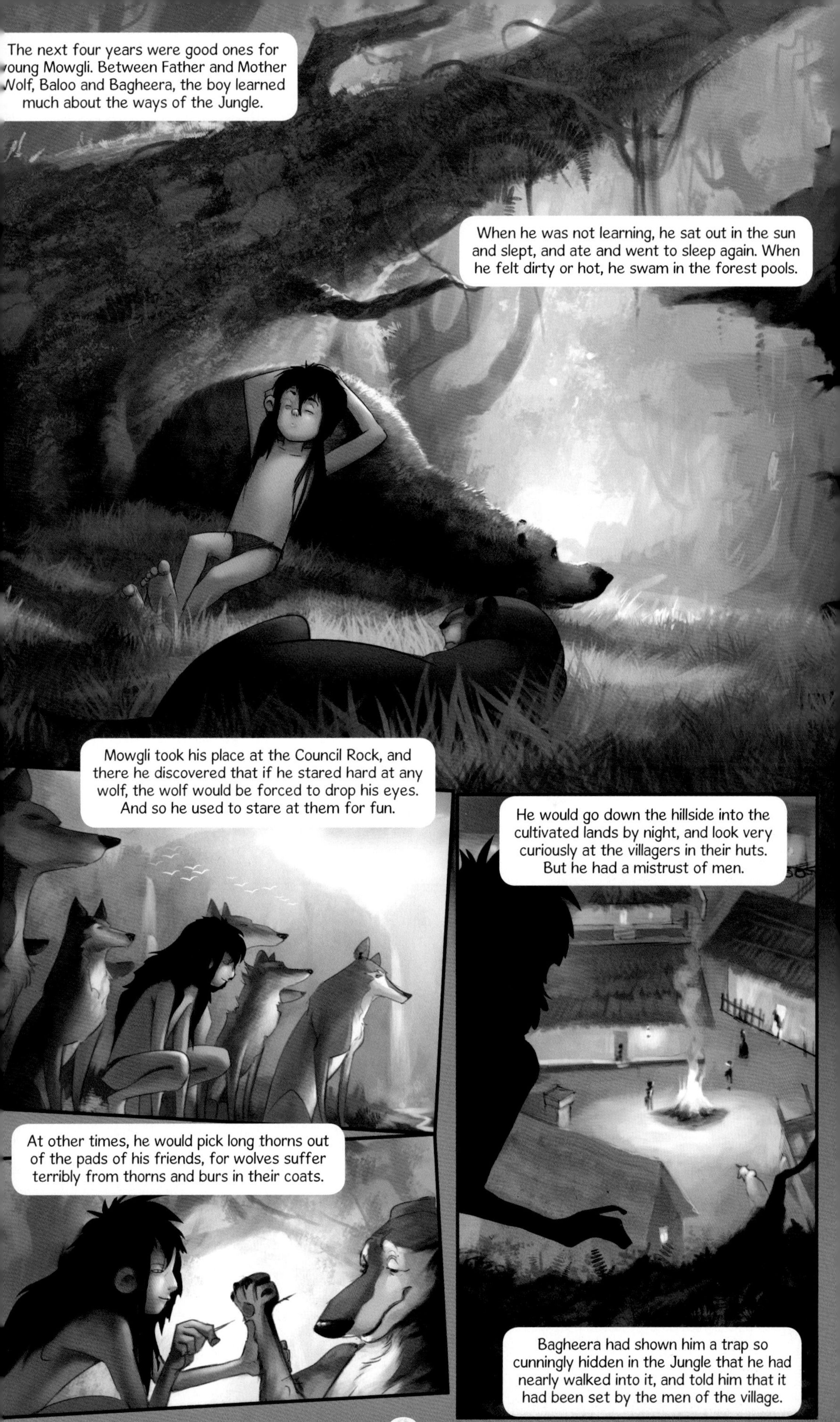

The next four years were good ones for young Mowgli. Between Father and Mother Wolf, Baloo and Bagheera, the boy learned much about the ways of the Jungle.
When he was not learning, he sat out in the sun and slept, and ate and went to sleep again. When he felt dirty or hot, he swam in the forest pools.
Mowgli took his place at the Council Rock, and there he discovered that if he stared hard at any wolf, the wolf would be forced to drop his eyes. And so he used to stare at them for fun.
At other times, he would pick long thorns out of the pads of his friends, for wolves suffer terribly from thorns and burs in their coats.
He would go down the hillside into the cultivated lands by night, and look very curiously at the villagers in their huts. But he had a mistrust of men.
Bagheera had shown him a trap so cunningly hidden in the Jungle that he had nearly walked into it, and told him that it had been set by the men of the village.

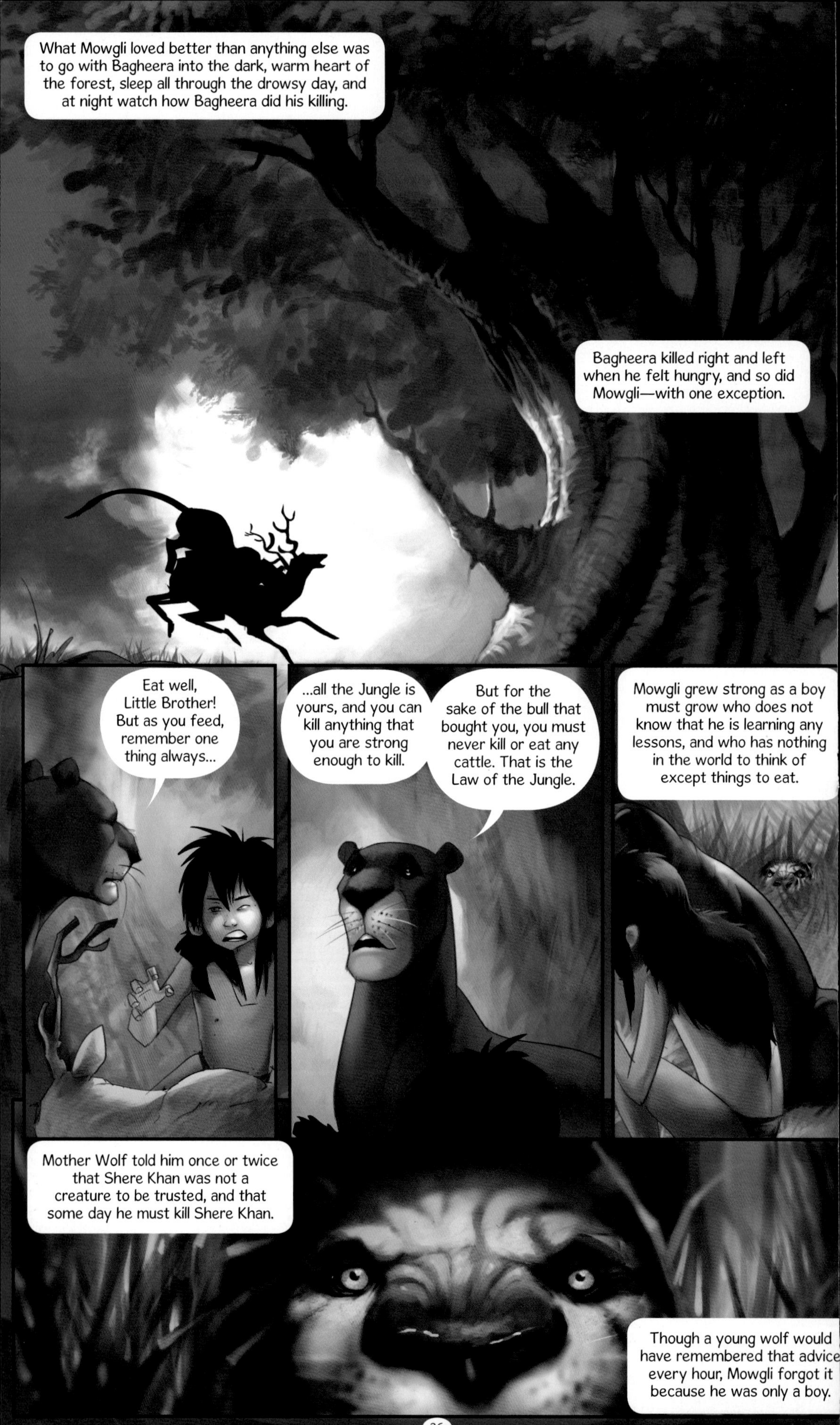
What Mowgli loved better than anything else was to go with Bagheera into the dark, warm heart of the forest, sleep all through the drowsy day, and at night watch how Bagheera did his killing.
Bagheera killed right and left when he felt hungry, and so did Mowgli—with one exception.
Eat well, Little Brother! But as you feed, remember one thing always...
...all the Jungle is yours, and you can kill anything that you are strong enough to kill.
But for the sake of the bull that bought you, you must never kill or eat any cattle. That is the Law of the Jungle.
Mowgli grew strong as a boy must grow who does not know that he is learning any lessons, and who has nothing in the world to think of except things to eat.
Mother Wolf told him once or twice that Shere Khan was not a creature to be trusted, and that some day he must kill Shere Khan.
Though a young wolf would have remembered that advic every hour, Mowgli forgot it because he was only a boy.

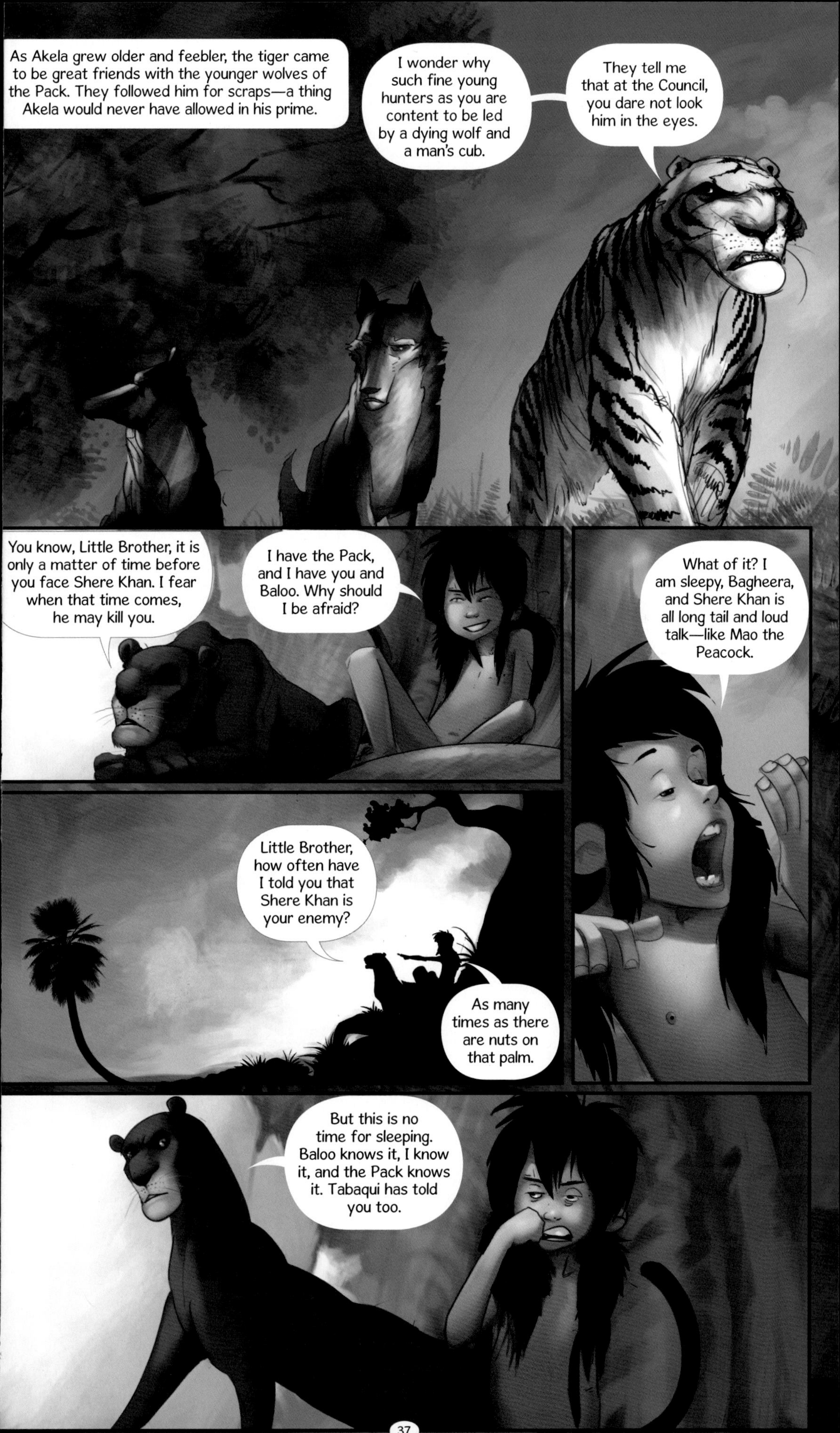

As Akela grew older and feebler, the tiger came to be great friends with the younger wolves of the Pack. They followed him for scraps—a thing Akela would never have allowed in his prime.
I wonder why such fine young hunters as you are content to be led by a dying wolf and a man's cub.
They tell me that at the Council, you dare not look him in the eyes.
You know, Little Brother, it is only a matter of time before you face Shere Khan. I fear when that time comes, he may kill you.
I have the Pack, and I have you and Baloo. Why should I be afraid?
Little Brother, how often have I told you that Shere Khan is your enemy?
As many times as there are nuts on that palm.
What of it? I am sleepy, Bagheera, and Shere Khan is all long tail and loud talk—like Mao the Peacock.
But this is no time for sleeping. Baloo knows it, I know it, and the Pack knows it. Tabaqui has told you too.

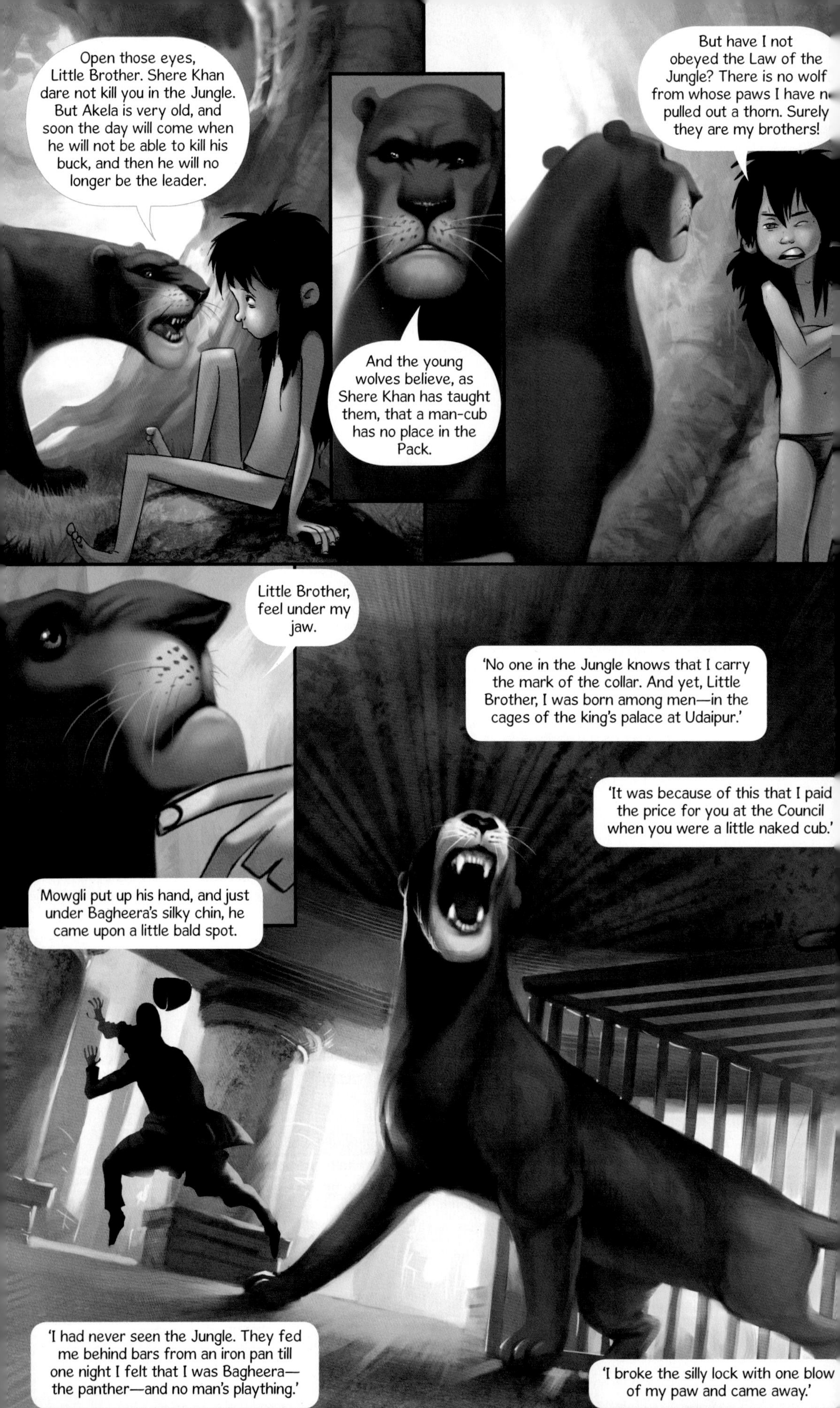
Open those eyes, Little Brother. Shere Khan dare not kill you in the Jungle. But Akela is very old, and soon the day will come when he will not be able to kill his buck, and then he will no longer be the leader.
And the young wolves believe, as Shere Khan has taught them, that a man-cub has no place in the Pack.
But have I not obeyed the Law of the Jungle? There is no wolf from whose paws I have n pulled out a thorn. Surely they are my brothers!
Little Brother, feel under my jaw.
Mowgli put up his hand, and just under Bagheera's silky chin, he came upon a little bald spot.
'No one in the Jungle knows that I carry the mark of the collar. And yet, Little Brother, I was born among men—in the cages of the king's palace at Udaipur.'
'It was because of this that I paid the price for you at the Council when you were a little naked cub.'
'I had never seen the Jungle. They fed me behind bars from an iron pan till one night I felt that I was Bagheera—the panther—and no man's plaything.'
'I broke the silly lock with one blow of my paw and came away.'

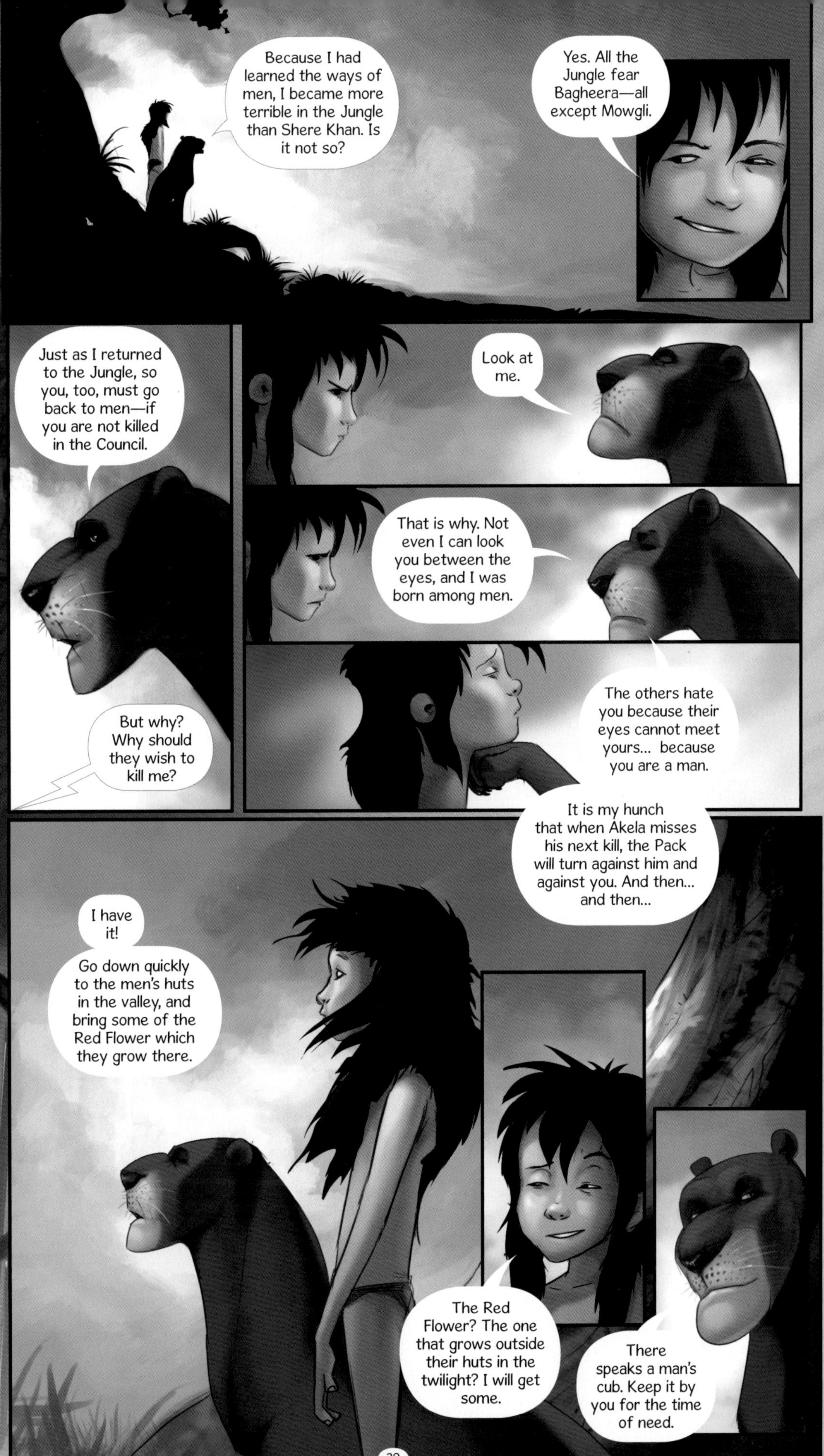

Because I had learned the ways of men, I became more terrible in the Jungle than Shere Khan. Is it not so?
Yes. All the Jungle fear Bagheera—all except Mowgli.
Just as I returned to the Jungle, so you, too, must go back to men—if you are not killed in the Council.
But why? Why should they wish to kill me?
Look at me.
That is why. Not even I can look you between the eyes, and I was born among men.
The others hate you because their eyes cannot meet yours... because you are a man.
It is my hunch that when Akela misses his next kill, the Pack will turn against him and against you. And then... and then...
I have it!
Go down quickly to the men's huts in the valley, and bring some of the Red Flower which they grow there.
The Red Flower? The one that grows outside their huts in the twilight? I will get some.
There speaks a man's cub. Keep it by you for the time of need.

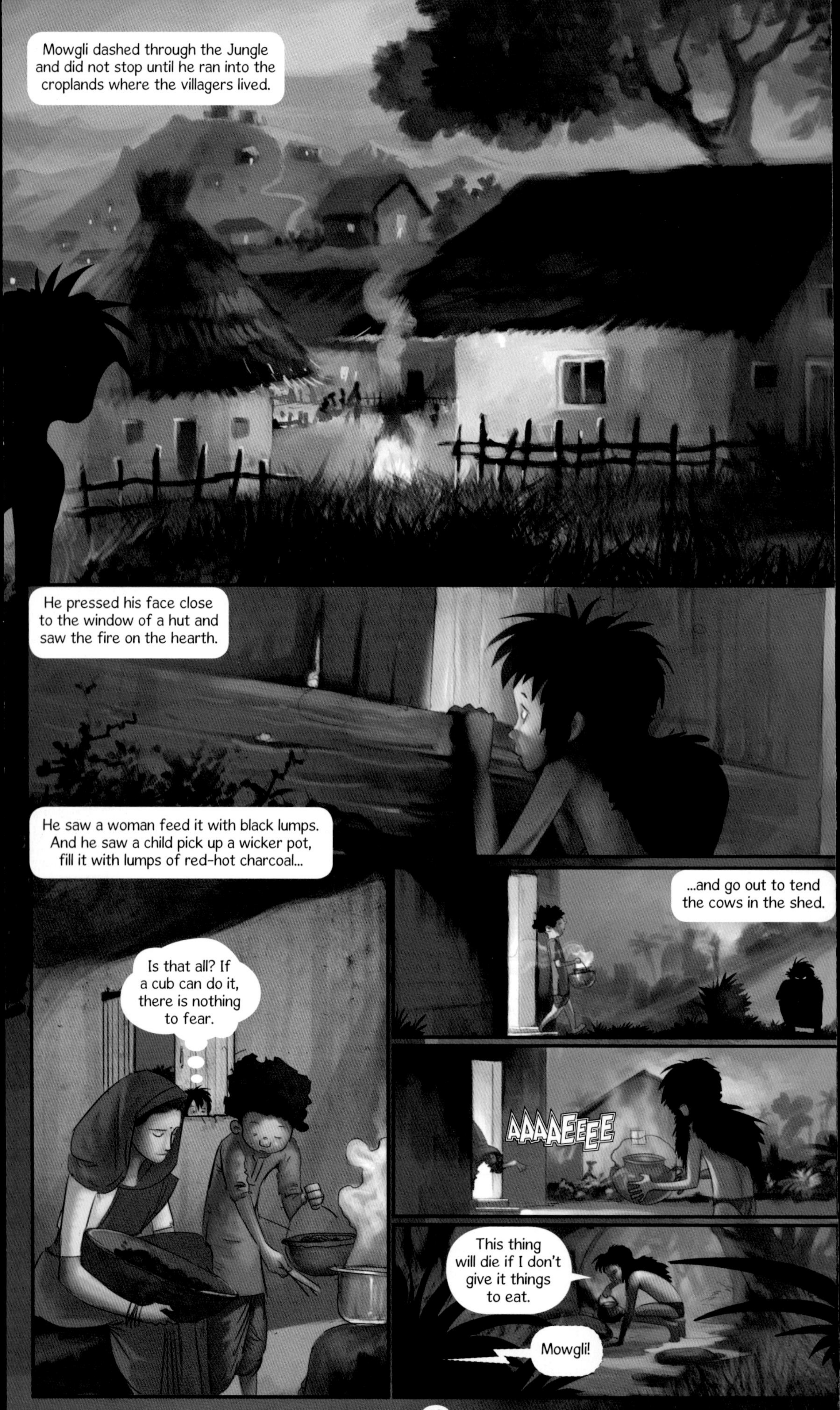
Mowgli dashed through the Jungle and did not stop until he ran into the croplands where the villagers lived.
He pressed his face close to the window of a hut and saw the fire on the hearth.
He saw a woman feed it with black lumps. And he saw a child pick up a wicker pot, fill it with lumps of red-hot charcoal...
Is that all? If a cub can do it, there is nothing to fear.
...and go out to tend the cows in the shed.
AAAAEEEE
This thing will die if I don't give it things to eat.
Mowgli!

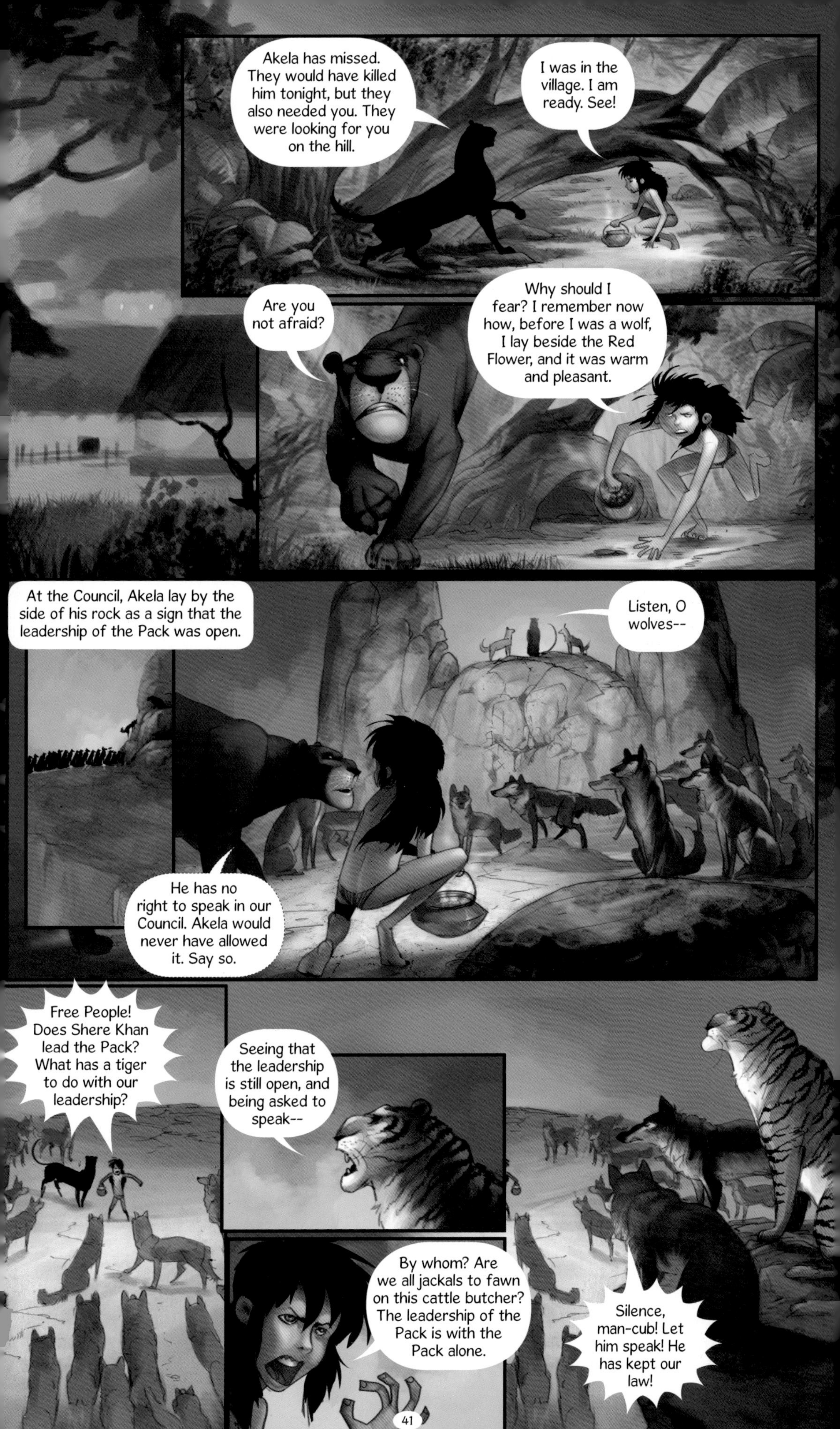
Akela has missed. They would have killed him tonight, but they also needed you. They were looking for you on the hill.
I was in the village. I am ready. See!
Are you not afraid?
Why should I fear? I remember now how, before I was a wolf, I lay beside the Red Flower, and it was warm and pleasant.
At the Council, Akela lay by the side of his rock as a sign that the leadership of the Pack was open.
Listen, O wolves--
He has no right to speak in our Council. Akela would never have allowed it. Say so.
Free People! Does Shere Khan lead the Pack? What has a tiger to do with our leadership?
Seeing that the leadership is still open, and being asked to speak--
By whom? Are we all jackals to fawn on this cattle butcher? The leadership of the Pack is with the Pack alone.
Silence, man-cub! Let him speak! He has kept our law!

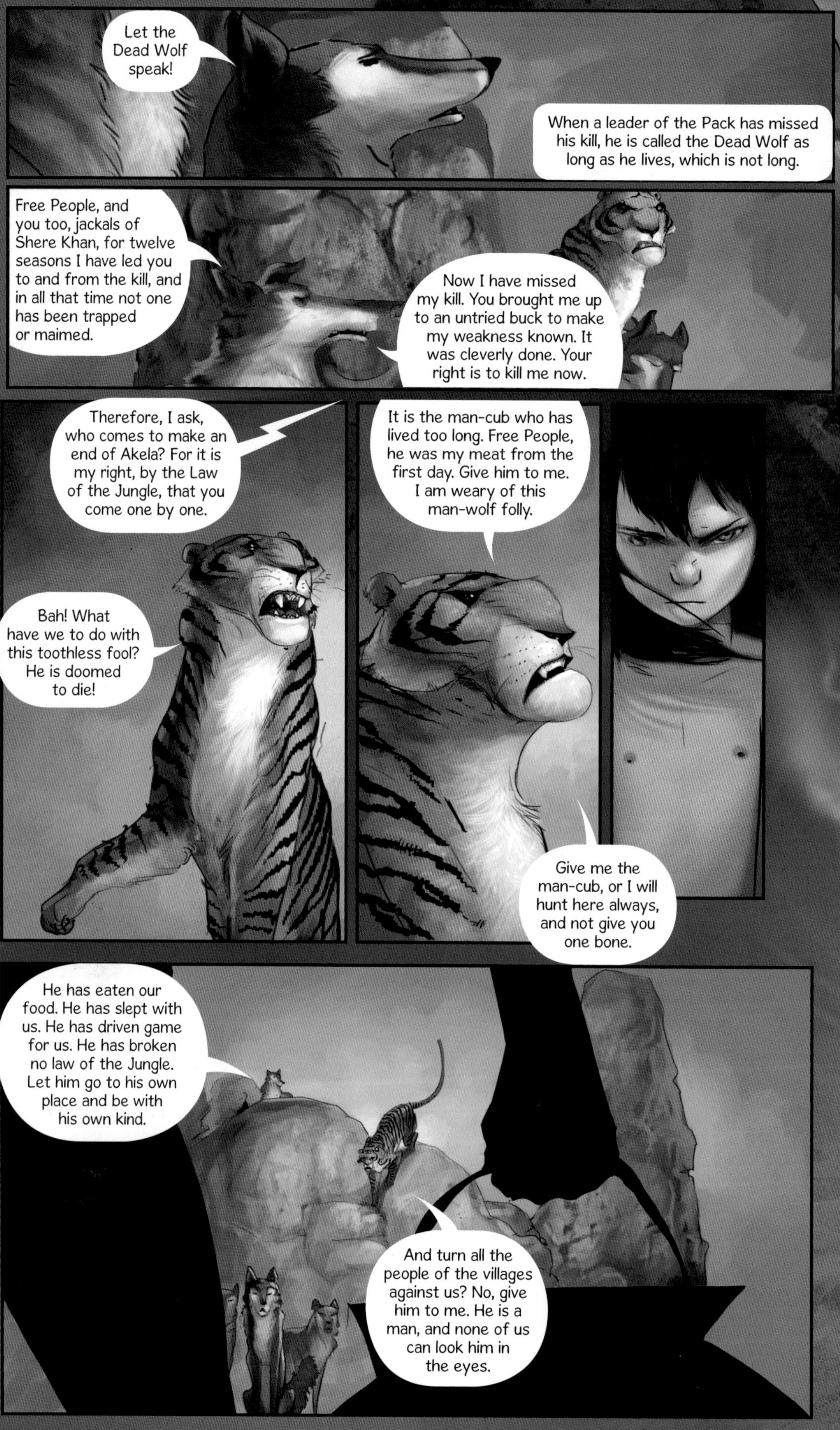
Let the Dead Wolf speak!
When a leader of the Pack has missed his kill, he is called the Dead Wolf as long as he lives, which is not long.
Free People, and you too, jackals of Shere Khan, for twelve seasons I have led you to and from the kill, and in all that time not one has been trapped or maimed.
Now I have missed my kill. You brought me up to an untried buck to make my weakness known. It was cleverly done. Your right is to kill me now.
Therefore, I ask, who comes to make an end of Akela? For it is my right, by the Law of the Jungle, that you come one by one.
Bah! What have we to do with this toothless fool? He is doomed to die!
It is the man-cub who has lived too long. Free People, he was my meat from the first day. Give him to me. I am weary of this man-wolf folly.
Give me the man-cub, or I will hunt here always, and not give you one bone.
He has eaten our food. He has slept with us. He has driven game for us. He has broken no law of the Jungle. Let him go to his own place and be with his own kind.
And turn all the people of the villages against us? No, give him to me. He is a man, and none of us can look him in the eyes.

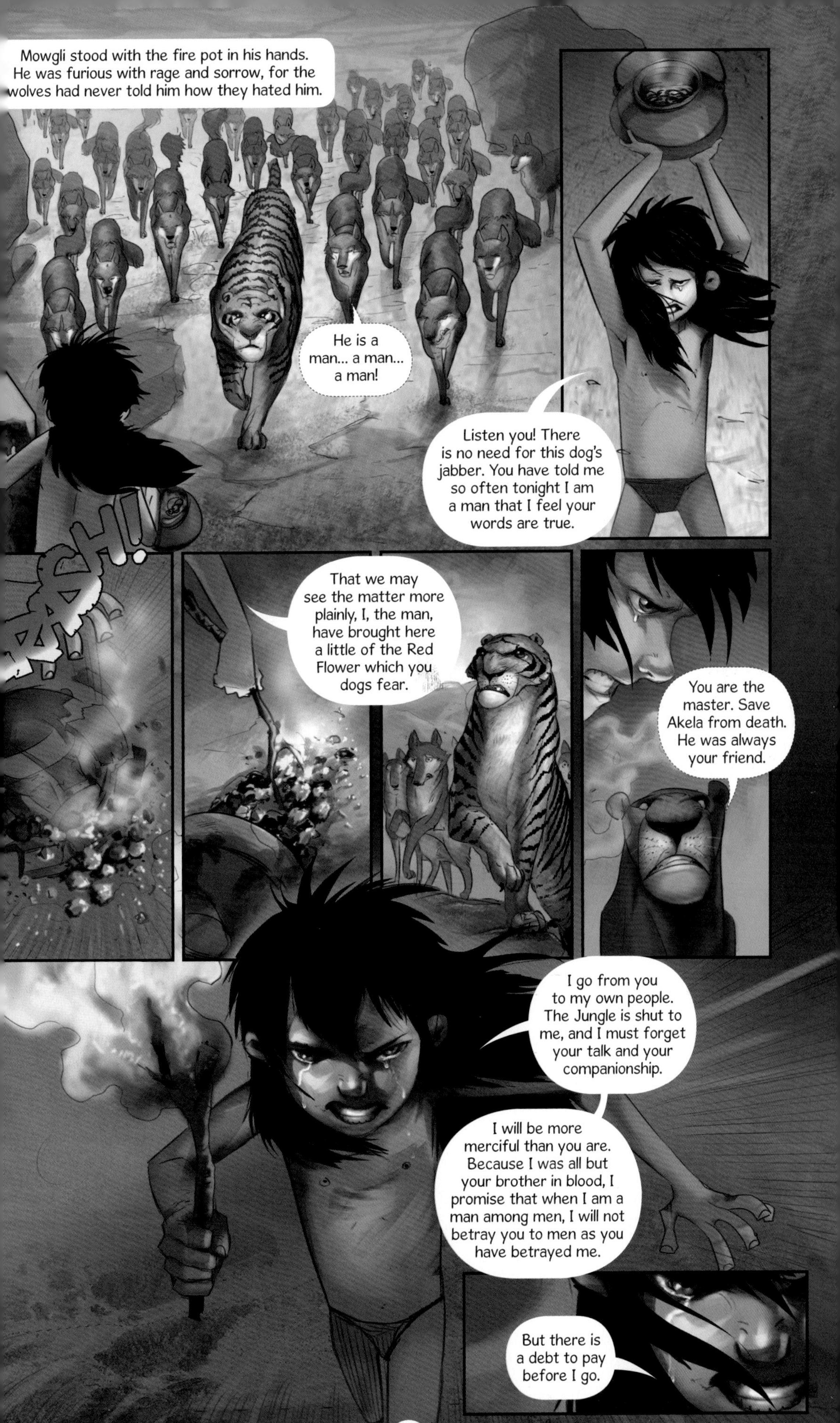

Mowgli stood with the fire pot in his hands. He was furious with rage and sorrow, for the wolves had never told him how they hated him.
He is a man... a man... a man!
Listen you! There is no need for this dog's jabber. You have told me so often tonight I am a man that I feel your words are true.
That we may see the matter more plainly, I, the man, have brought here a little of the Red Flower which you dogs fear.
You are the master. Save Akela from death. He was always your friend.
I go from you to my own people. The Jungle is shut to me, and I must forget your talk and your companionship.
I will be more merciful than you are. Because I was all but your brother in blood, I promise that when I am a man among men, I will not betray you to men as you have betrayed me.
But there is a debt to pay before I go.

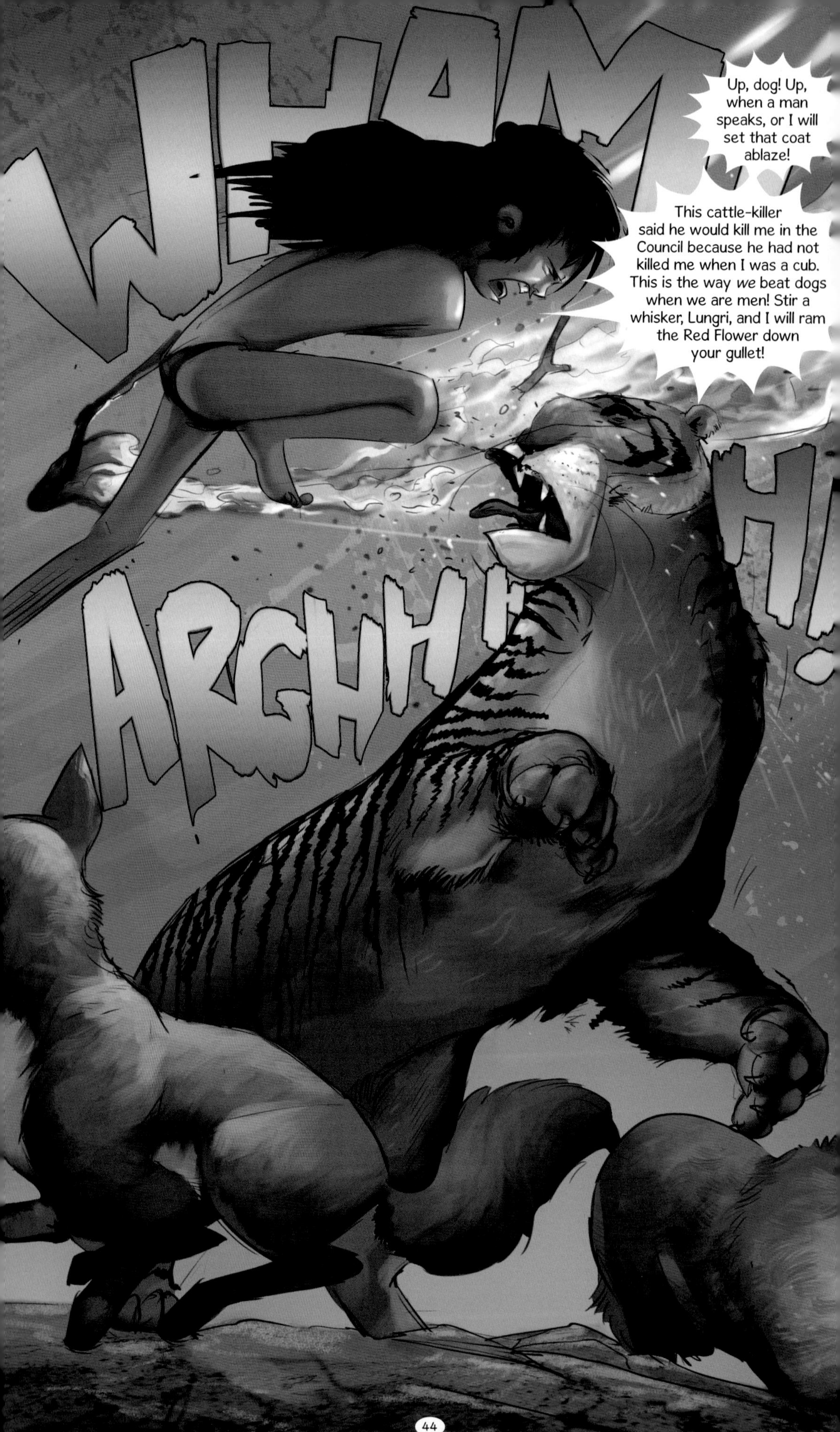
WHAM
Up, dog! Up, when a man speaks, or I will set that coat ablaze!
This cattle-killer said he would kill me in the Council because he had not killed me when I was a cub. This is the way *we* beat dogs when we are men! Stir a whisker, Lungri, and I will ram the Red Flower down your gullet!
ARGHH!!

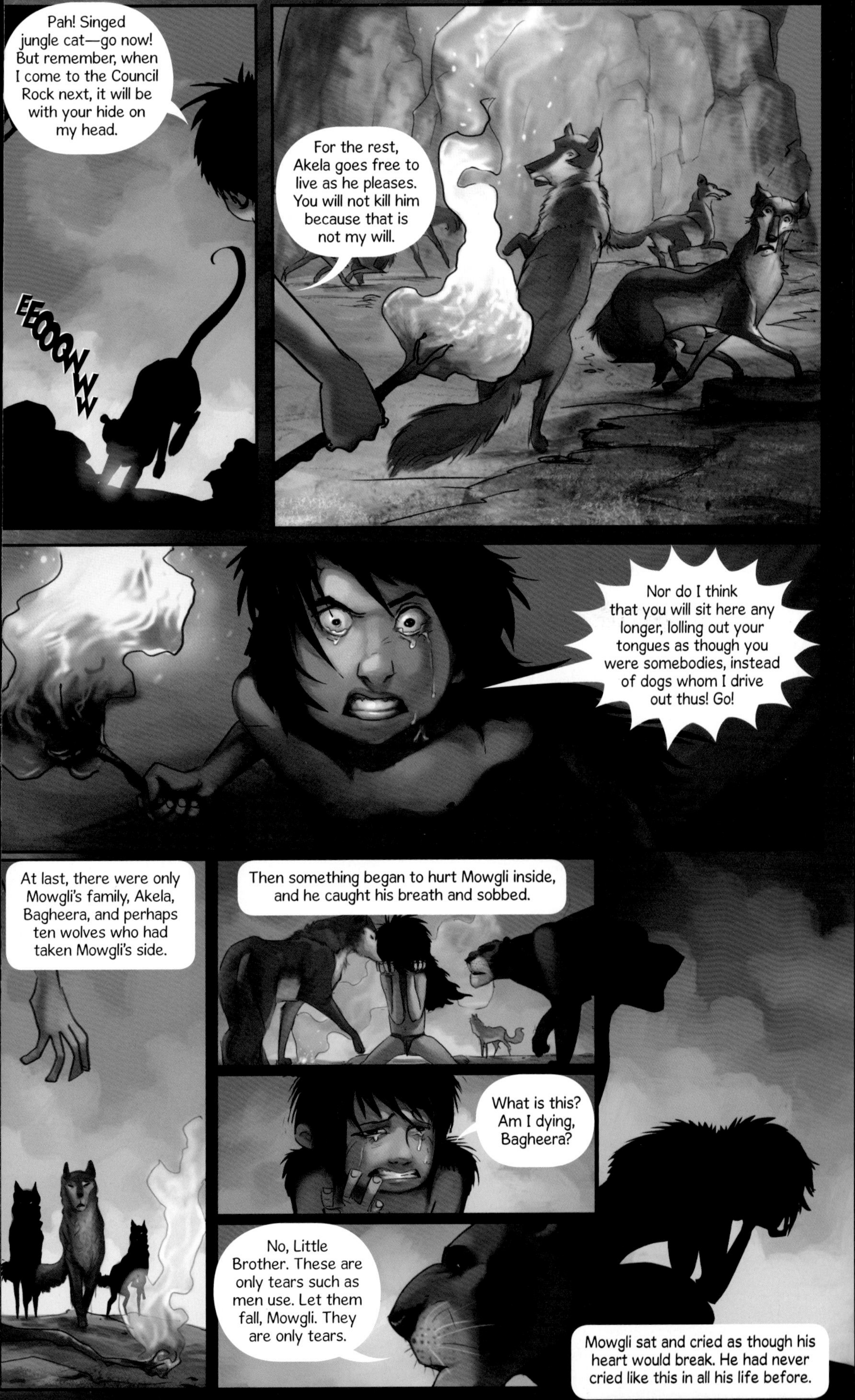
Pah! Singed jungle cat—go now! But remember, when I come to the Council Rock next, it will be with your hide on my head.
EEOOOWWW
For the rest, Akela goes free to live as he pleases. You will not kill him because that is not my will.
Nor do I think that you will sit here any longer, lolling out your tongues as though you were somebodies, instead of dogs whom I drive out thus! Go!
At last, there were only Mowgli's family, Akela, Bagheera, and perhaps ten wolves who had taken Mowgli's side.
Then something began to hurt Mowgli inside, and he caught his breath and sobbed.
What is this? Am I dying, Bagheera?
No, Little Brother. These are only tears such as men use. Let them fall, Mowgli. They are only tears.
Mowgli sat and cried as though his heart would break. He had never cried like this in all his life before.

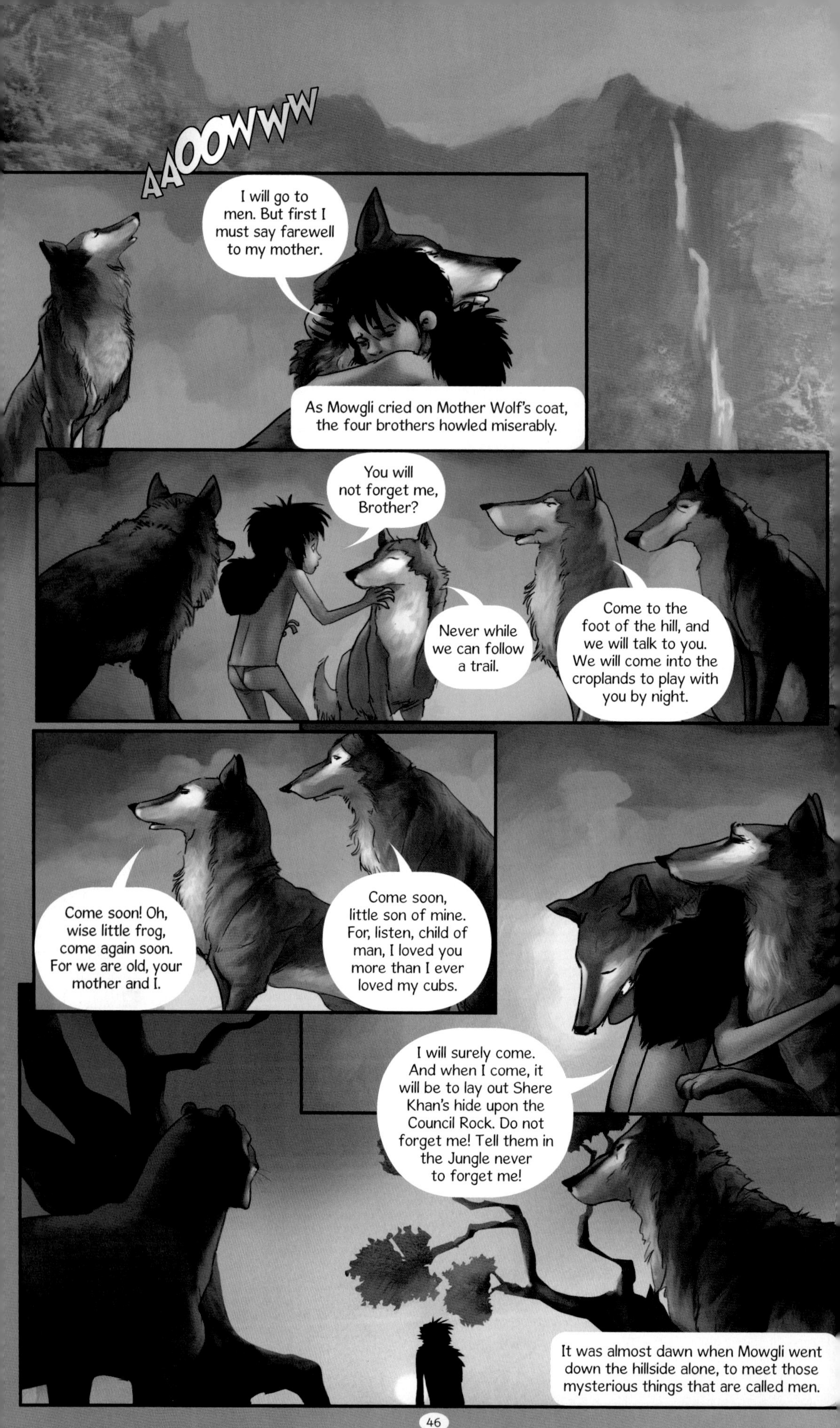

AAOOWWW
I will go to men. But first I must say farewell to my mother.
As Mowgli cried on Mother Wolf's coat, the four brothers howled miserably.
You will not forget me, Brother?
Never while we can follow a trail.
Come to the foot of the hill, and we will talk to you. We will come into the croplands to play with you by night.
Come soon! Oh, wise little frog, come again soon. For we are old, your mother and I.
Come soon, little son of mine. For, listen, child of man, I loved you more than I ever loved my cubs.
I will surely come. And when I come, it will be to lay out Shere Khan's hide upon the Council Rock. Do not forget me! Tell them in the Jungle never to forget me!
It was almost dawn when Mowgli went down the hillside alone, to meet those mysterious things that are called men.

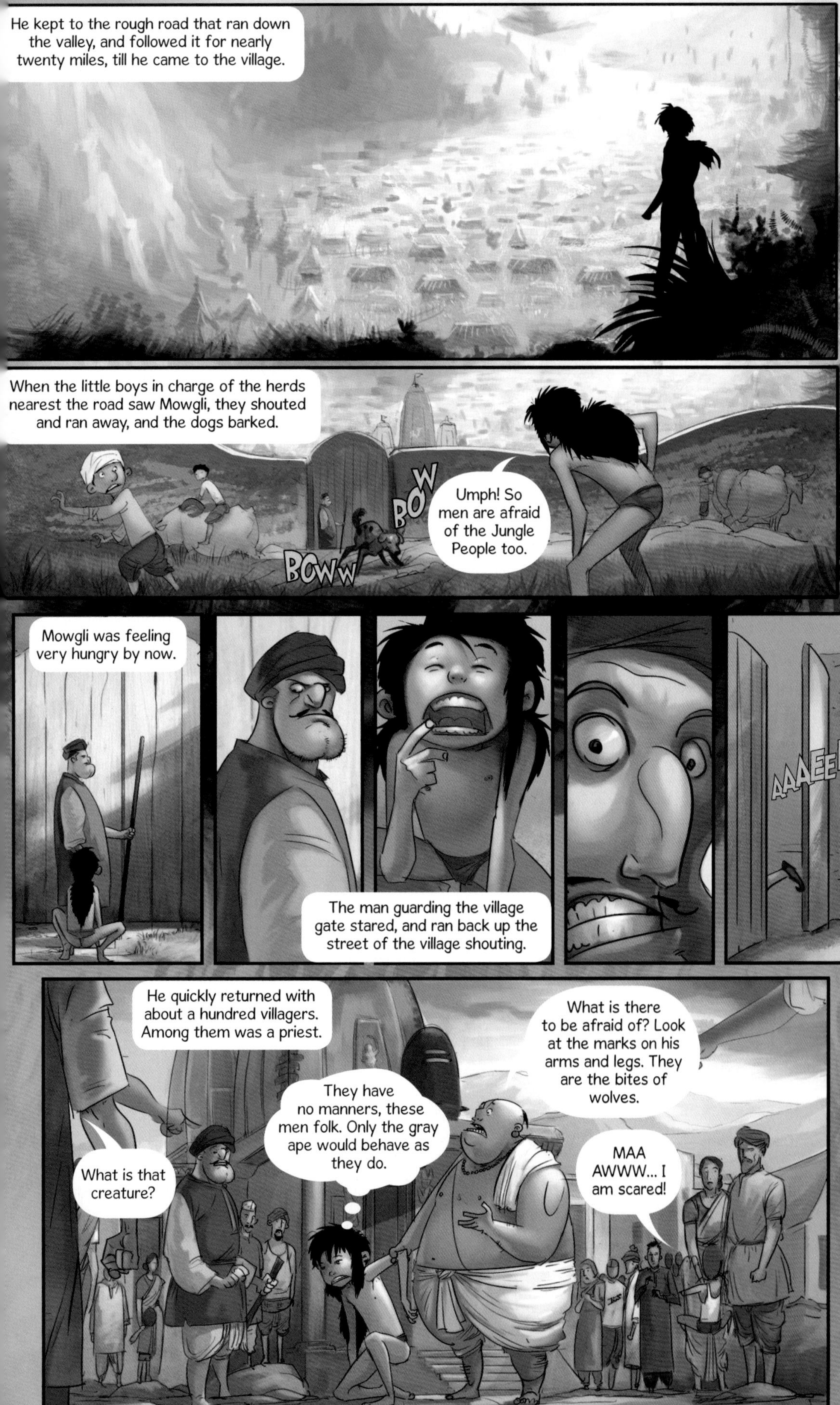
He kept to the rough road that ran down the valley, and followed it for nearly twenty miles, till he came to the village.
When the little boys in charge of the herds nearest the road saw Mowgli, they shouted and ran away, and the dogs barked.
BOW
BOWW
Umph! So men are afraid of the Jungle People too.
Mowgli was feeling very hungry by now.
The man guarding the village gate stared, and ran back up the street of the village shouting.
AAAEEE
He quickly returned with about a hundred villagers. Among them was a priest.
What is that creature?
They have no manners, these men folk. Only the gray ape would behave as they do.
What is there to be afraid of? Look at the marks on his arms and legs. They are the bites of wolves.
MAA AWWW... I am scared!

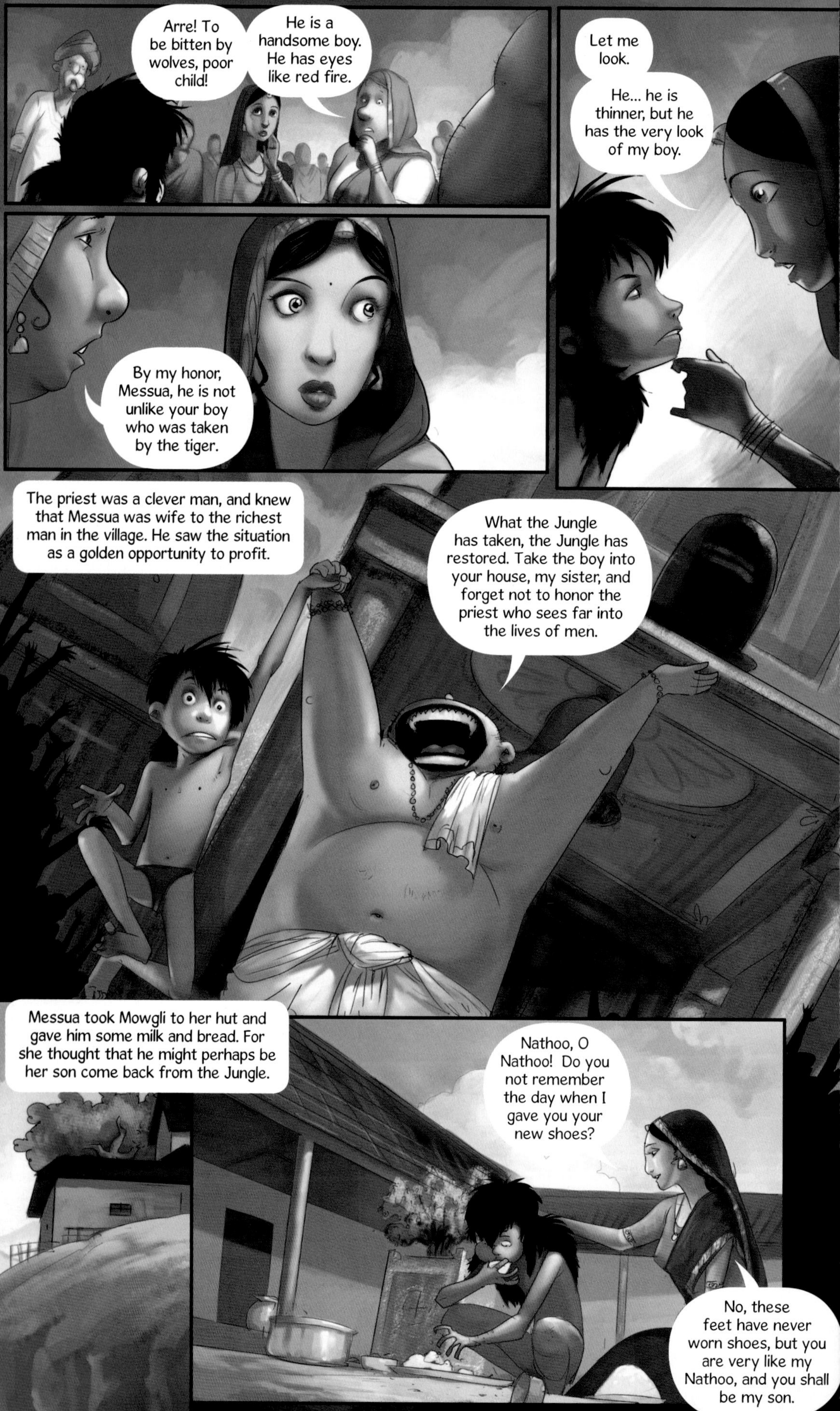
Arre! To be bitten by wolves, poor child!
He is a handsome boy. He has eyes like red fire.
By my honor, Messua, he is not unlike your boy who was taken by the tiger.
Let me look.
He... he is thinner, but he has the very look of my boy.
The priest was a clever man, and knew that Messua was wife to the richest man in the village. He saw the situation as a golden opportunity to profit.
What the Jungle has taken, the Jungle has restored. Take the boy into your house, my sister, and forget not to honor the priest who sees far into the lives of men.
Messua took Mowgli to her hut and gave him some milk and bread. For she thought that he might perhaps be her son come back from the Jungle.
Nathoo, O Nathoo! Do you not remember the day when I gave you your new shoes?
No, these feet have never worn shoes, but you are very like my Nathoo, and you shall be my son.

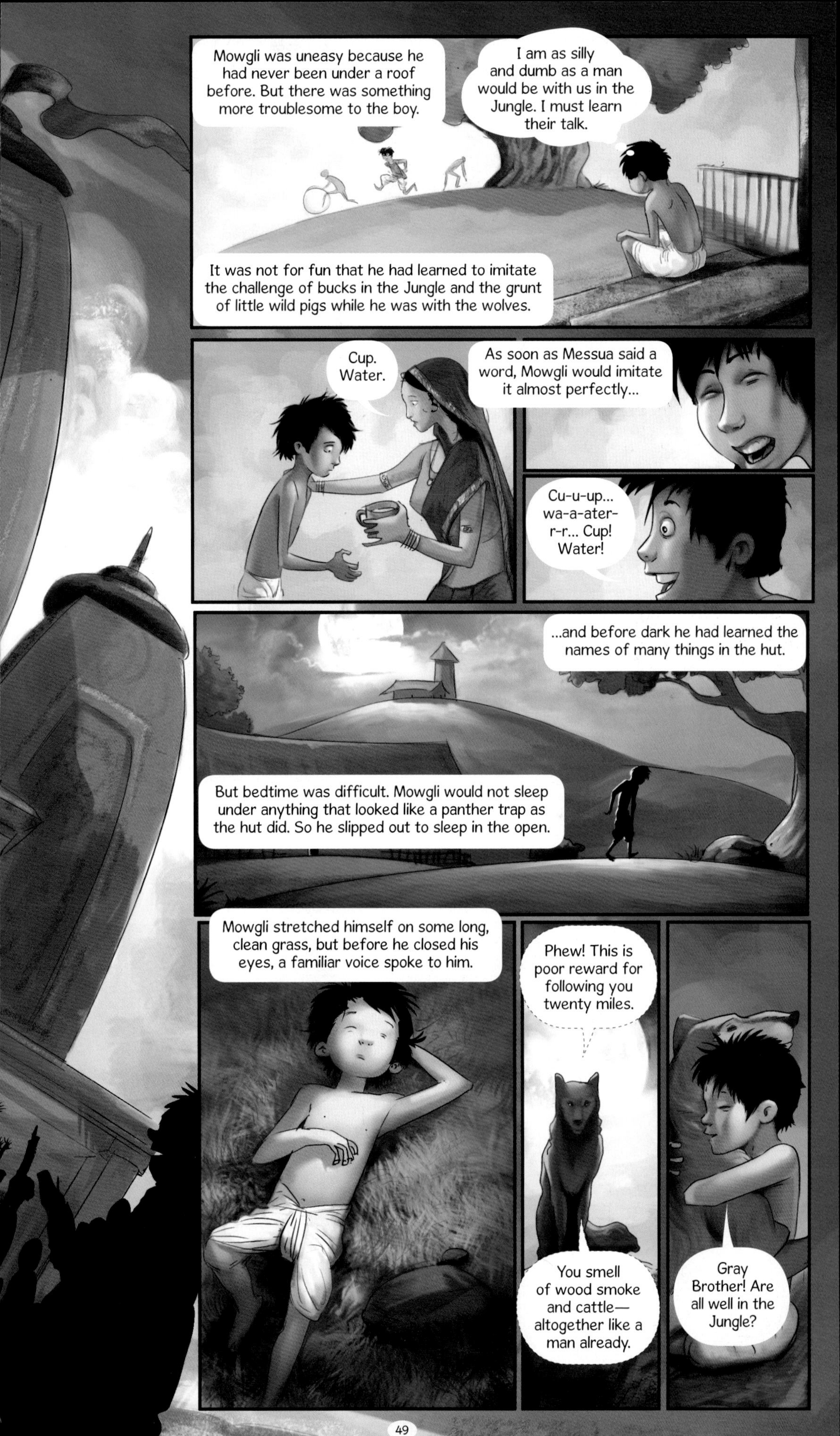
Mowgli was uneasy because he had never been under a roof before. But there was something more troublesome to the boy.
I am as silly and dumb as a man would be with us in the Jungle. I must learn their talk.
It was not for fun that he had learned to imitate the challenge of bucks in the Jungle and the grunt of little wild pigs while he was with the wolves.
Cup. Water.
As soon as Messua said a word, Mowgli would imitate it almost perfectly...
Cu-u-up... wa-a-ater-r-r... Cup! Water!
...and before dark he had learned the names of many things in the hut.
But bedtime was difficult. Mowgli would not sleep under anything that looked like a panther trap as the hut did. So he slipped out to sleep in the open.
Mowgli stretched himself on some long, clean grass, but before he closed his eyes, a familiar voice spoke to him.
Phew! This is poor reward for following you twenty miles.
You smell of wood smoke and cattle— altogether like a man already.
Gray Brother! Are all well in the Jungle?

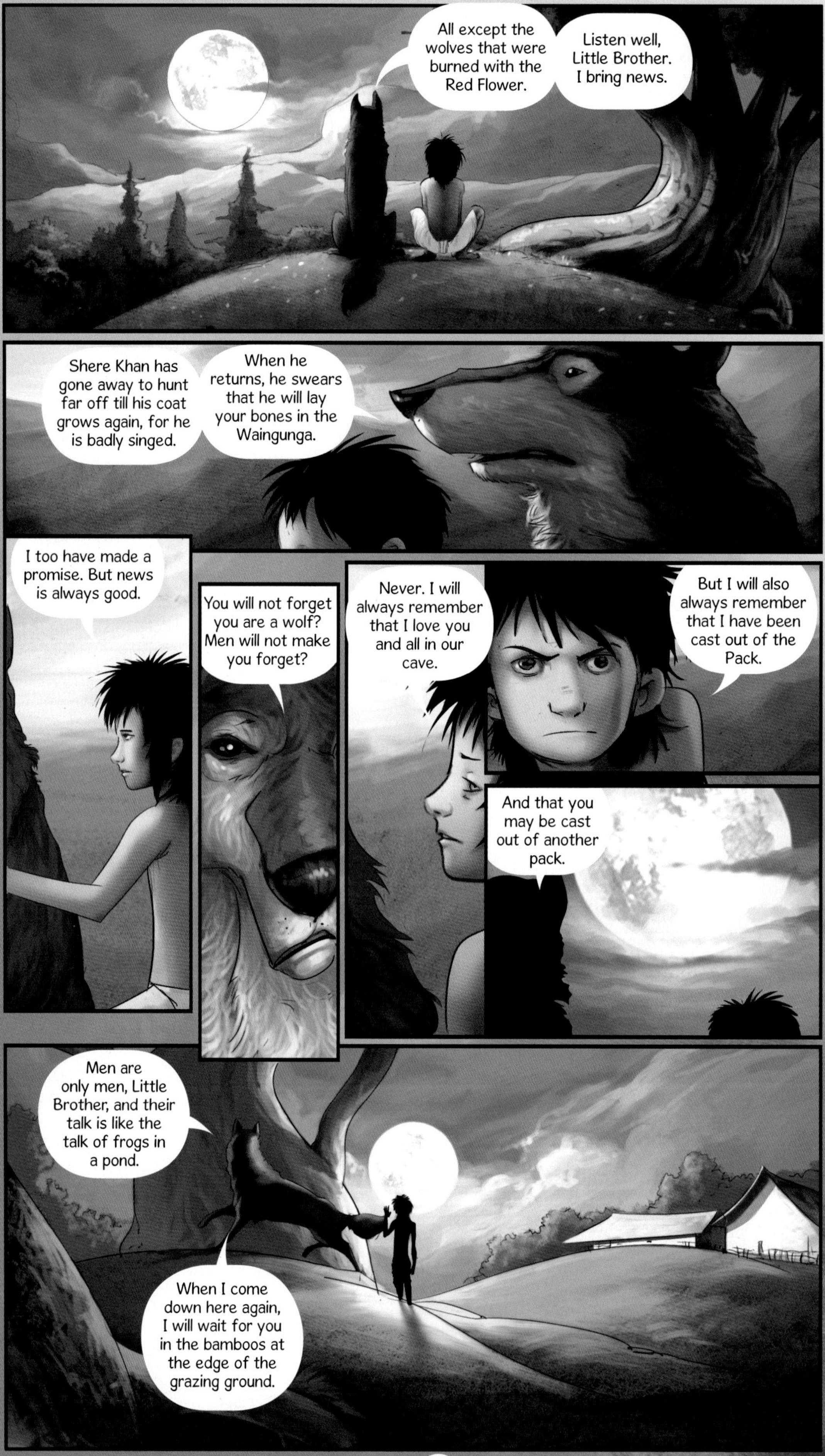
All except the wolves that were burned with the Red Flower.
Listen well, Little Brother. I bring news.
Shere Khan has gone away to hunt far off till his coat grows again, for he is badly singed.
When he returns, he swears that he will lay your bones in the Waingunga.
I too have made a promise. But news is always good.
You will not forget you are a wolf? Men will not make you forget?
Never. I will always remember that I love you and all in our cave.
But I will also always remember that I have been cast out of the Pack.
And that you may be cast out of another pack.
Men are only men, Little Brother, and their talk is like the talk of frogs in a pond.
When I come down here again, I will wait for you in the bamboos at the edge of the grazing ground.

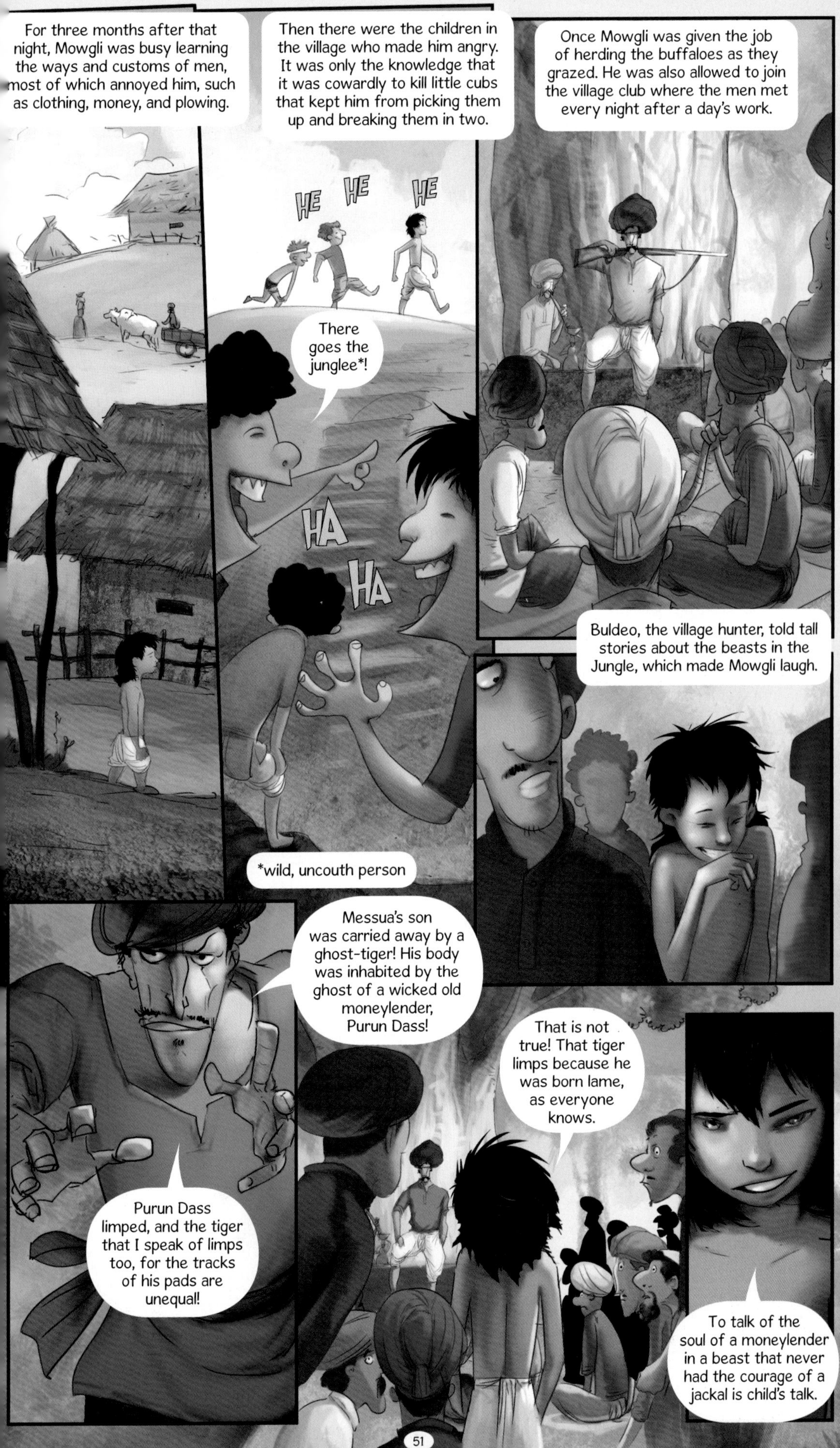
For three months after that night, Mowgli was busy learning the ways and customs of men, most of which annoyed him, such as clothing, money, and plowing.
Then there were the children in the village who made him angry. It was only the knowledge that it was cowardly to kill little cubs that kept him from picking them up and breaking them in two.
HE HE HE
There goes the junglee*!
HA HA
*wild, uncouth person
Once Mowgli was given the job of herding the buffaloes as they grazed. He was also allowed to join the village club where the men met every night after a day's work.
Buldeo, the village hunter, told tall stories about the beasts in the Jungle, which made Mowgli laugh.
Messua's son was carried away by a ghost-tiger! His body was inhabited by the ghost of a wicked old moneylender, Purun Dass!
Purun Dass limped, and the tiger that I speak of limps too, for the tracks of his pads are unequal!
That is not true! That tiger limps because he was born lame, as everyone knows.
To talk of the soul of a moneylender in a beast that never had the courage of a jackal is child's talk.

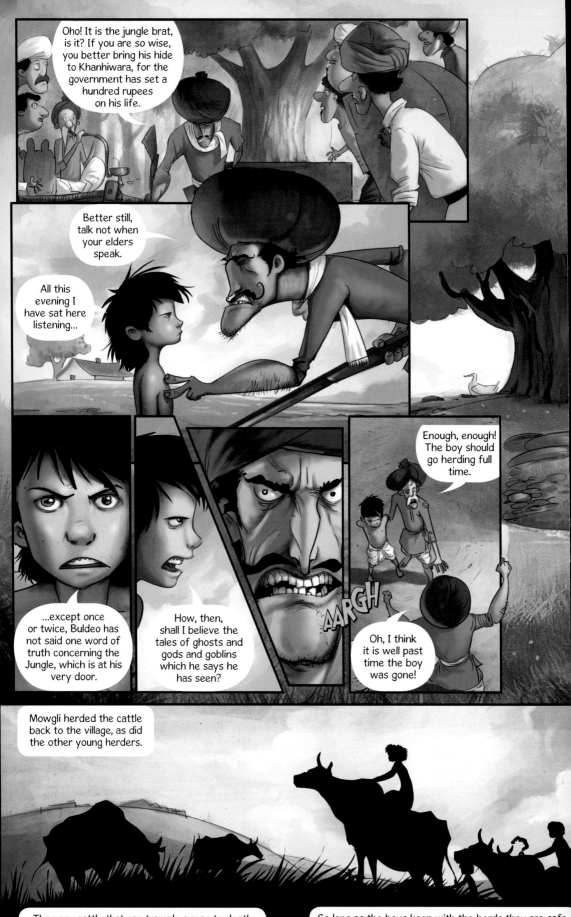

Oho! It is the jungle brat, is it? If you are so wise, you better bring his hide to Khanhiwara, for the government has set a hundred rupees on his life.

Better still, talk not when your elders speak.

All this evening I have sat here listening...

...except once or twice, Buldeo has not said one word of truth concerning the Jungle, which is at his very door.

How, then, shall I believe the tales of ghosts and gods and goblins which he says he has seen?

AARGH

Enough, enough! The boy should go herding full time.

Oh, I think it is well past time the boy was gone!

Mowgli herded the cattle back to the village, as did the other young herders.

The very cattle that can trample a man to death allow themselves to be banged and shouted at by children who hardly come up to their noses.

So long as the boys keep with the herds they are safe, for not even the tiger will charge a mob of cattle. But if they fall behind, they are sometimes carried off.

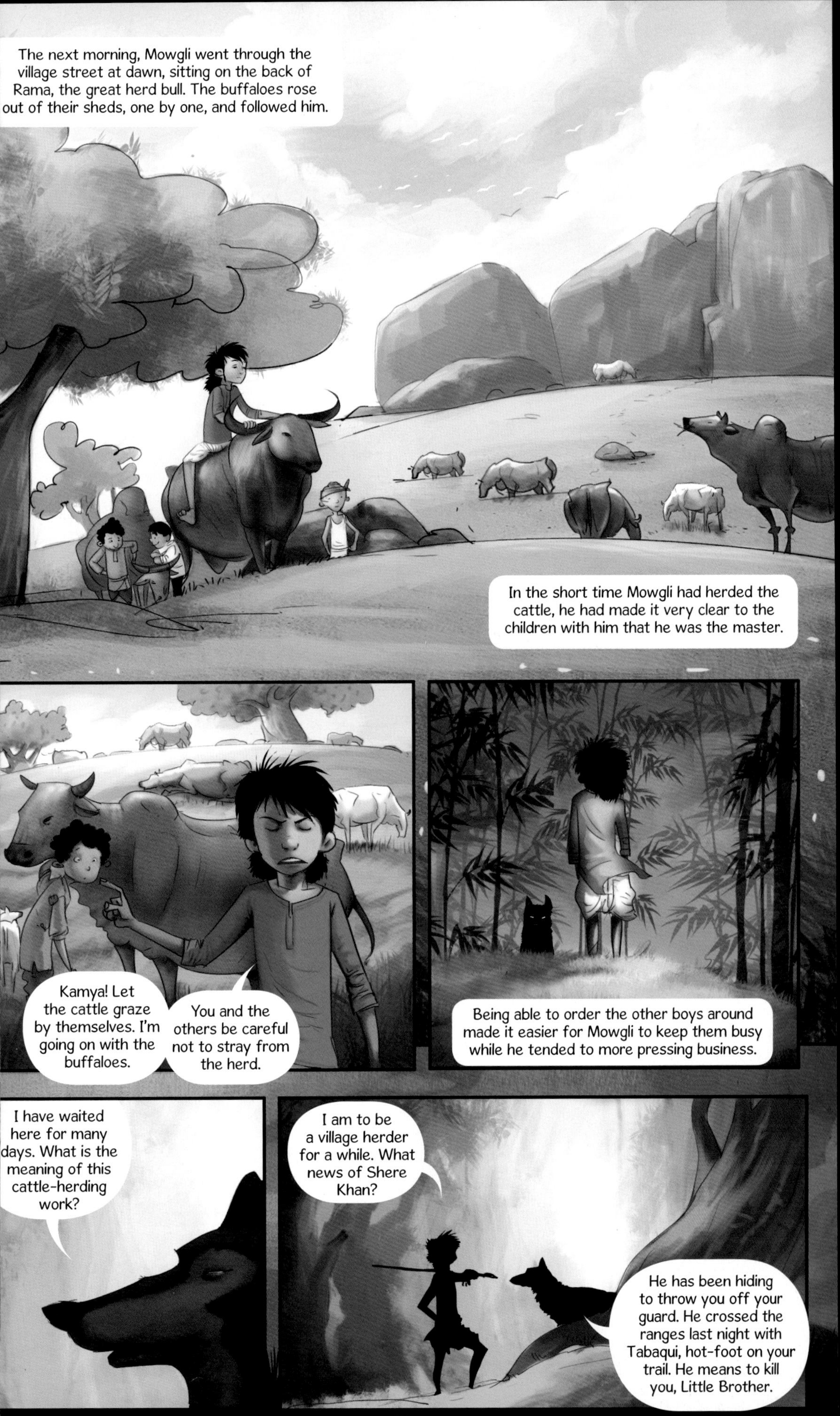
The next morning, Mowgli went through the village street at dawn, sitting on the back of Rama, the great herd bull. The buffaloes rose out of their sheds, one by one, and followed him.
In the short time Mowgli had herded the cattle, he had made it very clear to the children with him that he was the master.
Kamya! Let the cattle graze by themselves. I'm going on with the buffaloes.
You and the others be careful not to stray from the herd.
Being able to order the other boys around made it easier for Mowgli to keep them busy while he tended to more pressing business.
I have waited here for many days. What is the meaning of this cattle-herding work?
I am to be a village herder for a while. What news of Shere Khan?
He has been hiding to throw you off your guard. He crossed the ranges last night with Tabaqui, hot-foot on your trail. He means to kill you, Little Brother.

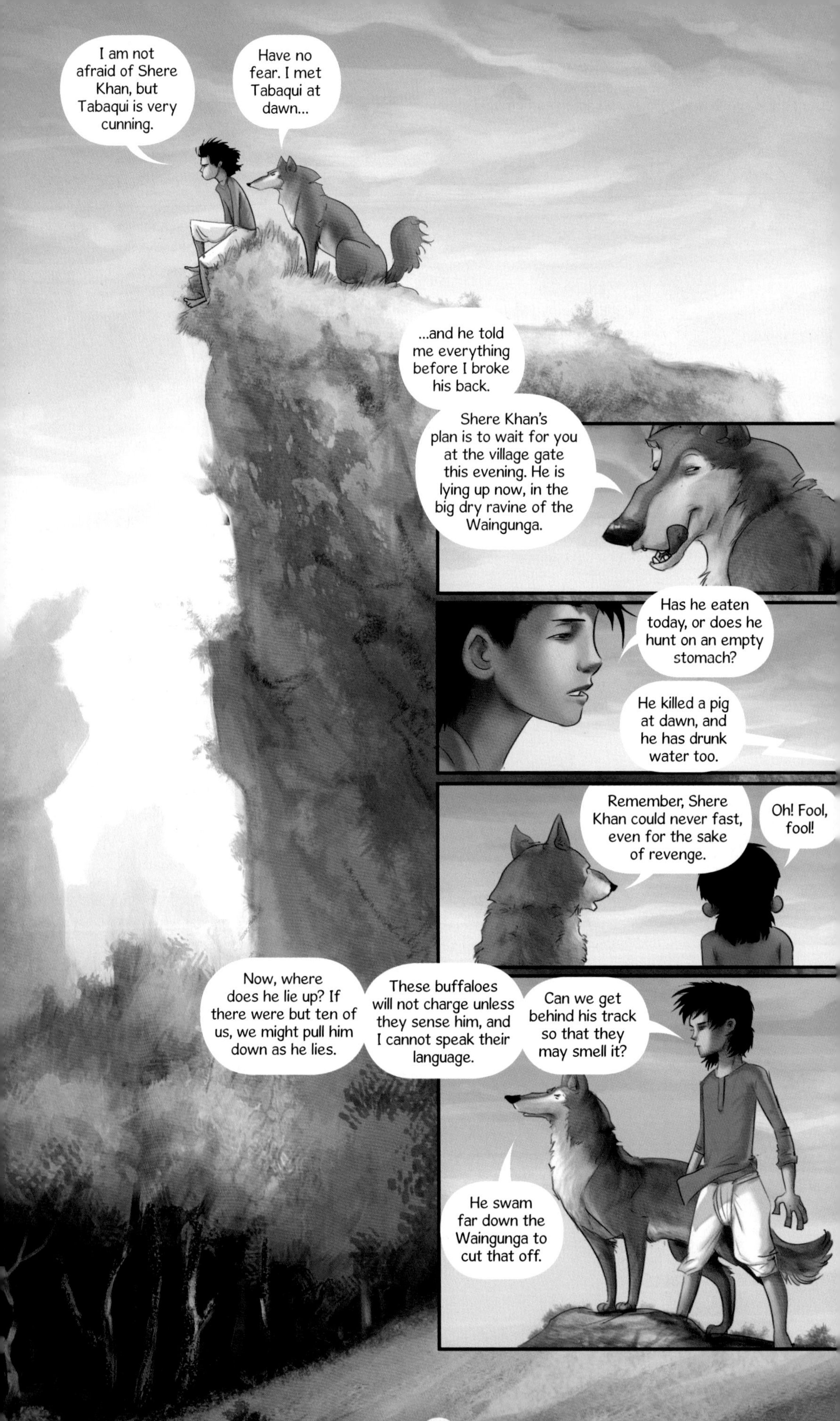

I am not afraid of Shere Khan, but Tabaqui is very cunning.
Have no fear. I met Tabaqui at dawn...
...and he told me everything before I broke his back.
Shere Khan's plan is to wait for you at the village gate this evening. He is lying up now, in the big dry ravine of the Waingunga.
Has he eaten today, or does he hunt on an empty stomach?
He killed a pig at dawn, and he has drunk water too.
Remember, Shere Khan could never fast, even for the sake of revenge.
Oh! Fool, fool!
Now, where does he lie up? If there were but ten of us, we might pull him down as he lies.
These buffaloes will not charge unless they sense him, and I cannot speak their language.
Can we get behind his track so that they may smell it?
He swam far down the Waingunga to cut that off.

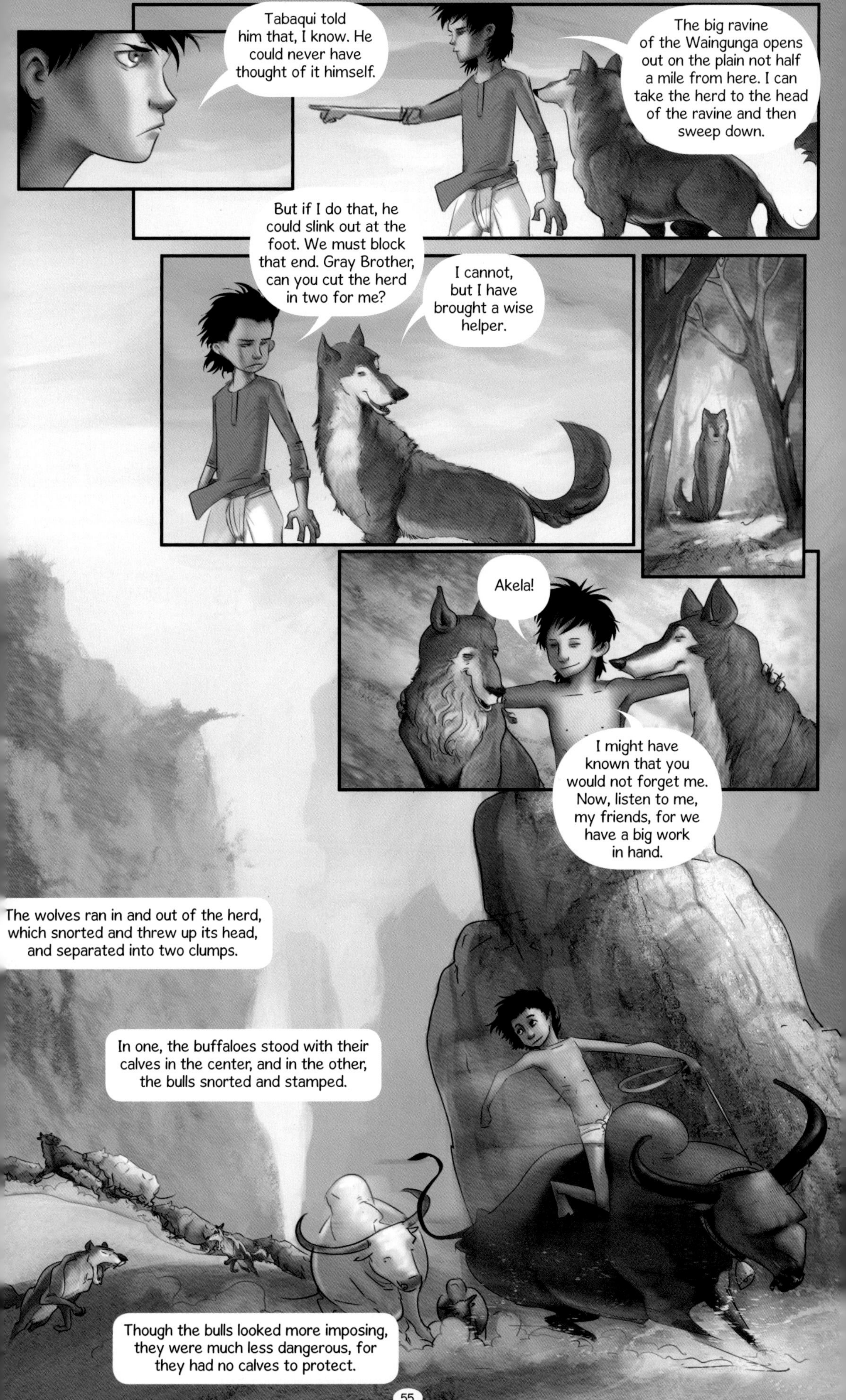

Tabaqui told him that, I know. He could never have thought of it himself.
The big ravine of the Waingunga opens out on the plain not half a mile from here. I can take the herd to the head of the ravine and then sweep down.
But if I do that, he could slink out at the foot. We must block that end. Gray Brother, can you cut the herd in two for me?
I cannot, but I have brought a wise helper.
Akela!
I might have known that you would not forget me. Now, listen to me, my friends, for we have a big work in hand.
The wolves ran in and out of the herd, which snorted and threw up its head, and separated into two clumps.
In one, the buffaloes stood with their calves in the center, and in the other, the bulls snorted and stamped.
Though the bulls looked more imposing, they were much less dangerous, for they had no calves to protect.

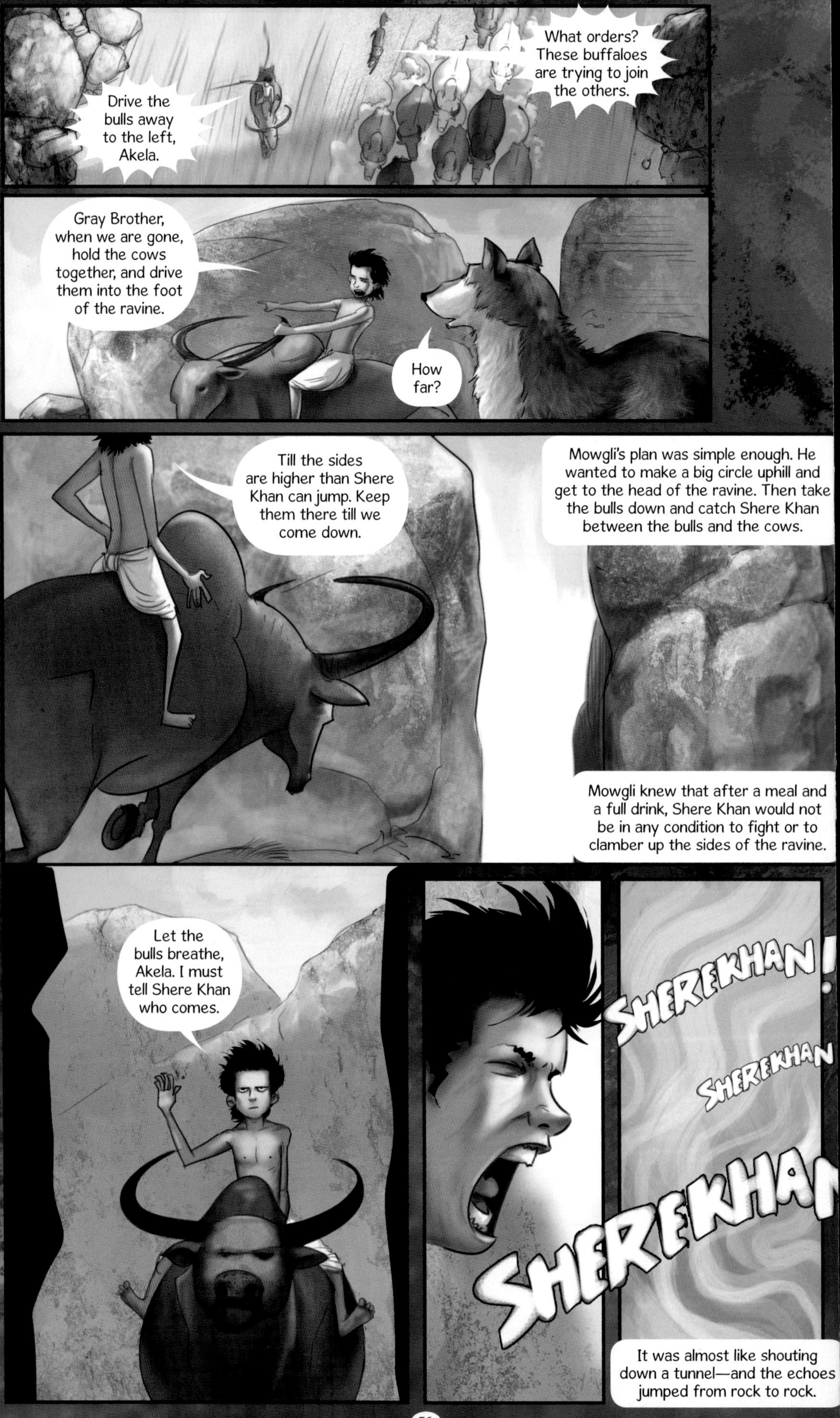

Drive the bulls away to the left, Akela.
What orders? These buffaloes are trying to join the others.
Gray Brother, when we are gone, hold the cows together, and drive them into the foot of the ravine.
How far?
Till the sides are higher than Shere Khan can jump. Keep them there till we come down.
Mowgli's plan was simple enough. He wanted to make a big circle uphill and get to the head of the ravine. Then take the bulls down and catch Shere Khan between the bulls and the cows.
Mowgli knew that after a meal and a full drink, Shere Khan would not be in any condition to fight or to clamber up the sides of the ravine.
Let the bulls breathe, Akela. I must tell Shere Khan who comes.
SHEREKHAN!
SHEREKHAN
SHEREKHAN
SHEREKHAN
It was almost like shouting down a tunnel—and the echoes jumped from rock to rock.

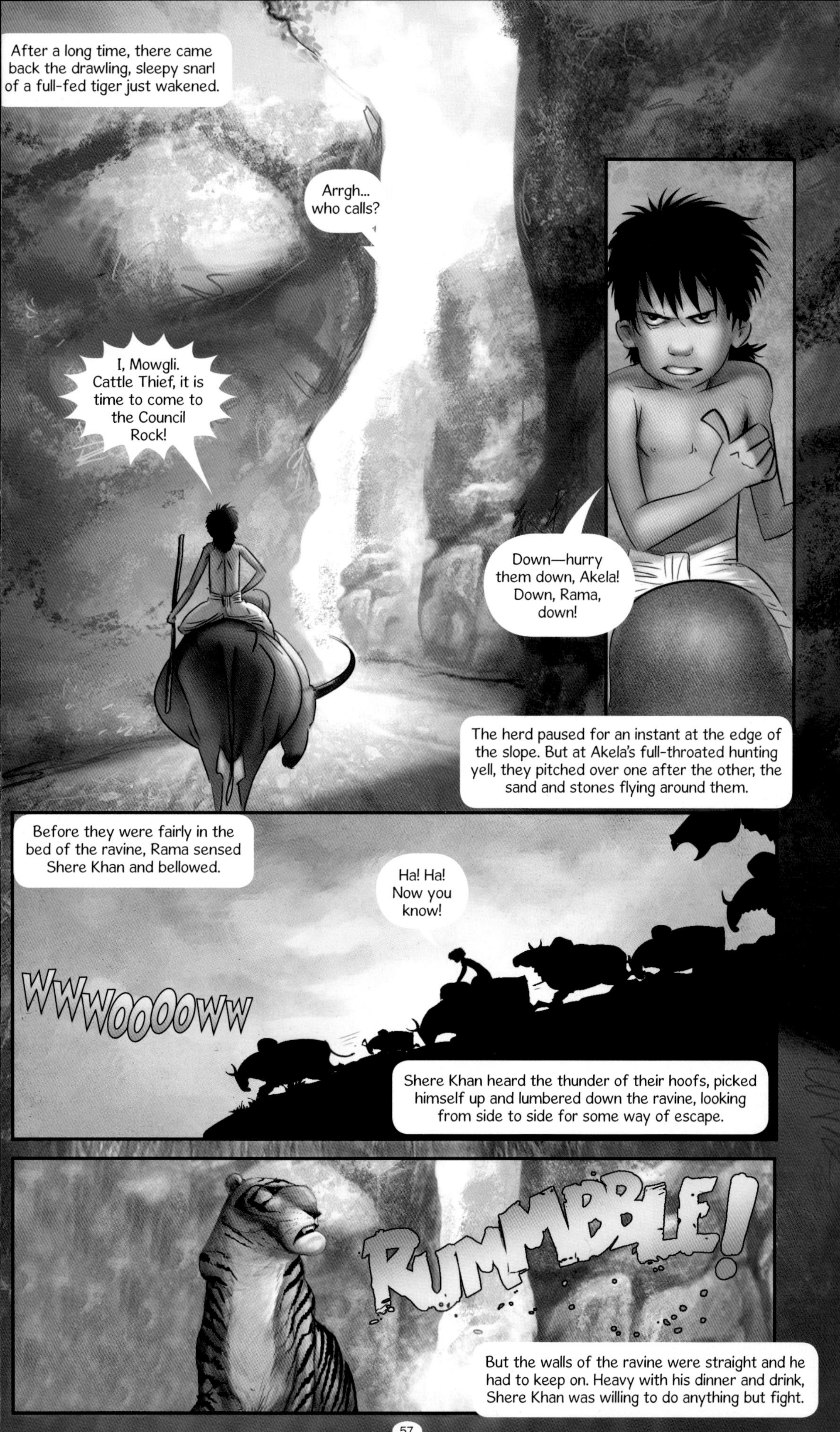
After a long time, there came back the drawling, sleepy snarl of a full-fed tiger just wakened.
Arrgh... who calls?
I, Mowgli. Cattle Thief, it is time to come to the Council Rock!
Down—hurry them down, Akela! Down, Rama, down!
The herd paused for an instant at the edge of the slope. But at Akela's full-throated hunting yell, they pitched over one after the other, the sand and stones flying around them.
Before they were fairly in the bed of the ravine, Rama sensed Shere Khan and bellowed.
Ha! Ha! Now you know!
WWWOOOOOWW
Shere Khan heard the thunder of their hoofs, picked himself up and lumbered down the ravine, looking from side to side for some way of escape.
RUMMBBLE!
But the walls of the ravine were straight and he had to keep on. Heavy with his dinner and drink, Shere Khan was willing to do anything but fight.

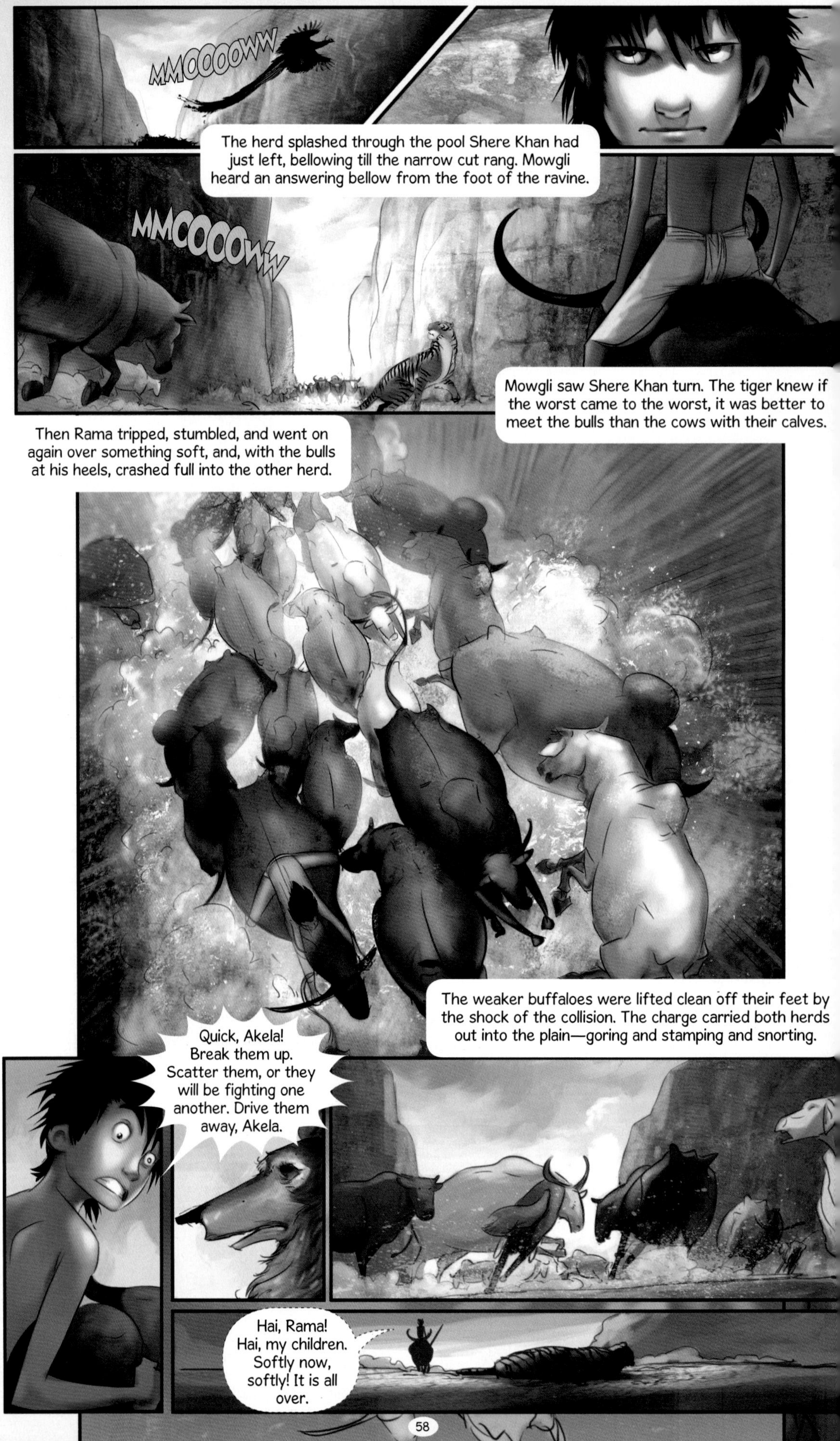
MMOOOOWW
The herd splashed through the pool Shere Khan had just left, bellowing till the narrow cut rang. Mowgli heard an answering bellow from the foot of the ravine.
MMCOOOOWW
Mowgli saw Shere Khan turn. The tiger knew if the worst came to the worst, it was better to meet the bulls than the cows with their calves.
Then Rama tripped, stumbled, and went on again over something soft, and, with the bulls at his heels, crashed full into the other herd.
The weaker buffaloes were lifted clean off their feet by the shock of the collision. The charge carried both herds out into the plain—goring and stamping and snorting.
Quick, Akela! Break them up. Scatter them, or they will be fighting one another. Drive them away, Akela.
Hai, Rama! Hai, my children. Softly now, softly! It is all over.

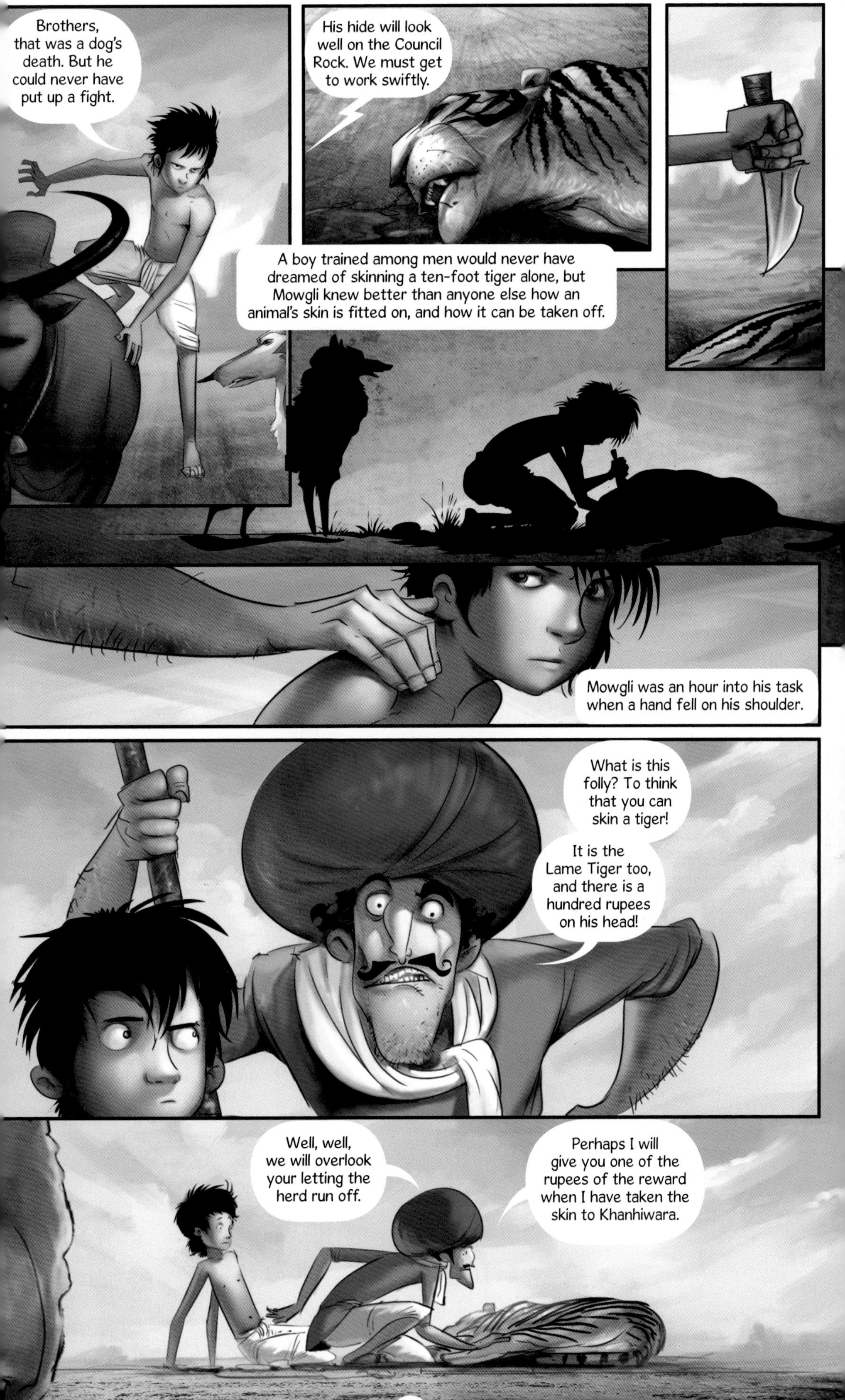
Brothers, that was a dog's death. But he could never have put up a fight.
His hide will look well on the Council Rock. We must get to work swiftly.
A boy trained among men would never have dreamed of skinning a ten-foot tiger alone, but Mowgli knew better than anyone else how an animal's skin is fitted on, and how it can be taken off.
Mowgli was an hour into his task when a hand fell on his shoulder.
What is this folly? To think that you can skin a tiger!
It is the Lame Tiger too, and there is a hundred rupees on his head!
Well, well, we will overlook your letting the herd run off.
Perhaps I will give you one of the rupees of the reward when I have taken the skin to Khanhiwara.

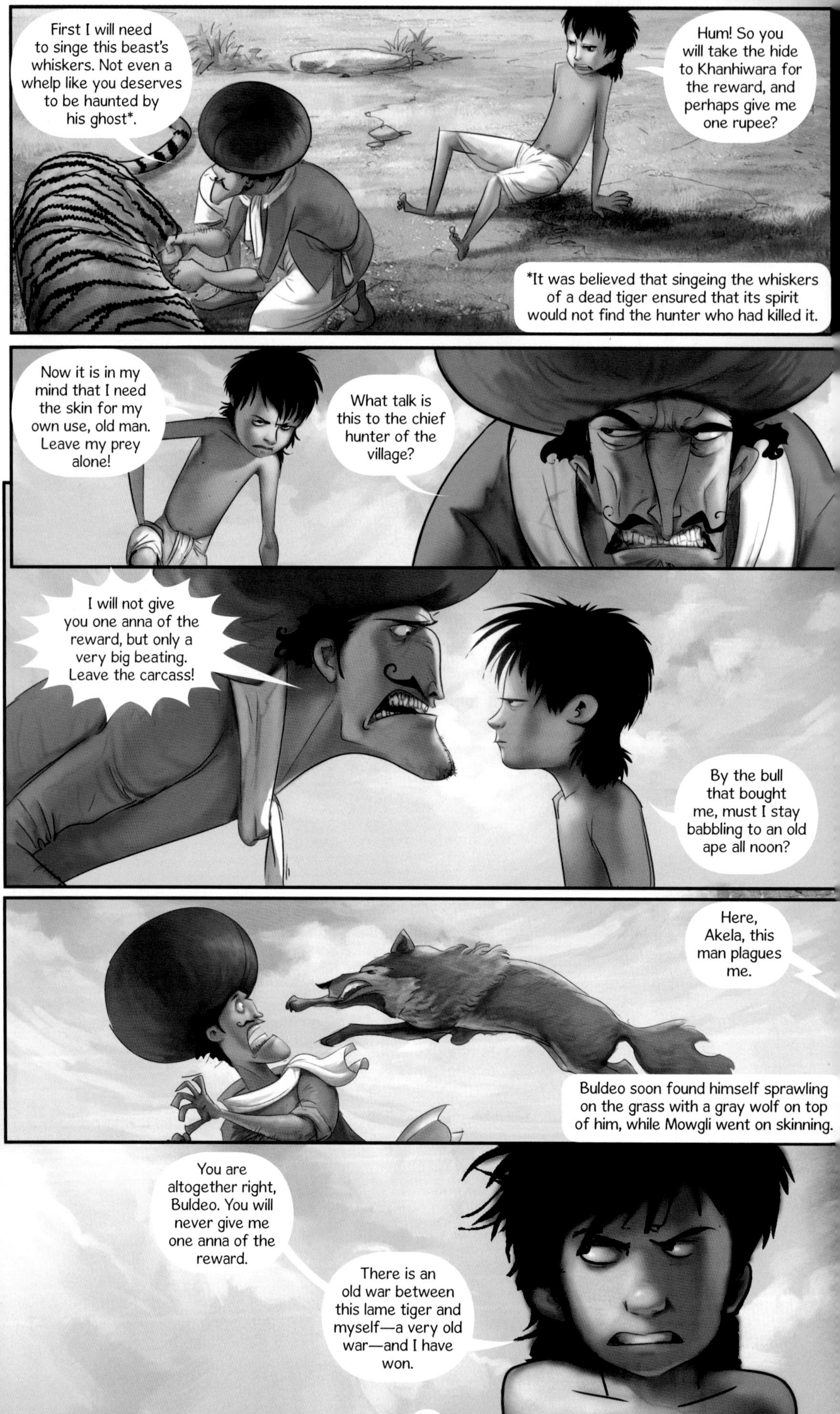
First I will need to singe this beast's whiskers. Not even a whelp like you deserves to be haunted by his ghost*.
Hum! So you will take the hide to Khanhiwara for the reward, and perhaps give me one rupee?
*It was believed that singeing the whiskers of a dead tiger ensured that its spirit would not find the hunter who had killed it.
Now it is in my mind that I need the skin for my own use, old man. Leave my prey alone!
What talk is this to the chief hunter of the village?
I will not give you one anna of the reward, but only a very big beating. Leave the carcass!
By the bull that bought me, must I stay babbling to an old ape all noon?
Here, Akela, this man plagues me.
Buldeo soon found himself sprawling on the grass with a gray wolf on top of him, while Mowgli went on skinning.
You are altogether right, Buldeo. You will never give me one anna of the reward.
There is an old war between this lame tiger and myself—a very old war—and I have won.

If Buldeo had been younger, he would have taken his chance with Akela. But a wolf who obeyed the orders of this boy, who had private wars with man-eating tigers, was not a common animal.

Maharaj! Great king! I am an old man. May I rise up and go away, or will your servant tear me to pieces?

Go! But do not meddle with my game again. Let him go, Akela.

Buldeo hobbled away to the village as fast as he could, looking over his shoulder in case Mowgli should change into something terrible.

Mowgli went on with his work, but it was nearly twilight before he had drawn the skin clear of the body.

After hiding Shere Khan's skin, Mowgli gathered the herd and returned to the village. When he arrived, half the village seemed to be waiting for him by the gate.

Mowgli thought that they had gathered to greet him because he had killed Shere Khan. But he was shocked when they began to attack and scream at him.

Sorcerer!

Wolf's brat!

Jungle demon!

Go away!

Get away from here quickly, or the priest will turn you into a wolf again!

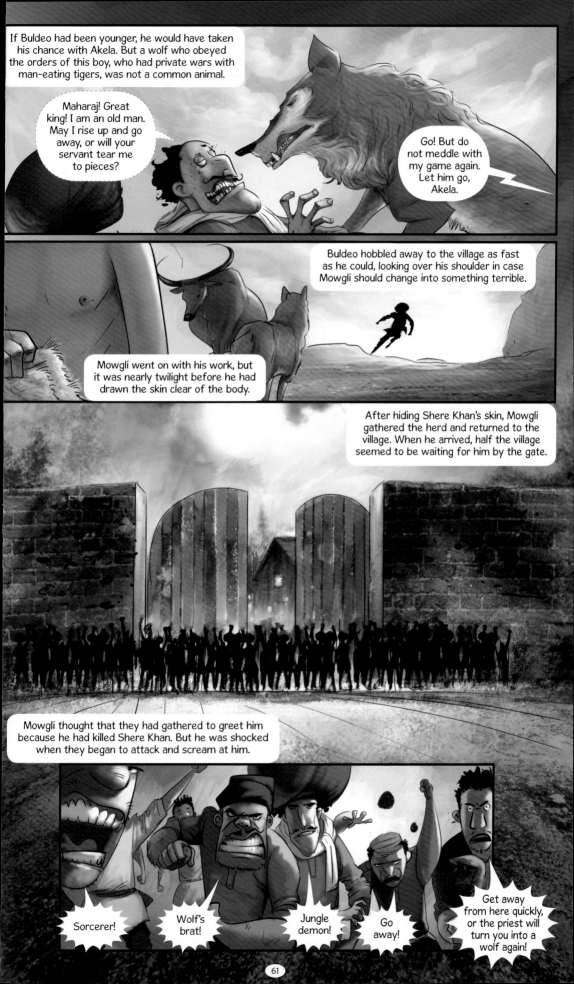

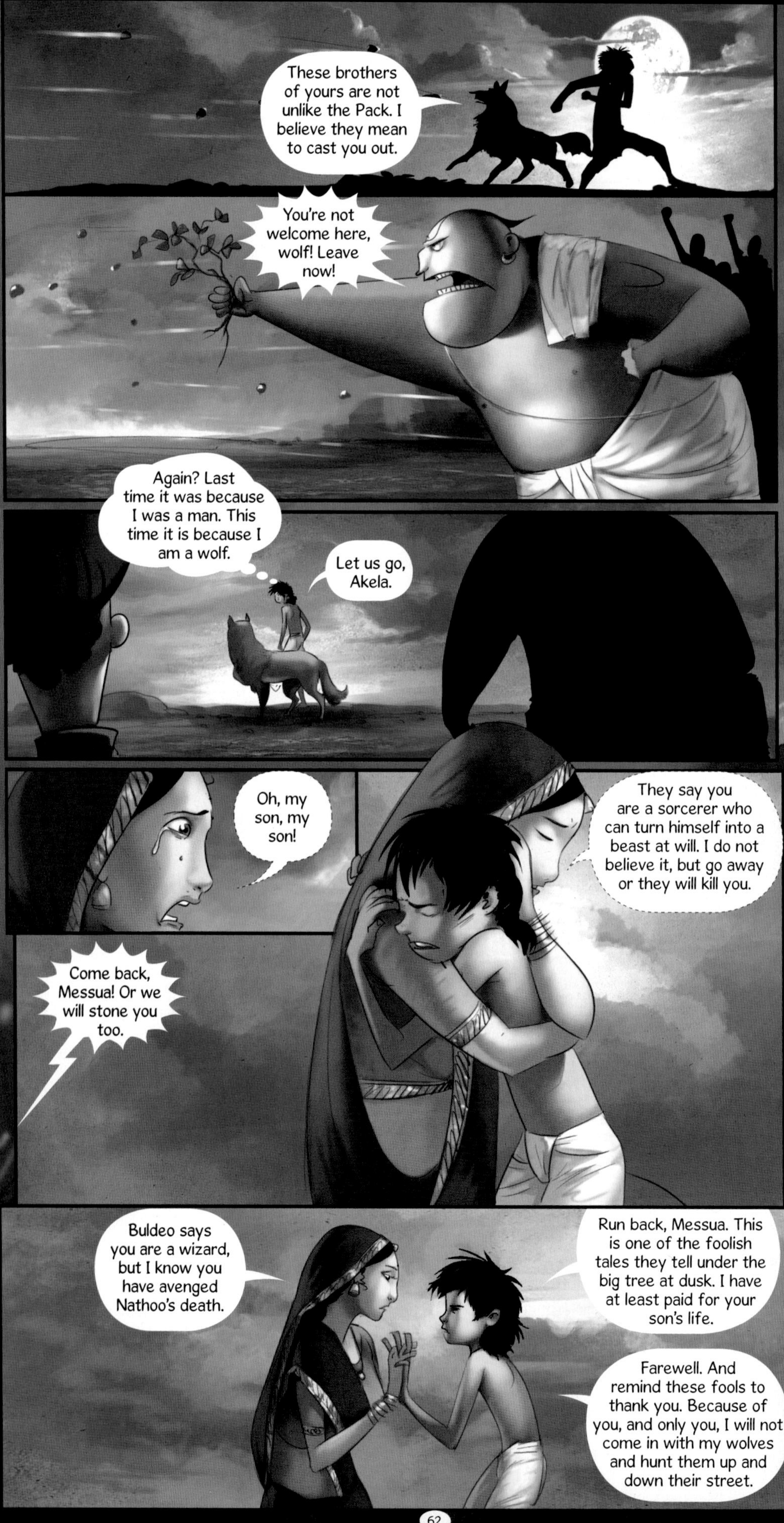
These brothers of yours are not unlike the Pack. I believe they mean to cast you out.
You're not welcome here, wolf! Leave now!
Again? Last time it was because I was a man. This time it is because I am a wolf.
Let us go, Akela.
Oh, my son, my son!
They say you are a sorcerer who can turn himself into a beast at will. I do not believe it, but go away or they will kill you.
Come back, Messua! Or we will stone you too.
Buldeo says you are a wizard, but I know you have avenged Nathoo's death.
Run back, Messua. This is one of the foolish tales they tell under the big tree at dusk. I have at least paid for your son's life.
Farewell. And remind these fools to thank you. Because of you, and only you, I will not come in with my wolves and hunt them up and down their street.

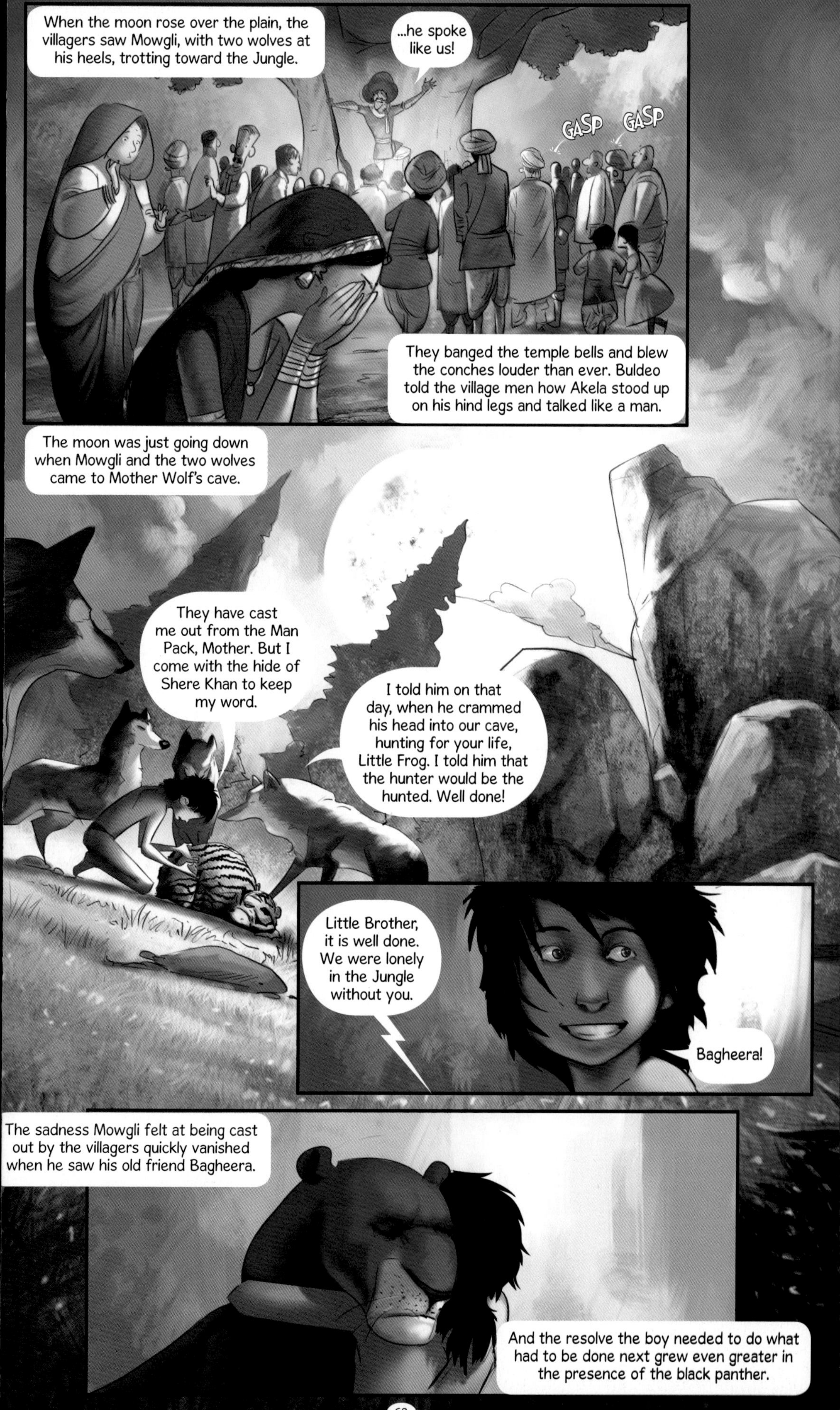
When the moon rose over the plain, the villagers saw Mowgli, with two wolves at his heels, trotting toward the Jungle.
...he spoke like us!
GASP
GASP
They banged the temple bells and blew the conches louder than ever. Buldeo told the village men how Akela stood up on his hind legs and talked like a man.
The moon was just going down when Mowgli and the two wolves came to Mother Wolf's cave.
They have cast me out from the Man Pack, Mother. But I come with the hide of Shere Khan to keep my word.
I told him on that day, when he crammed his head into our cave, hunting for your life, Little Frog. I told him that the hunter would be the hunted. Well done!
Little Brother, it is well done. We were lonely in the Jungle without you.
Bagheera!
The sadness Mowgli felt at being cast out by the villagers quickly vanished when he saw his old friend Bagheera.
And the resolve the boy needed to do what had to be done next grew even greater in the presence of the black panther.

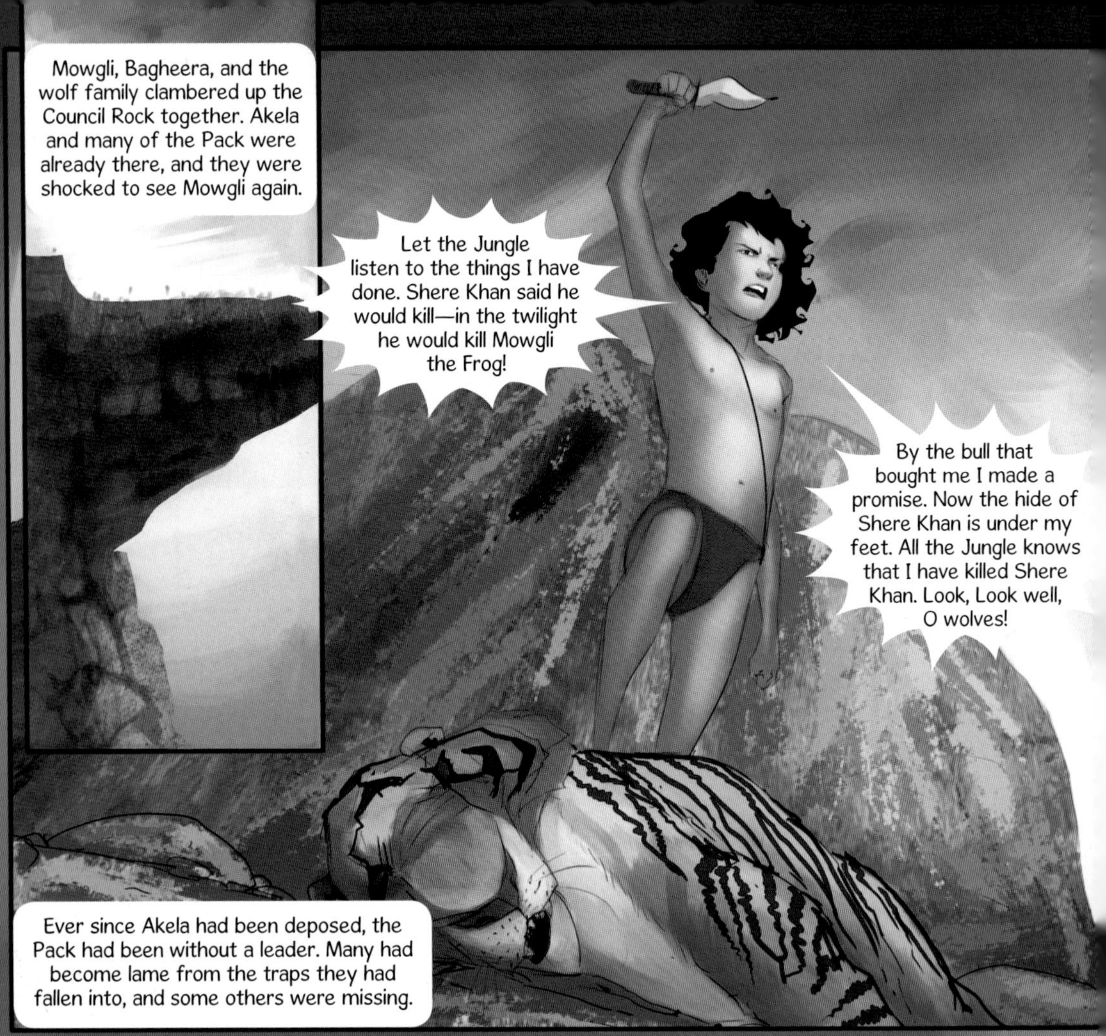
Mowgli, Bagheera, and the wolf family clambered up the Council Rock together. Akela and many of the Pack were already there, and they were shocked to see Mowgli again.
Let the Jungle listen to the things I have done. Shere Khan said he would kill—in the twilight he would kill Mowgli the Frog!
By the bull that bought me I made a promise. Now the hide of Shere Khan is under my feet. All the Jungle knows that I have killed Shere Khan. Look, Look well, O wolves!
Ever since Akela had been deposed, the Pack had been without a leader. Many had become lame from the traps they had fallen into, and some others were missing.

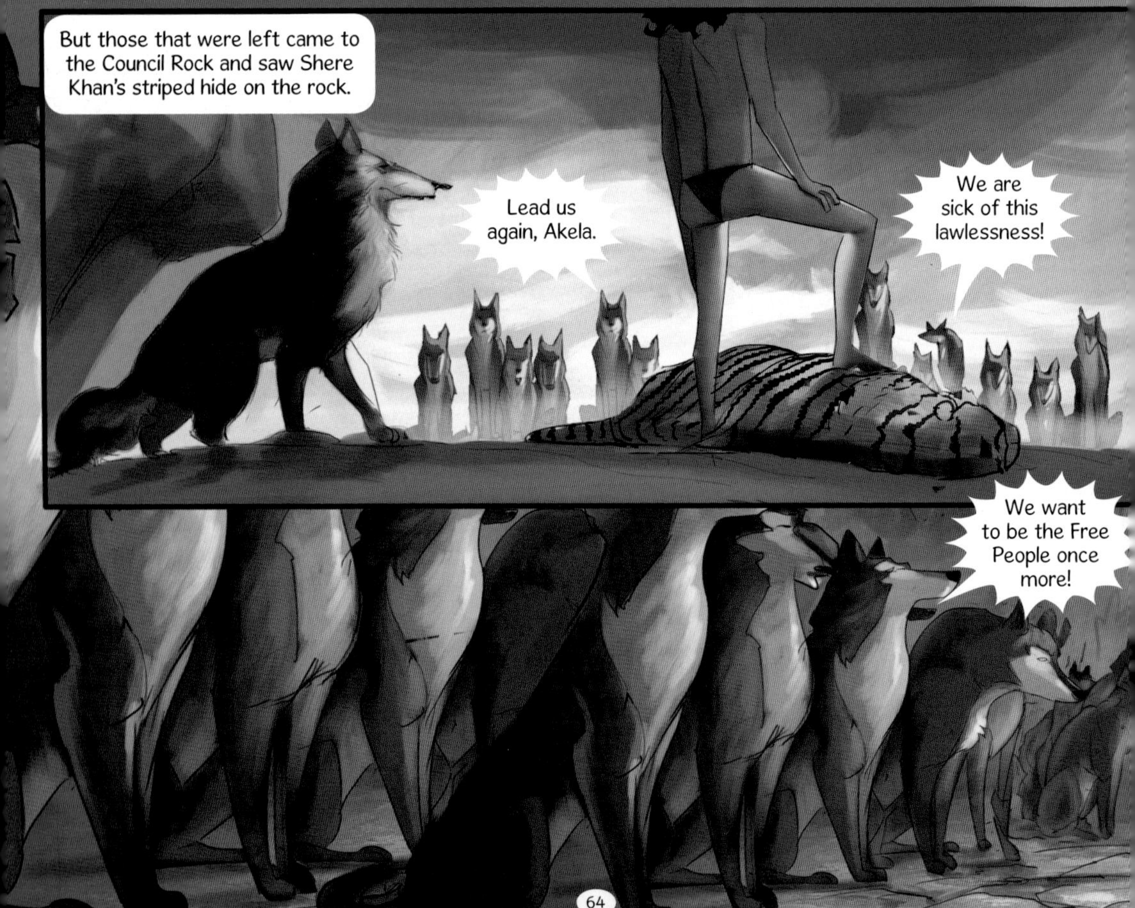
But those that were left came to the Council Rock and saw Shere Khan's striped hide on the rock.
Lead us again, Akela.
We are sick of this lawlessness!
We want to be the Free People once more!

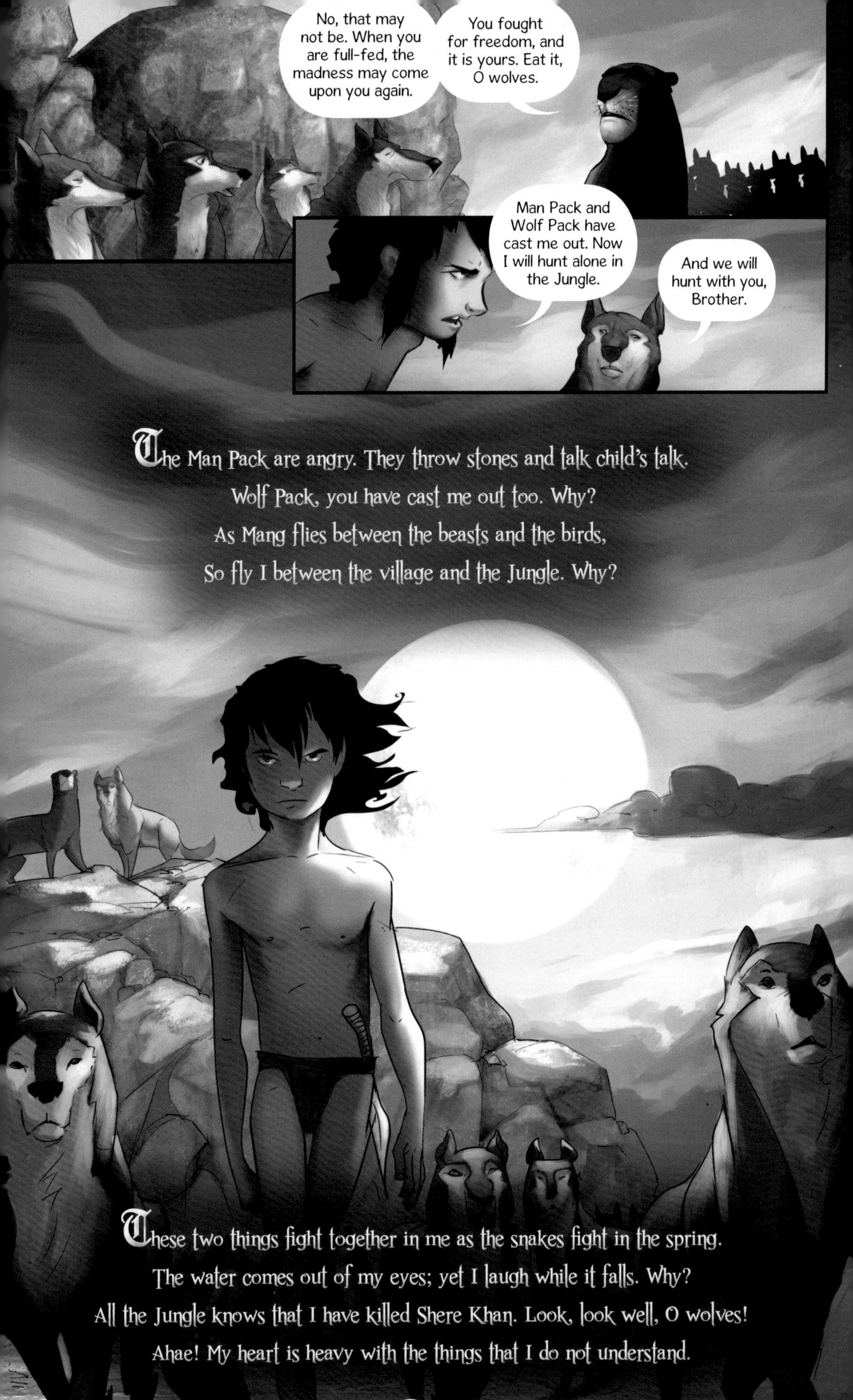
No, that may not be. When you are full-fed, the madness may come upon you again.
You fought for freedom, and it is yours. Eat it, O wolves.
Man Pack and Wolf Pack have cast me out. Now I will hunt alone in the Jungle.
And we will hunt with you, Brother.
The Man Pack are angry. They throw stones and talk child's talk.
Wolf Pack, you have cast me out too. Why?
As Mang flies between the beasts and the birds,
So fly I between the village and the Jungle. Why?
These two things fight together in me as the snakes fight in the spring.
The water comes out of my eyes; yet I laugh while it falls. Why?
All the Jungle knows that I have killed Shere Khan. Look, look well, O wolves!
Ahae! My heart is heavy with the things that I do not understand.

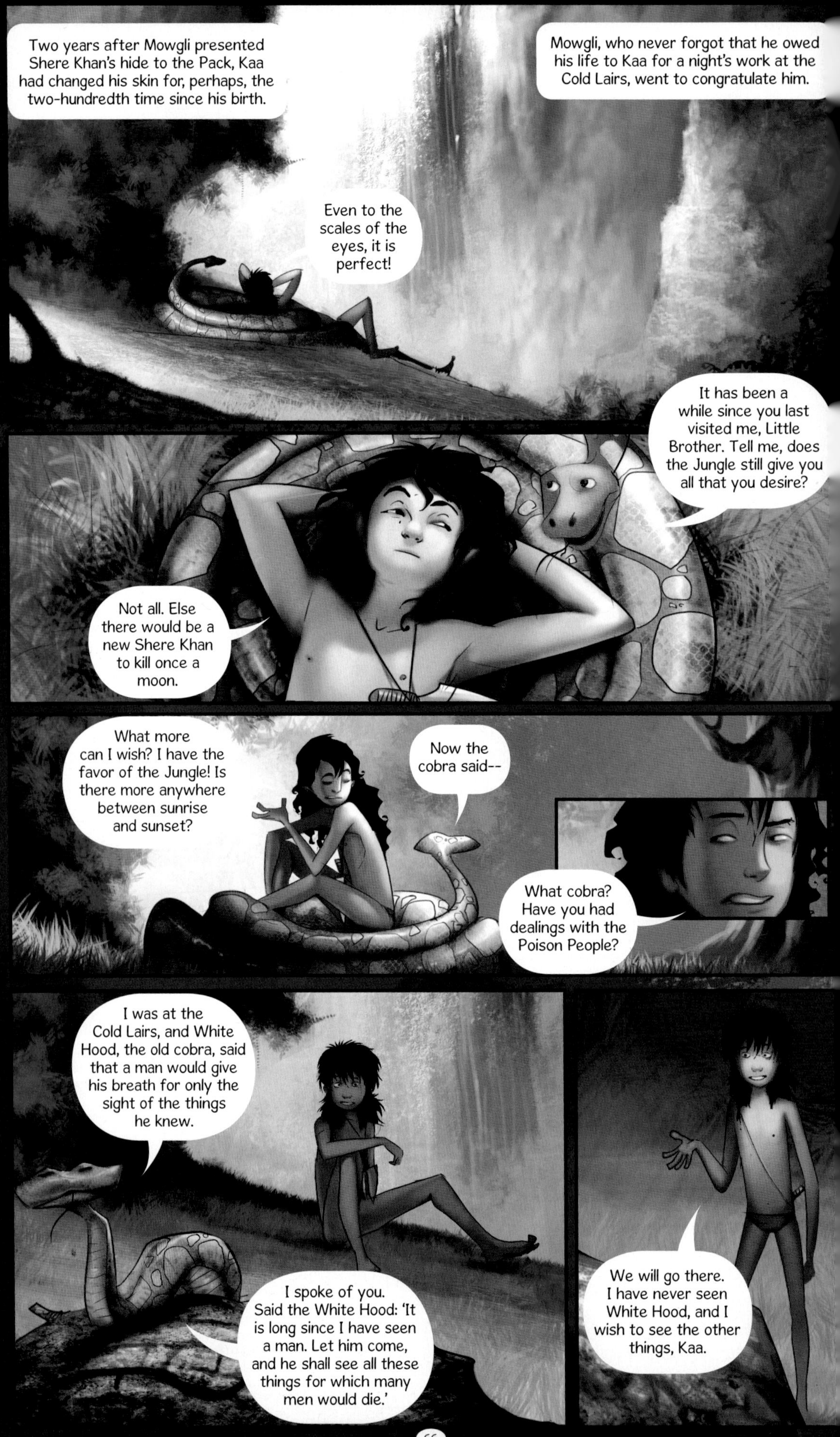

Two years after Mowgli presented Shere Khan's hide to the Pack, Kaa had changed his skin for, perhaps, the two-hundredth time since his birth.
Mowgli, who never forgot that he owed his life to Kaa for a night's work at the Cold Lairs, went to congratulate him.
Even to the scales of the eyes, it is perfect!
It has been a while since you last visited me, Little Brother. Tell me, does the Jungle still give you all that you desire?
Not all. Else there would be a new Shere Khan to kill once a moon.
What more can I wish? I have the favor of the Jungle! Is there more anywhere between sunrise and sunset?
Now the cobra said--
What cobra? Have you had dealings with the Poison People?
I was at the Cold Lairs, and White Hood, the old cobra, said that a man would give his breath for only the sight of the things he knew.
I spoke of you. Said the White Hood: 'It is long since I have seen a man. Let him come, and he shall see all these things for which many men would die.'
We will go there. I have never seen White Hood, and I wish to see the other things, Kaa.

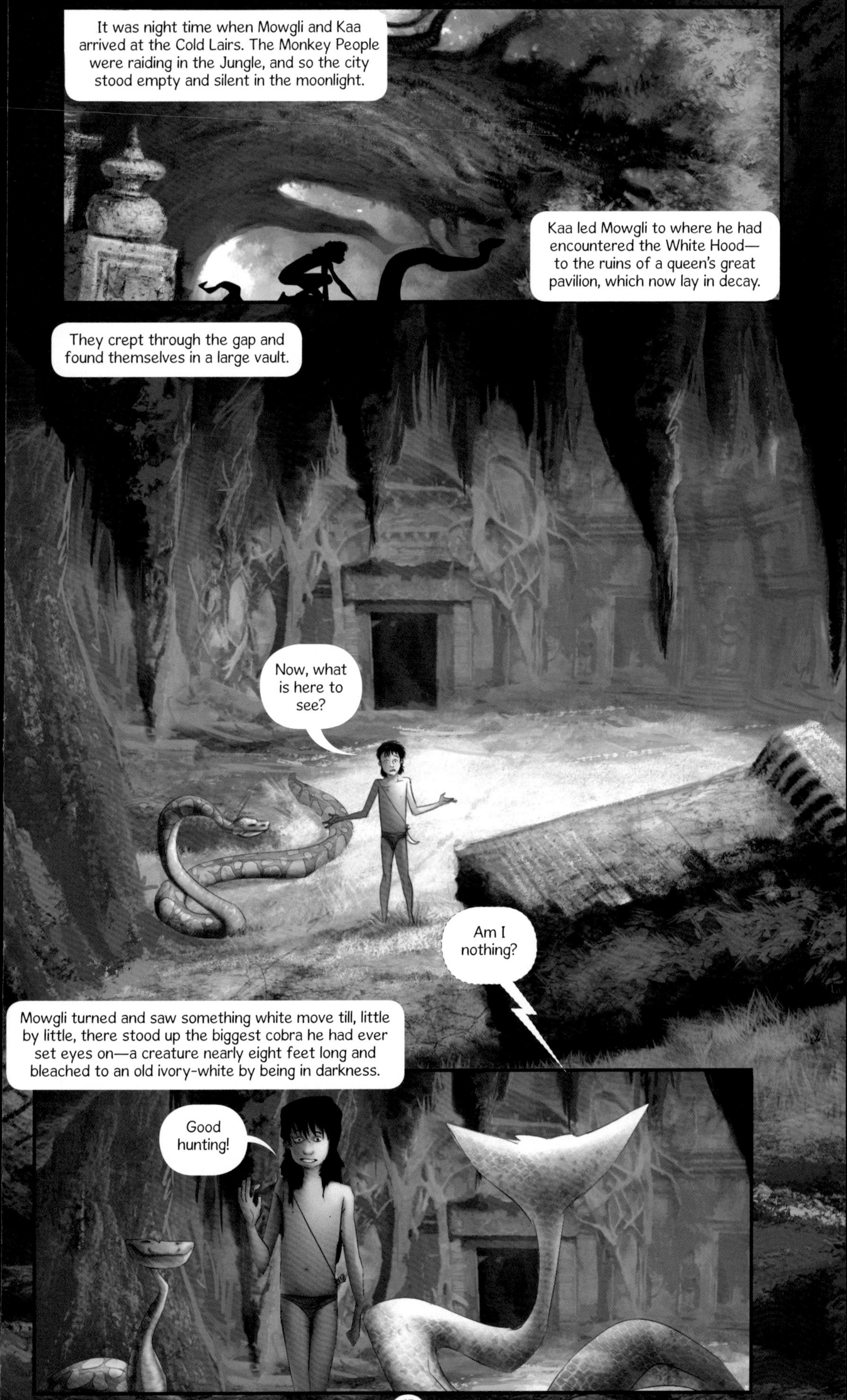
It was night time when Mowgli and Kaa arrived at the Cold Lairs. The Monkey People were raiding in the Jungle, and so the city stood empty and silent in the moonlight.
Kaa led Mowgli to where he had encountered the White Hood—to the ruins of a queen's great pavilion, which now lay in decay.
They crept through the gap and found themselves in a large vault.
Now, what is here to see?
Am I nothing?
Mowgli turned and saw something white move till, little by little, there stood up the biggest cobra he had ever set eyes on—a creature nearly eight feet long and bleached to an old ivory-white by being in darkness.
Good hunting!

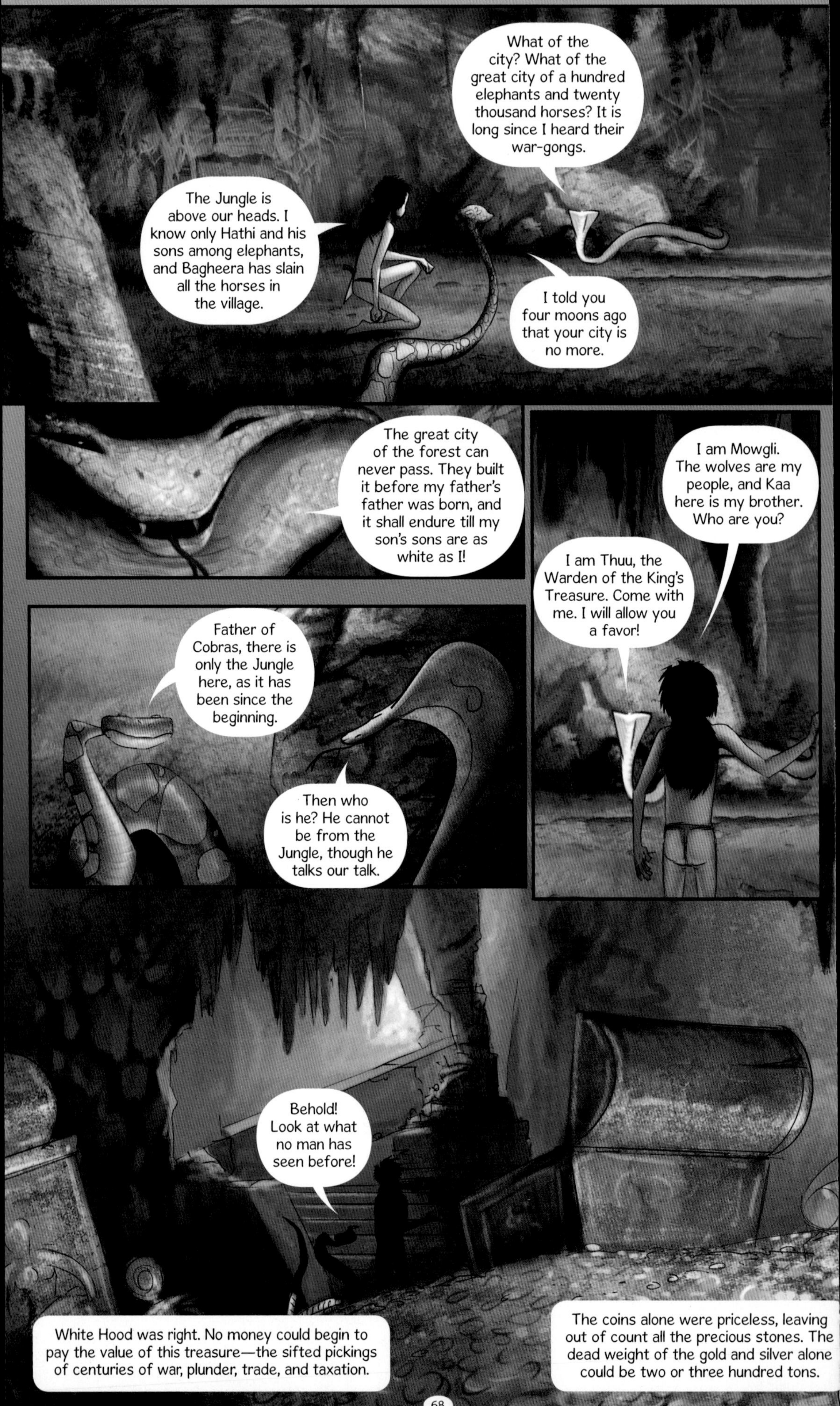

What of the city? What of the great city of a hundred elephants and twenty thousand horses? It is long since I heard their war-gongs.
The Jungle is above our heads. I know only Hathi and his sons among elephants, and Bagheera has slain all the horses in the village.
I told you four moons ago that your city is no more.
The great city of the forest can never pass. They built it before my father's father was born, and it shall endure till my son's sons are as white as I!
Father of Cobras, there is only the Jungle here, as it has been since the beginning.
Then who is he? He cannot be from the Jungle, though he talks our talk.
I am Mowgli. The wolves are my people, and Kaa here is my brother. Who are you?
I am Thuu, the Warden of the King's Treasure. Come with me. I will allow you a favor!
Behold! Look at what no man has seen before!
White Hood was right. No money could begin to pay the value of this treasure—the sifted pickings of centuries of war, plunder, trade, and taxation.
The coins alone were priceless, leaving out of count all the precious stones. The dead weight of the gold and silver alone could be two or three hundred tons.

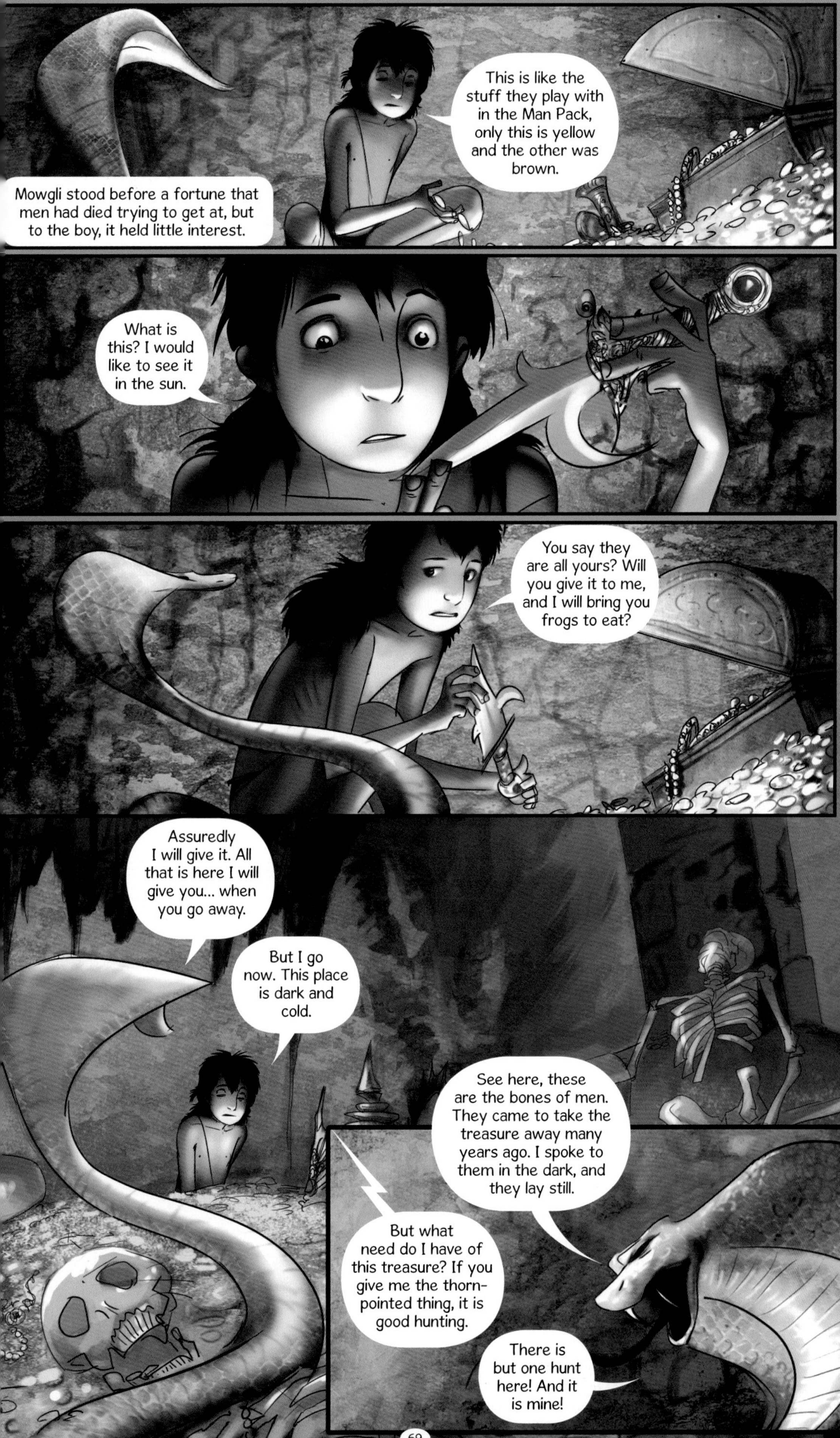
This is like the stuff they play with in the Man Pack, only this is yellow and the other was brown.
Mowgli stood before a fortune that men had died trying to get at, but to the boy, it held little interest.
What is this? I would like to see it in the sun.
You say they are all yours? Will you give it to me, and I will bring you frogs to eat?
Assuredly I will give it. All that is here I will give you... when you go away.
But I go now. This place is dark and cold.
See here, these are the bones of men. They came to take the treasure away many years ago. I spoke to them in the dark, and they lay still.
But what need do I have of this treasure? If you give me the thorn-pointed thing, it is good hunting.
There is but one hunt here! And it is mine!

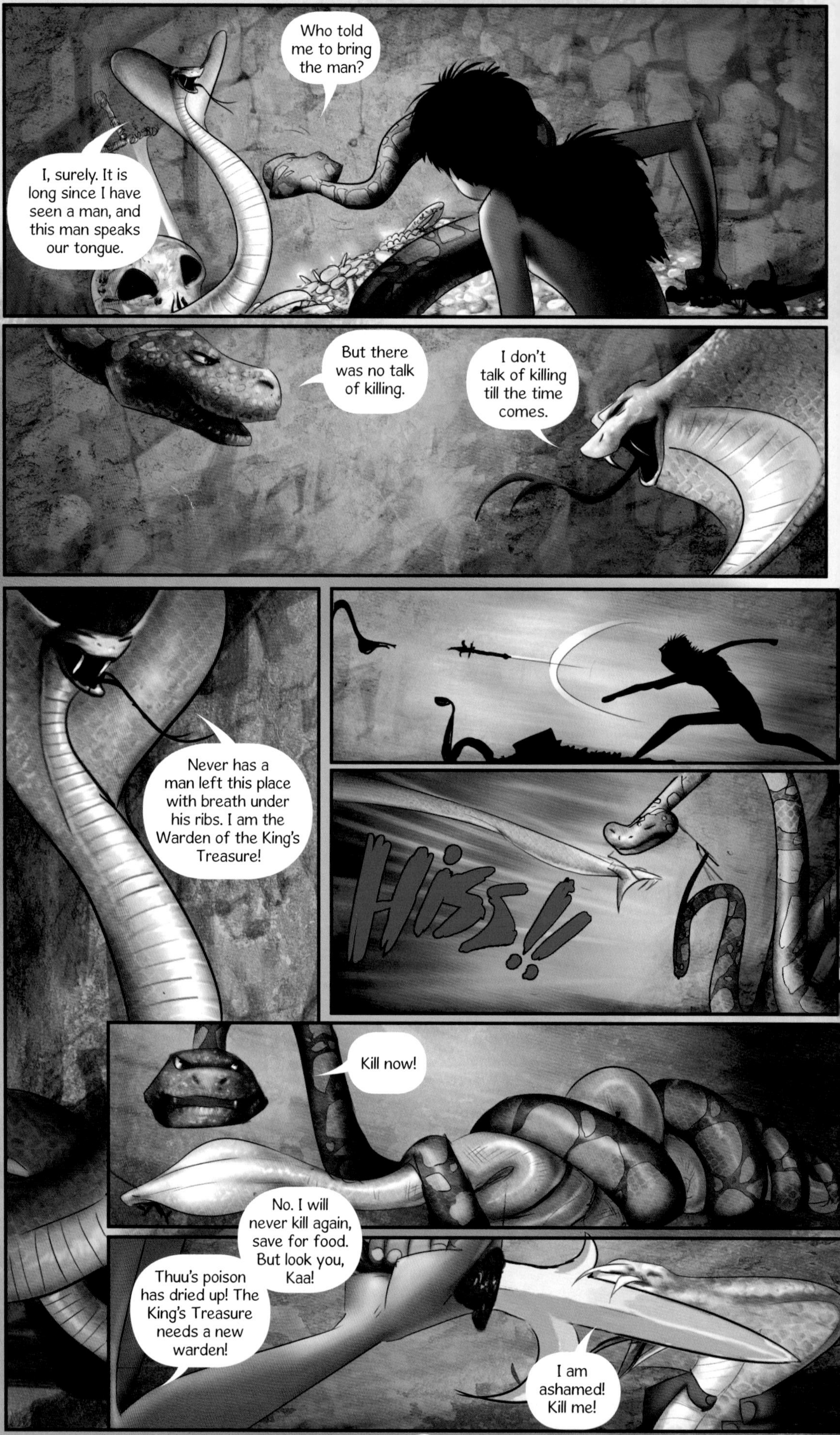
Who told me to bring the man?
I, surely. It is long since I have seen a man, and this man speaks our tongue.
But there was no talk of killing.
I don't talk of killing till the time comes.
Never has a man left this place with breath under his ribs. I am the Warden of the King's Treasure!
HISS!!
Kill now!
No. I will never kill again, save for food. But look you, Kaa!
Thuu's poison has dried up! The King's Treasure needs a new warden!
I am ashamed! Kill me!

There has been too much talk of killing. We will go now.

But I take the thorn-pointed thing, Thuu, because I have fought and beaten you.

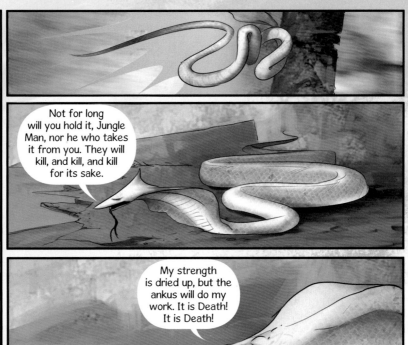

Not for long will you hold it, Jungle Man, nor he who takes it from you. They will kill, and kill, and kill for its sake.

My strength is dried up, but the ankus will do my work. It is Death! It is Death!

Mowgli and Kaa parted company after leaving the Cold Lairs. At dawn, Mowgli found Bagheera drinking after a heavy kill, and was eager to show him the prize he had taken from the white cobra.

I wonder what Thuu meant when he talked of death?

I know a little of men. Many men would kill thrice in a night for the sake of that one big red stone alone.

But the stone makes it heavy to the hand, and is not good to eat. My knife is better. Then why would they kill for it?

And I wonder for what use was this thorn-pointed thing made?

It was made by men to thrust into the heads of elephants. I have seen the like in the streets of Udaipur. That thing has tasted the blood of many elephants.

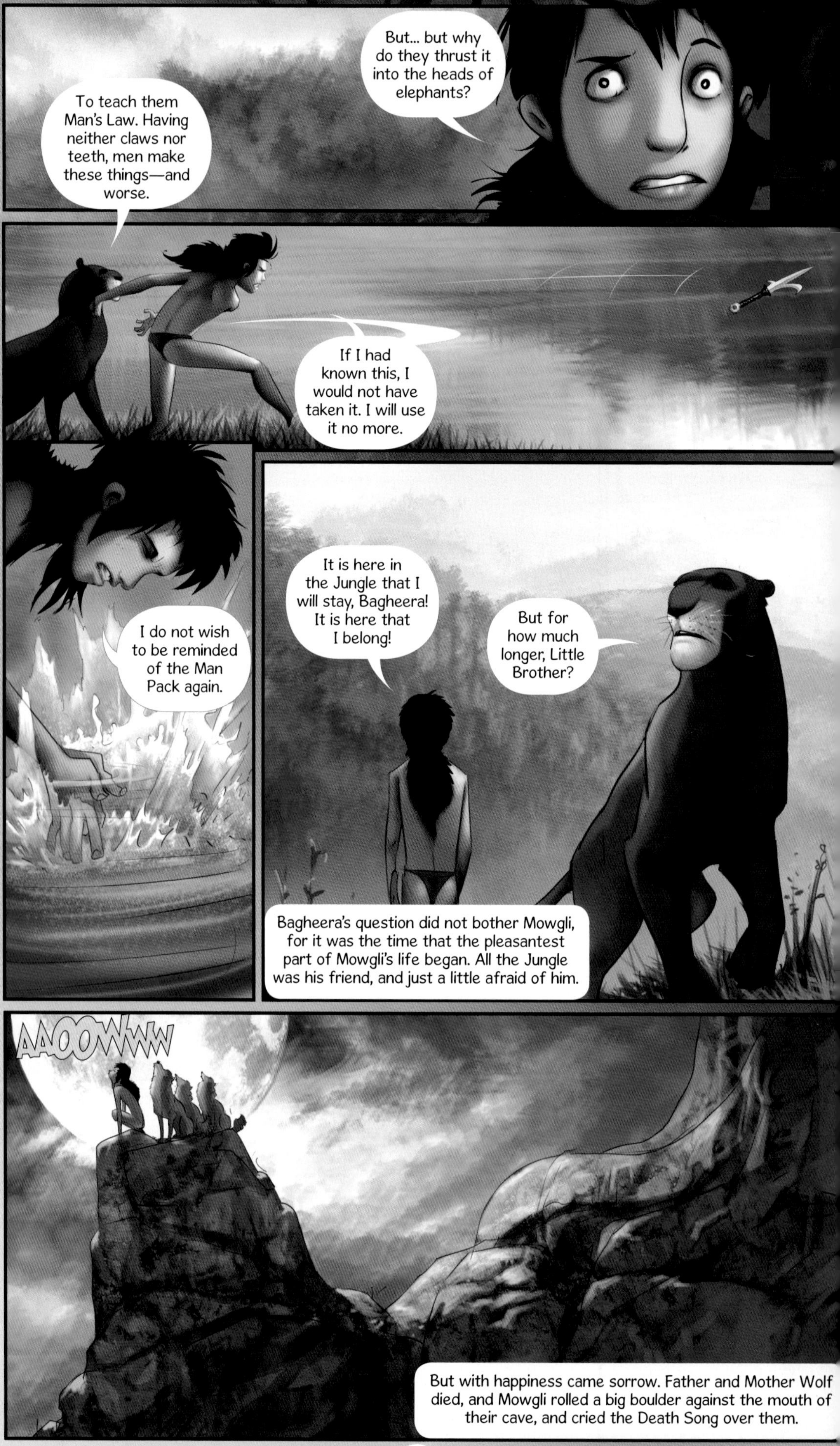
But... but why do they thrust it into the heads of elephants?
To teach them Man's Law. Having neither claws nor teeth, men make these things—and worse.
If I had known this, I would not have taken it. I will use it no more.
I do not wish to be reminded of the Man Pack again.
It is here in the Jungle that I will stay, Bagheera! It is here that I belong!
But for how much longer, Little Brother?
Bagheera's question did not bother Mowgli, for it was the time that the pleasantest part of Mowgli's life began. All the Jungle was his friend, and just a little afraid of him.
AAOOWWW
But with happiness came sorrow. Father and Mother Wolf died, and Mowgli rolled a big boulder against the mouth of their cave, and cried the Death Song over them.

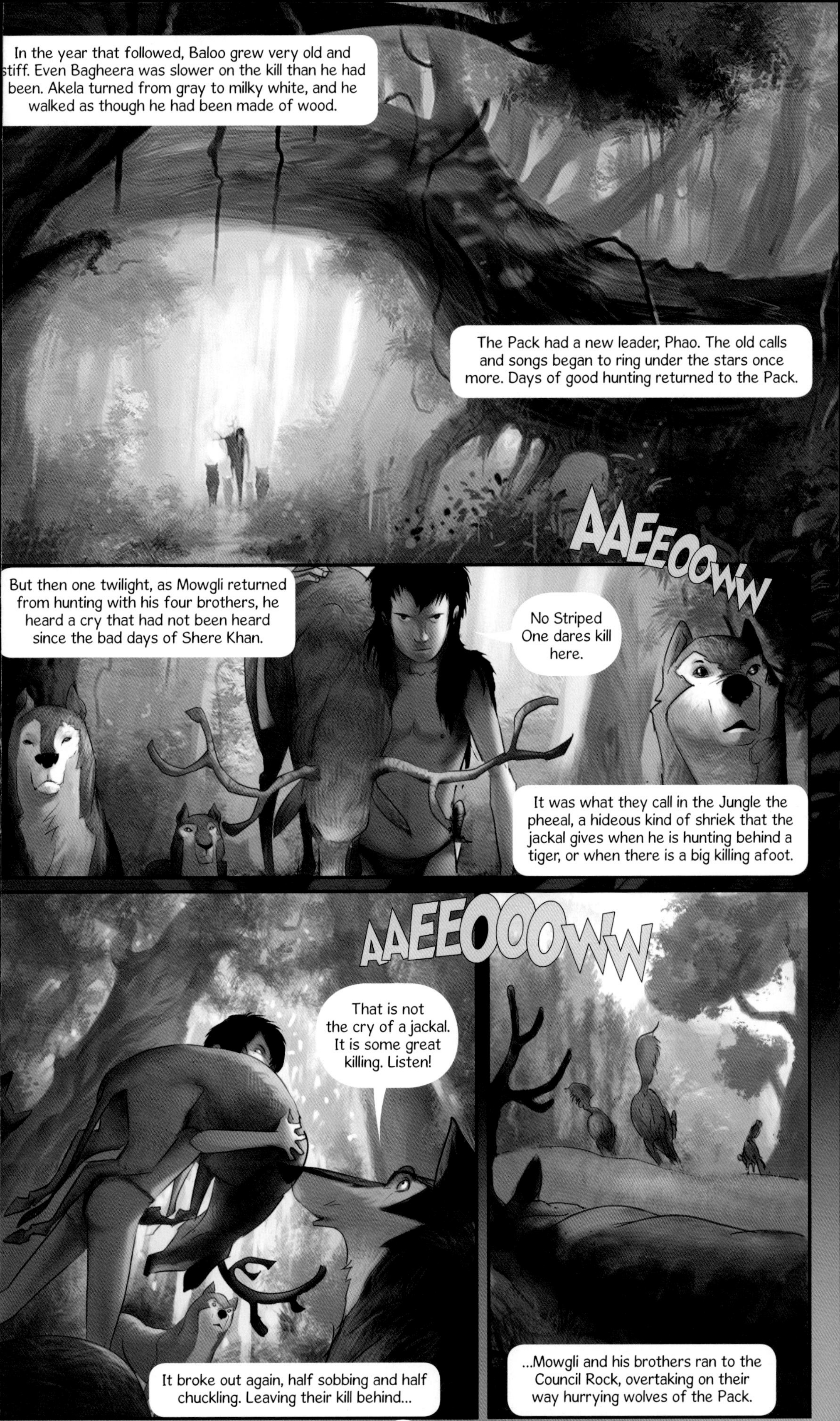
In the year that followed, Baloo grew very old and stiff. Even Bagheera was slower on the kill than he had been. Akela turned from gray to milky white, and he walked as though he had been made of wood.
The Pack had a new leader, Phao. The old calls and songs began to ring under the stars once more. Days of good hunting returned to the Pack.
AAEEOOWW
But then one twilight, as Mowgli returned from hunting with his four brothers, he heard a cry that had not been heard since the bad days of Shere Khan.
No Striped One dares kill here.
It was what they call in the Jungle the pheeal, a hideous kind of shriek that the jackal gives when he is hunting behind a tiger, or when there is a big killing afoot.
AAEEOOOWW
That is not the cry of a jackal. It is some great killing. Listen!
It broke out again, half sobbing and half chuckling. Leaving their kill behind...
...Mowgli and his brothers ran to the Council Rock, overtaking on their way hurrying wolves of the Pack.

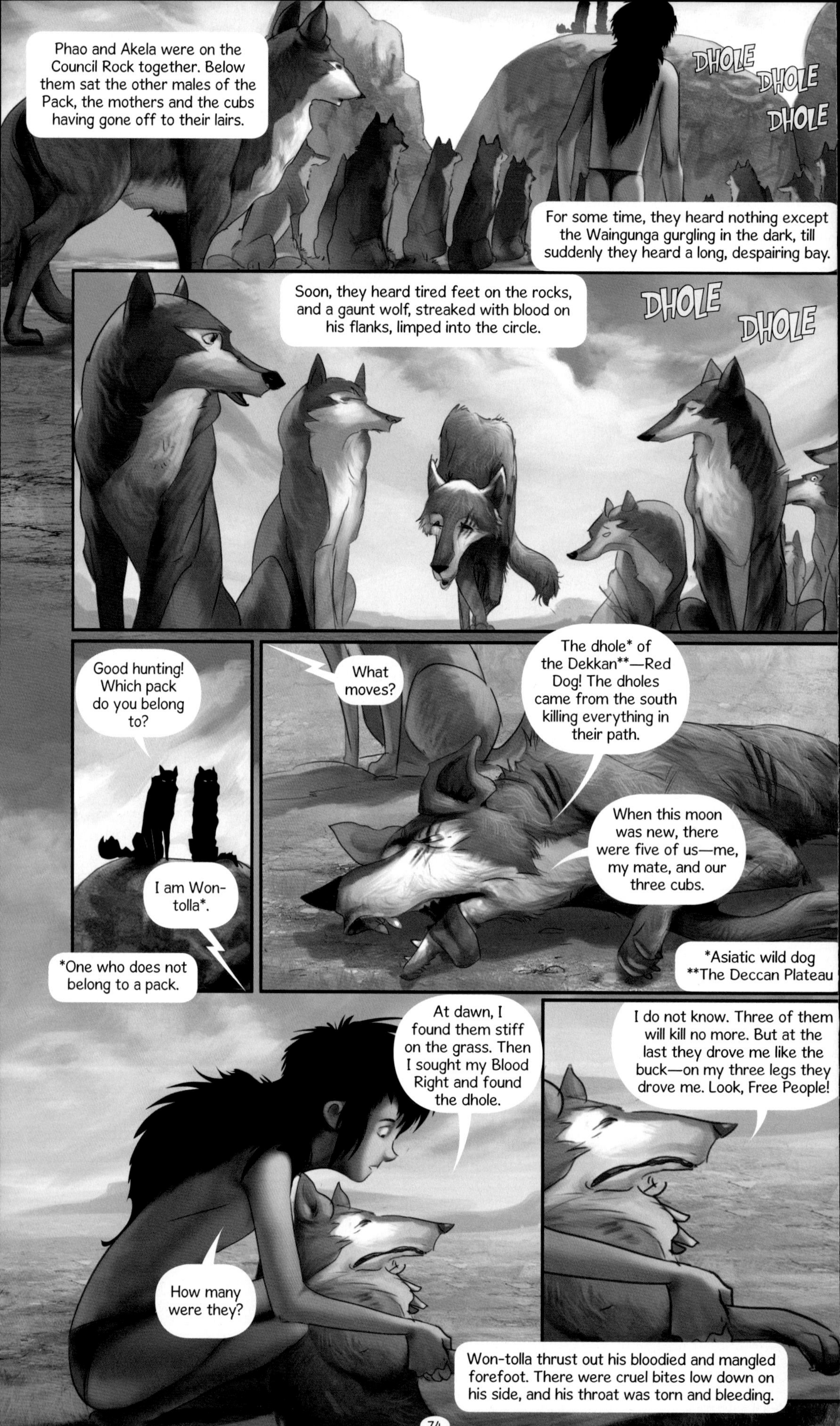

Phao and Akela were on the Council Rock together. Below them sat the other males of the Pack, the mothers and the cubs having gone off to their lairs.
DHOLE DHOLE DHOLE
For some time, they heard nothing except the Waingunga gurgling in the dark, till suddenly they heard a long, despairing bay.
Soon, they heard tired feet on the rocks, and a gaunt wolf, streaked with blood on his flanks, limped into the circle.
DHOLE DHOLE
Good hunting! Which pack do you belong to?
I am Won-tolla*.
*One who does not belong to a pack.
What moves?
The dhole* of the Dekkan**—Red Dog! The dholes came from the south killing everything in their path.
When this moon was new, there were five of us—me, my mate, and our three cubs.
*Asiatic wild dog
**The Deccan Plateau
At dawn, I found them stiff on the grass. Then I sought my Blood Right and found the dhole.
How many were they?
I do not know. Three of them will kill no more. But at the last they drove me like the buck—on my three legs they drove me. Look, Free People!
Won-tolla thrust out his bloodied and mangled forefoot. There were cruel bites low down on his side, and his throat was torn and bleeding.

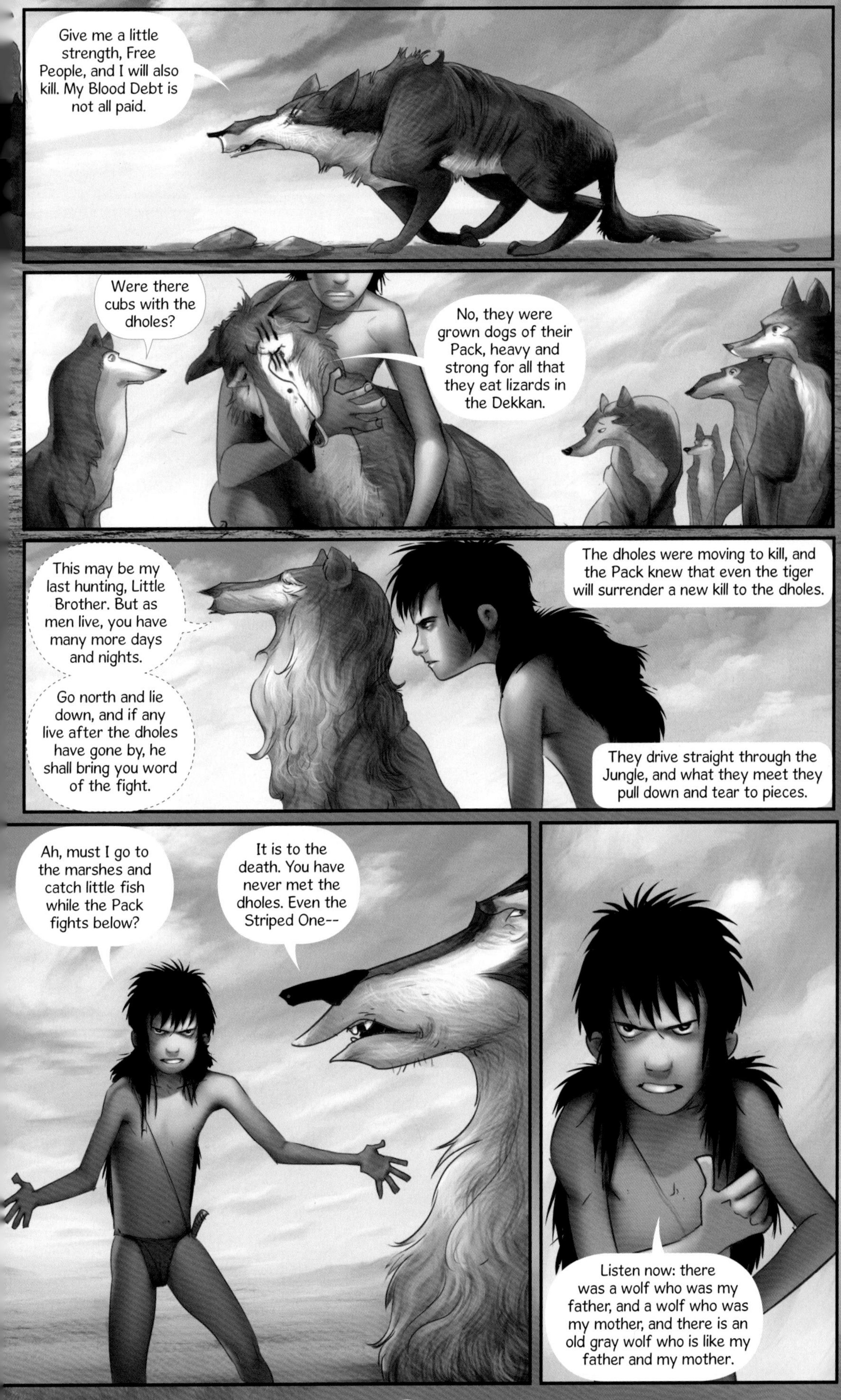
Give me a little strength, Free People, and I will also kill. My Blood Debt is not all paid.
Were there cubs with the dholes?
No, they were grown dogs of their Pack, heavy and strong for all that they eat lizards in the Dekkan.
This may be my last hunting, Little Brother. But as men live, you have many more days and nights.
Go north and lie down, and if any live after the dholes have gone by, he shall bring you word of the fight.
The dholes were moving to kill, and the Pack knew that even the tiger will surrender a new kill to the dholes.
They drive straight through the Jungle, and what they meet they pull down and tear to pieces.
Ah, must I go to the marshes and catch little fish while the Pack fights below?
It is to the death. You have never met the dholes. Even the Striped One--
Listen now: there was a wolf who was my father, and a wolf who was my mother, and there is an old gray wolf who is like my father and my mother.

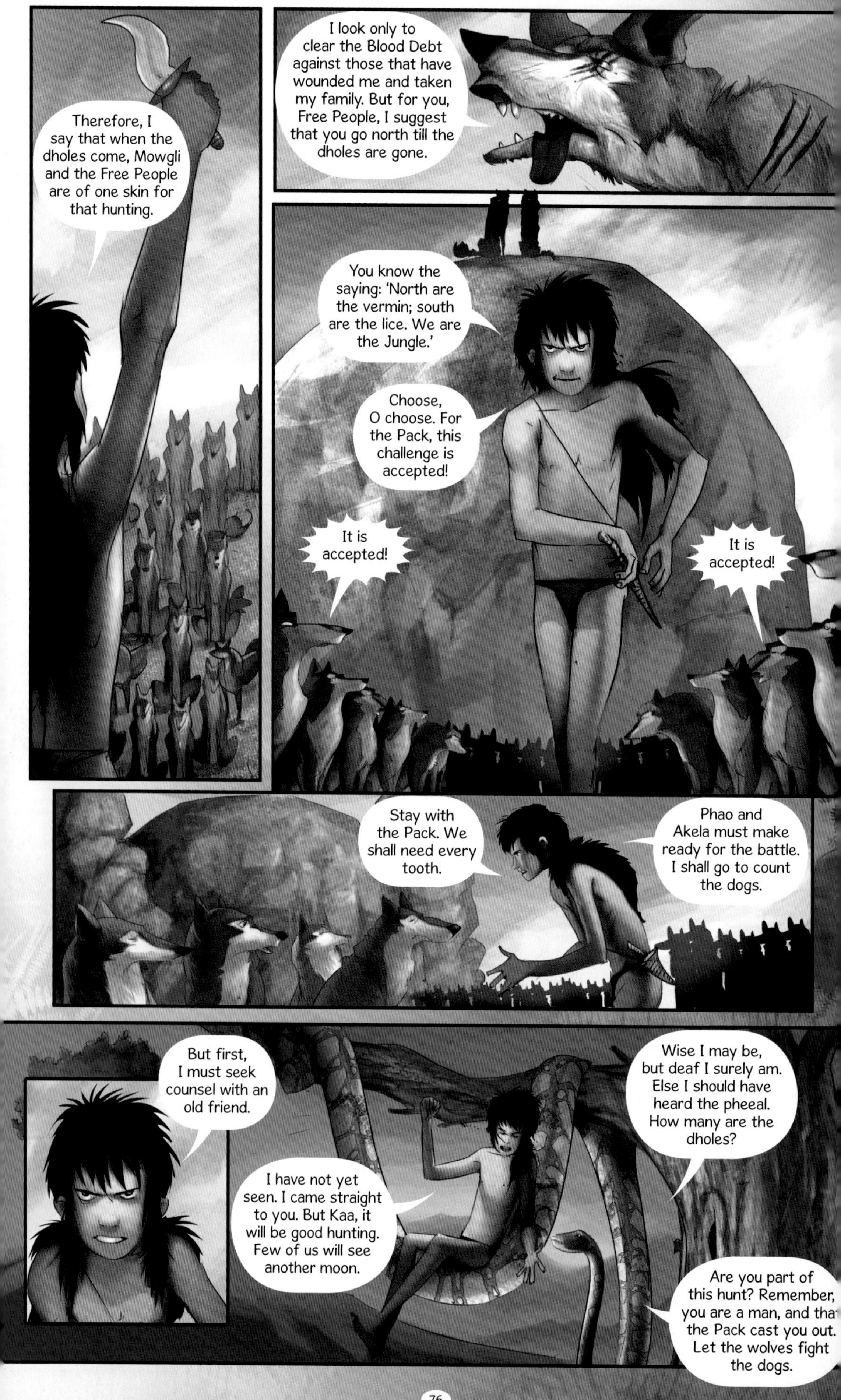

Therefore, I say that when the dholes come, Mowgli and the Free People are of one skin for that hunting.
I look only to clear the Blood Debt against those that have wounded me and taken my family. But for you, Free People, I suggest that you go north till the dholes are gone.
You know the saying: 'North are the vermin; south are the lice. We are the Jungle.'
Choose, O choose. For the Pack, this challenge is accepted!
It is accepted!
It is accepted!
Stay with the Pack. We shall need every tooth.
Phao and Akela must make ready for the battle. I shall go to count the dogs.
But first, I must seek counsel with an old friend.
Wise I may be, but deaf I surely am. Else I should have heard the pheeal. How many are the dholes?
I have not yet seen. I came straight to you. But Kaa, it will be good hunting. Few of us will see another moon.
Are you part of this hunt? Remember, you are a man, and tha the Pack cast you out. Let the wolves fight the dogs.

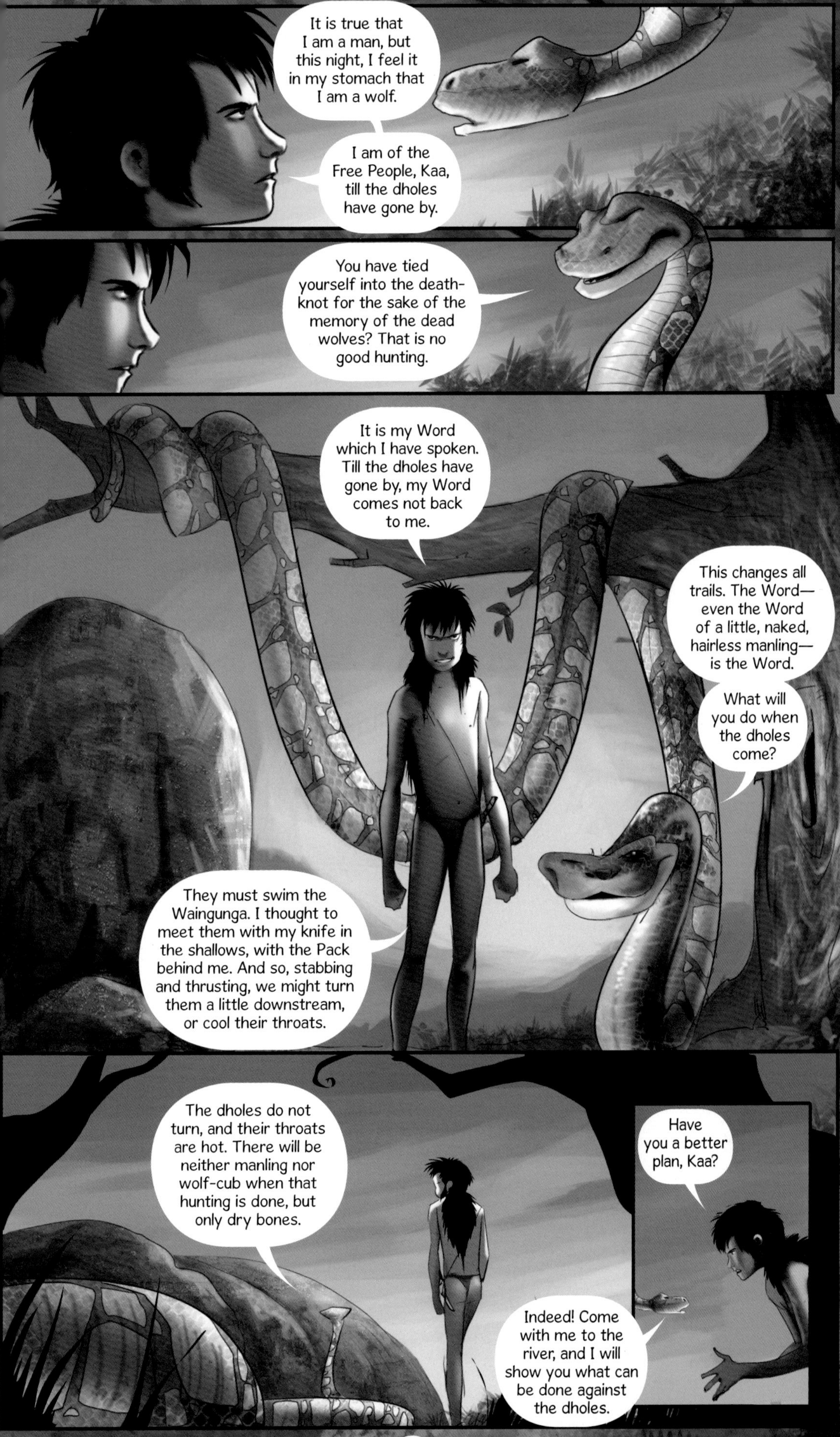
It is true that I am a man, but this night, I feel it in my stomach that I am a wolf.
I am of the Free People, Kaa, till the dholes have gone by.
You have tied yourself into the death-knot for the sake of the memory of the dead wolves? That is no good hunting.
It is my Word which I have spoken. Till the dholes have gone by, my Word comes not back to me.
This changes all trails. The Word—even the Word of a little, naked, hairless manling—is the Word.
What will you do when the dholes come?
They must swim the Waingunga. I thought to meet them with my knife in the shallows, with the Pack behind me. And so, stabbing and thrusting, we might turn them a little downstream, or cool their throats.
The dholes do not turn, and their throats are hot. There will be neither manling nor wolf-cub when that hunting is done, but only dry bones.
Have you a better plan, Kaa?
Indeed! Come with me to the river, and I will show you what can be done against the dholes.

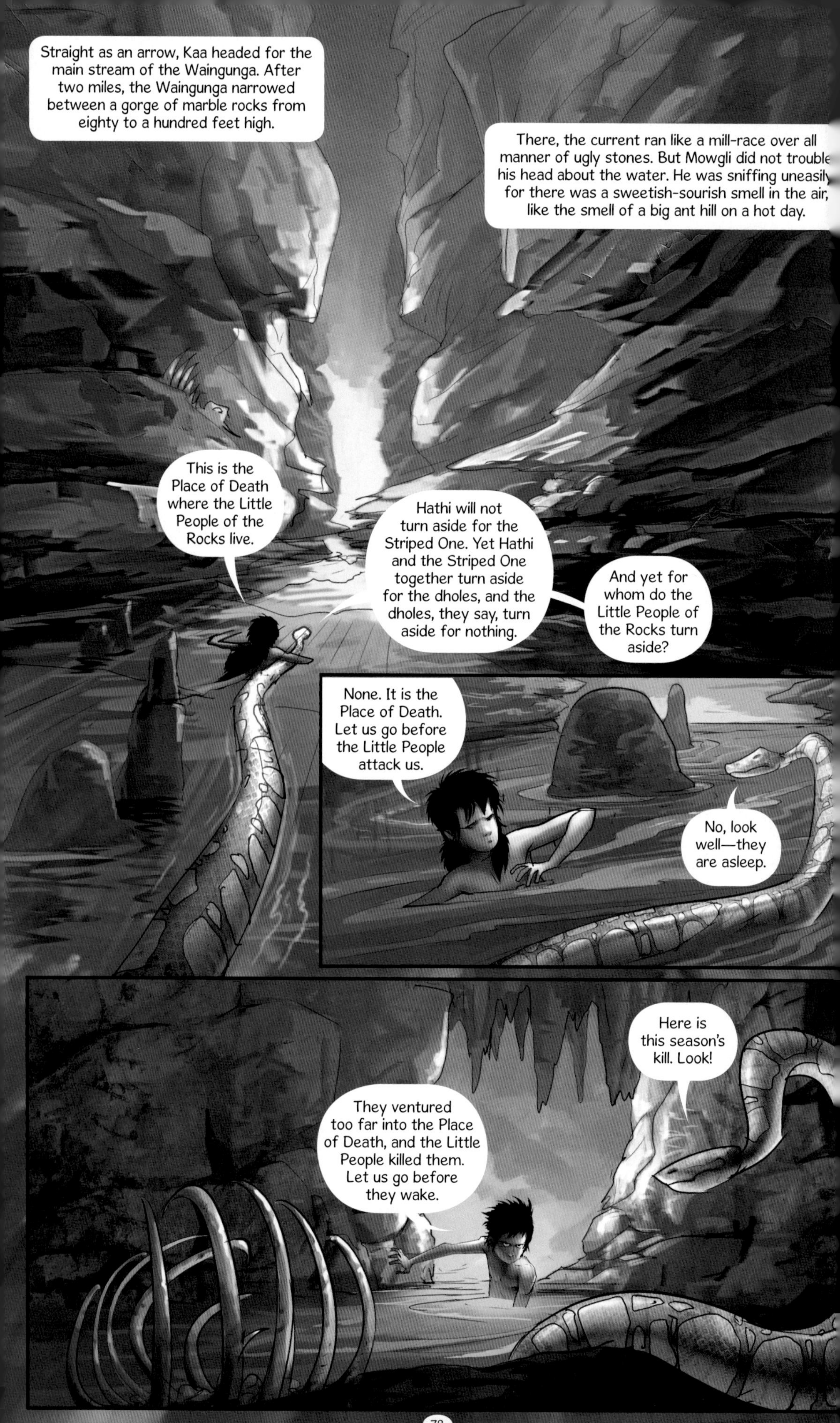

Straight as an arrow, Kaa headed for the main stream of the Waingunga. After two miles, the Waingunga narrowed between a gorge of marble rocks from eighty to a hundred feet high.
There, the current ran like a mill-race over all manner of ugly stones. But Mowgli did not trouble his head about the water. He was sniffing uneasily for there was a sweetish-sourish smell in the air, like the smell of a big ant hill on a hot day.
This is the Place of Death where the Little People of the Rocks live.
Hathi will not turn aside for the Striped One. Yet Hathi and the Striped One together turn aside for the dholes, and the dholes, they say, turn aside for nothing.
And yet for whom do the Little People of the Rocks turn aside?
None. It is the Place of Death. Let us go before the Little People attack us.
No, look well—they are asleep.
Here is this season's kill. Look!
They ventured too far into the Place of Death, and the Little People killed them. Let us go before they wake.

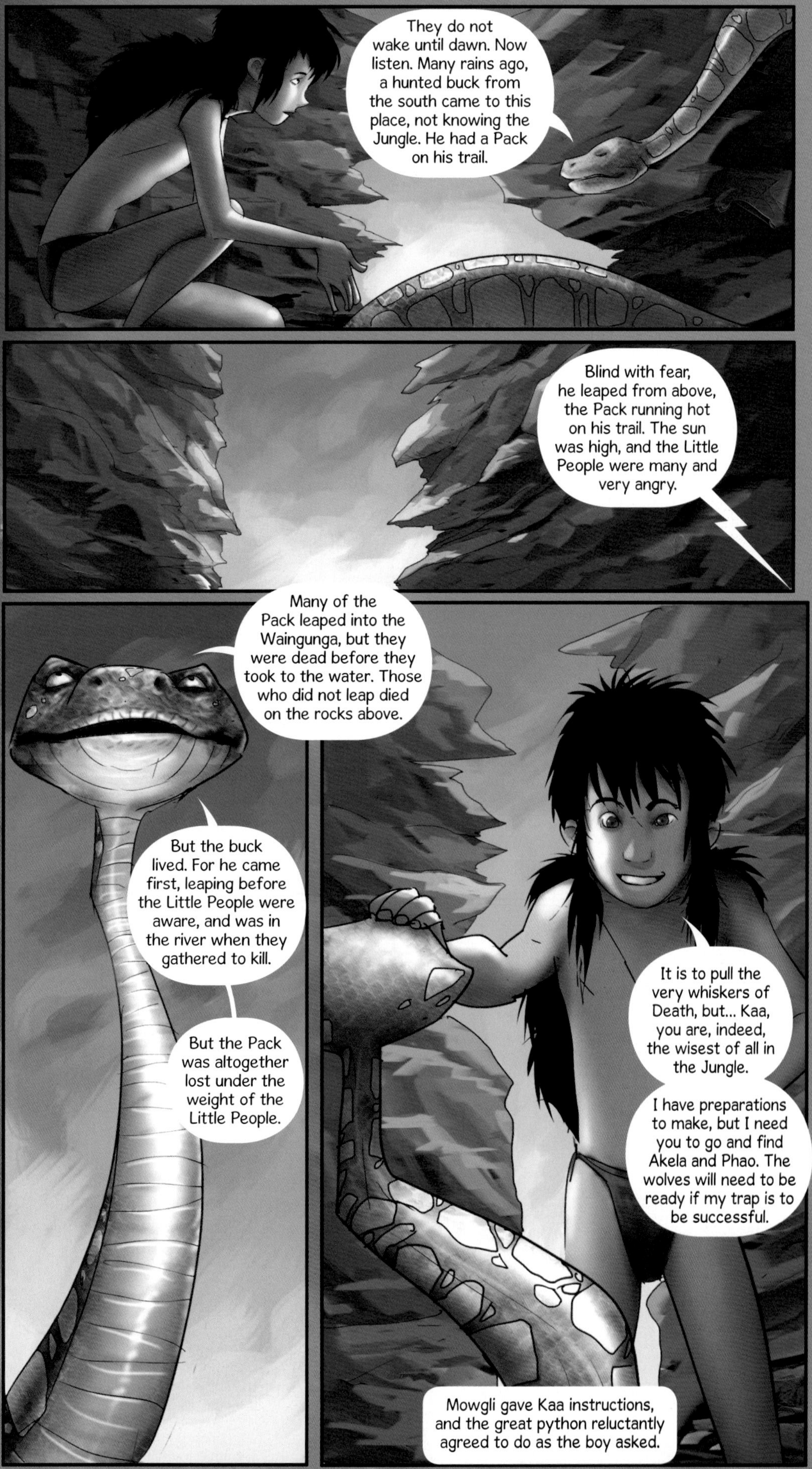
They do not wake until dawn. Now listen. Many rains ago, a hunted buck from the south came to this place, not knowing the Jungle. He had a Pack on his trail.
Blind with fear, he leaped from above, the Pack running hot on his trail. The sun was high, and the Little People were many and very angry.
Many of the Pack leaped into the Waingunga, but they were dead before they took to the water. Those who did not leap died on the rocks above.
But the buck lived. For he came first, leaping before the Little People were aware, and was in the river when they gathered to kill.
But the Pack was altogether lost under the weight of the Little People.
It is to pull the very whiskers of Death, but... Kaa, you are, indeed, the wisest of all in the Jungle.
I have preparations to make, but I need you to go and find Akela and Phao. The wolves will need to be ready if my trap is to be successful.
Mowgli gave Kaa instructions, and the great python reluctantly agreed to do as the boy asked.

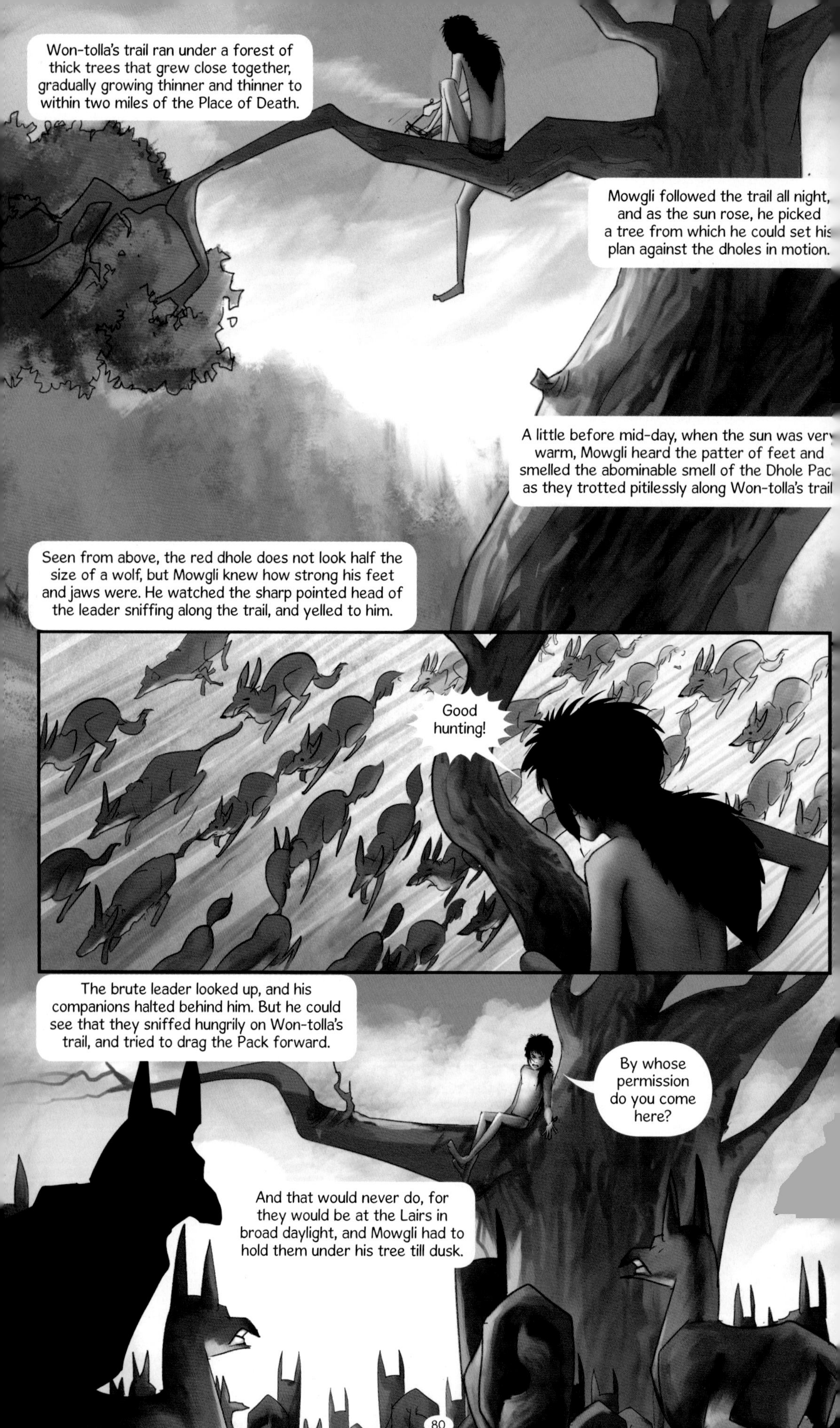
Won-tolla's trail ran under a forest of thick trees that grew close together, gradually growing thinner and thinner to within two miles of the Place of Death.
Mowgli followed the trail all night, and as the sun rose, he picked a tree from which he could set his plan against the dholes in motion.
A little before mid-day, when the sun was ver warm, Mowgli heard the patter of feet and smelled the abominable smell of the Dhole Pac as they trotted pitilessly along Won-tolla's trail
Seen from above, the red dhole does not look half the size of a wolf, but Mowgli knew how strong his feet and jaws were. He watched the sharp pointed head of the leader sniffing along the trail, and yelled to him.
Good hunting!
The brute leader looked up, and his companions halted behind him. But he could see that they sniffed hungrily on Won-tolla's trail, and tried to drag the Pack forward.
By whose permission do you come here?
And that would never do, for they would be at the Lairs in broad daylight, and Mowgli had to hold them under his tree till dusk.

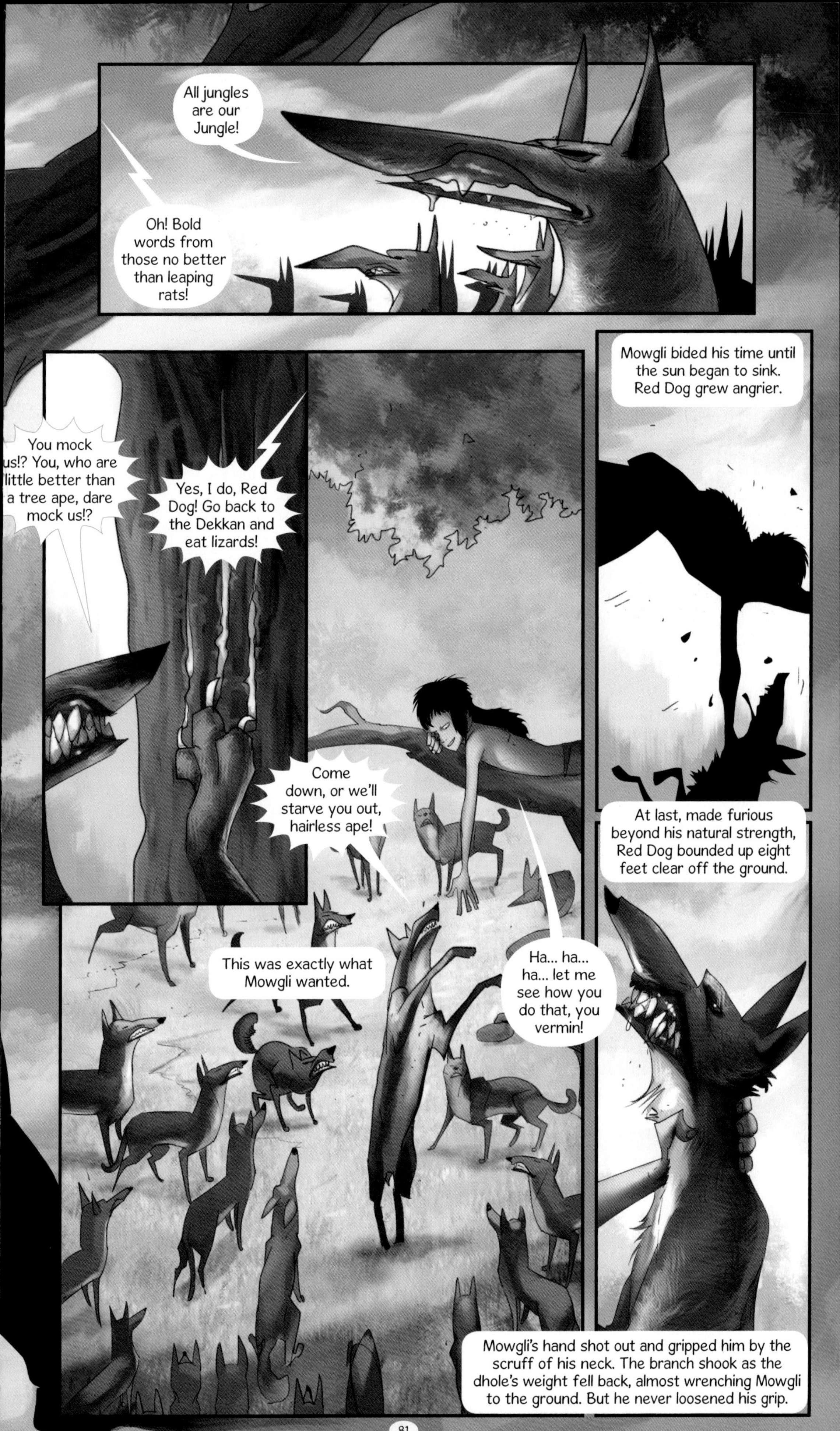

All jungles are our Jungle!
Oh! Bold words from those no better than leaping rats!
You mock us!? You, who are little better than a tree ape, dare mock us!?
Yes, I do, Red Dog! Go back to the Dekkan and eat lizards!
Come down, or we'll starve you out, hairless ape!
This was exactly what Mowgli wanted.
Ha... ha... ha... let me see how you do that, you vermin!
Mowgli bided his time until the sun began to sink. Red Dog grew angrier.
At last, made furious beyond his natural strength, Red Dog bounded up eight feet clear off the ground.
Mowgli's hand shot out and gripped him by the scruff of his neck. The branch shook as the dhole's weight fell back, almost wrenching Mowgli to the ground. But he never loosened his grip.

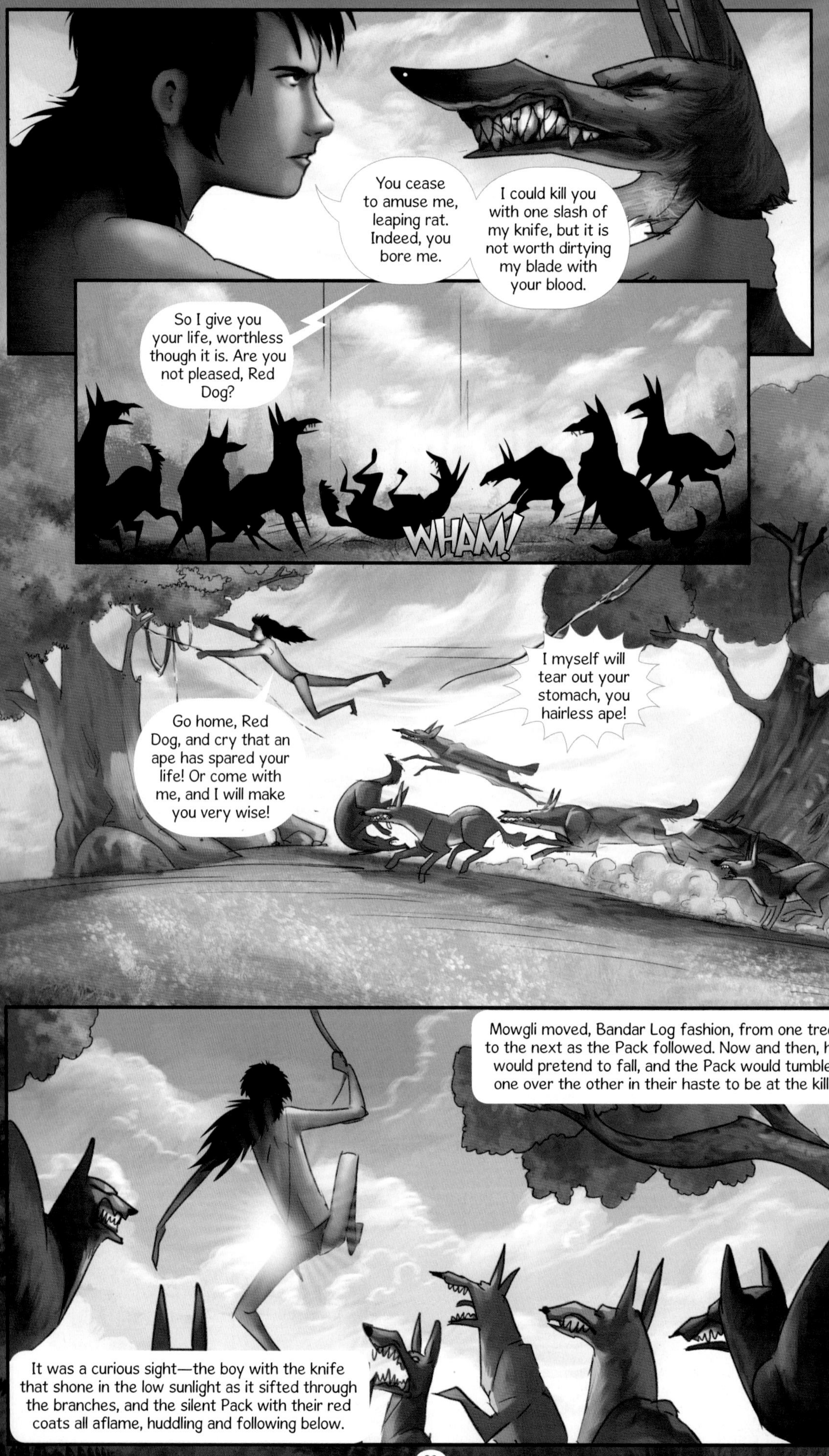
You cease to amuse me, leaping rat. Indeed, you bore me.
I could kill you with one slash of my knife, but it is not worth dirtying my blade with your blood.
So I give you your life, worthless though it is. Are you not pleased, Red Dog?
WHAM!
Go home, Red Dog, and cry that an ape has spared your life! Or come with me, and I will make you very wise!
I myself will tear out your stomach, you hairless ape!
Mowgli moved, Bandar Log fashion, from one tree to the next as the Pack followed. Now and then, he would pretend to fall, and the Pack would tumble one over the other in their haste to be at the kill.
It was a curious sight—the boy with the knife that shone in the low sunlight as it sifted through the branches, and the silent Pack with their red coats all aflame, huddling and following below.

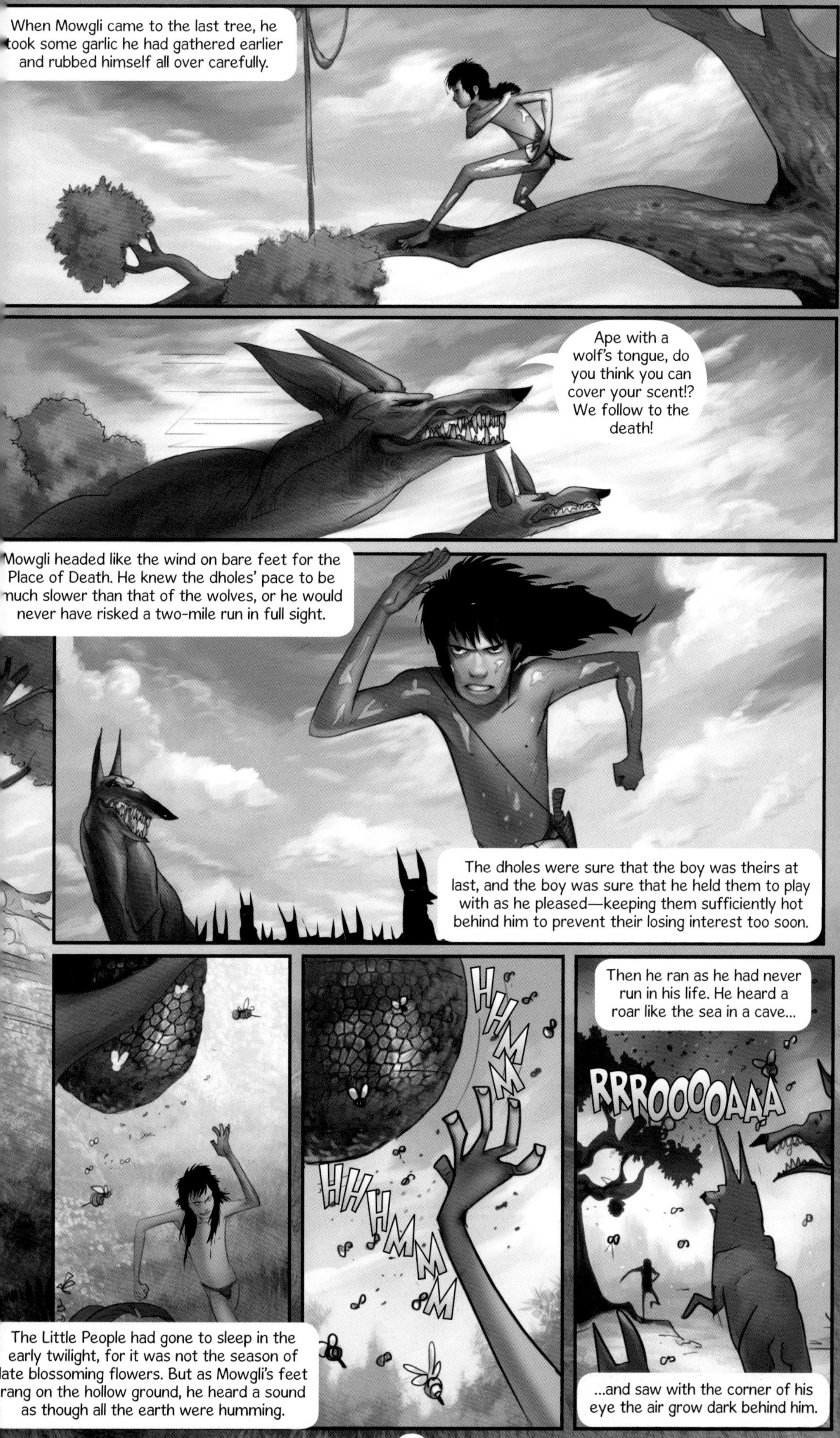

When Mowgli came to the last tree, he took some garlic he had gathered earlier and rubbed himself all over carefully.
Ape with a wolf's tongue, do you think you can cover your scent!? We follow to the death!
Mowgli headed like the wind on bare feet for the Place of Death. He knew the dholes' pace to be much slower than that of the wolves, or he would never have risked a two-mile run in full sight.
The dholes were sure that the boy was theirs at last, and the boy was sure that he held them to play with as he pleased—keeping them sufficiently hot behind him to prevent their losing interest too soon.
The Little People had gone to sleep in the early twilight, for it was not the season of late blossoming flowers. But as Mowgli's feet rang on the hollow ground, he heard a sound as though all the earth were humming.
HHMMM
HHHMMMMM
Then he ran as he had never run in his life. He heard a roar like the sea in a cave...
RRROOOOAAA
...and saw with the corner of his eye the air grow dark behind him.

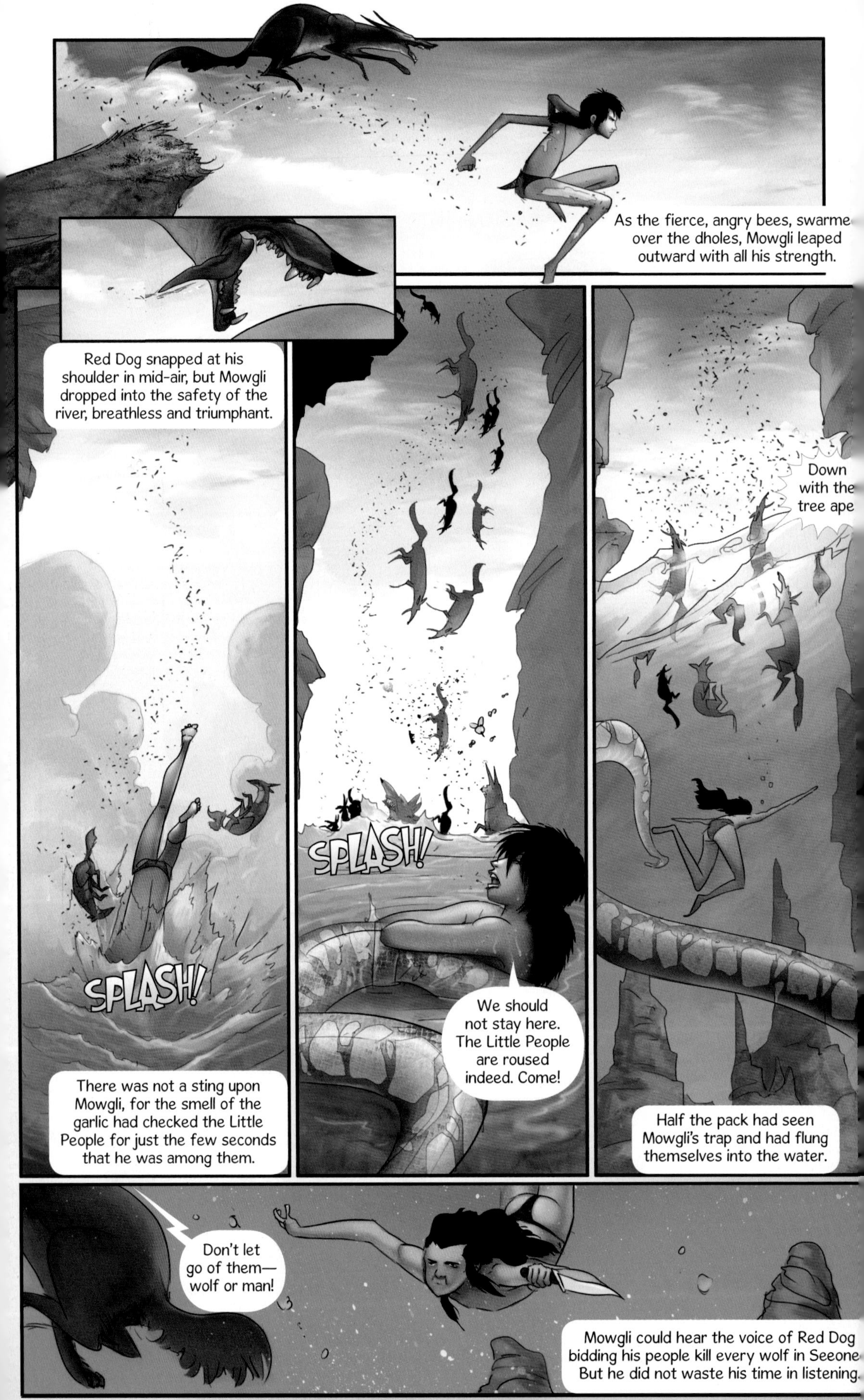
As the fierce, angry bees, swarme over the dholes, Mowgli leaped outward with all his strength.
Red Dog snapped at his shoulder in mid-air, but Mowgli dropped into the safety of the river, breathless and triumphant.
SPLASH!
There was not a sting upon Mowgli, for the smell of the garlic had checked the Little People for just the few seconds that he was among them.
SPLASH!
We should not stay here. The Little People are roused indeed. Come!
Down with the tree ape
Half the pack had seen Mowgli's trap and had flung themselves into the water.
Don't let go of them— wolf or man!
Mowgli could hear the voice of Red Dog bidding his people kill every wolf in Seone But he did not waste his time in listening.

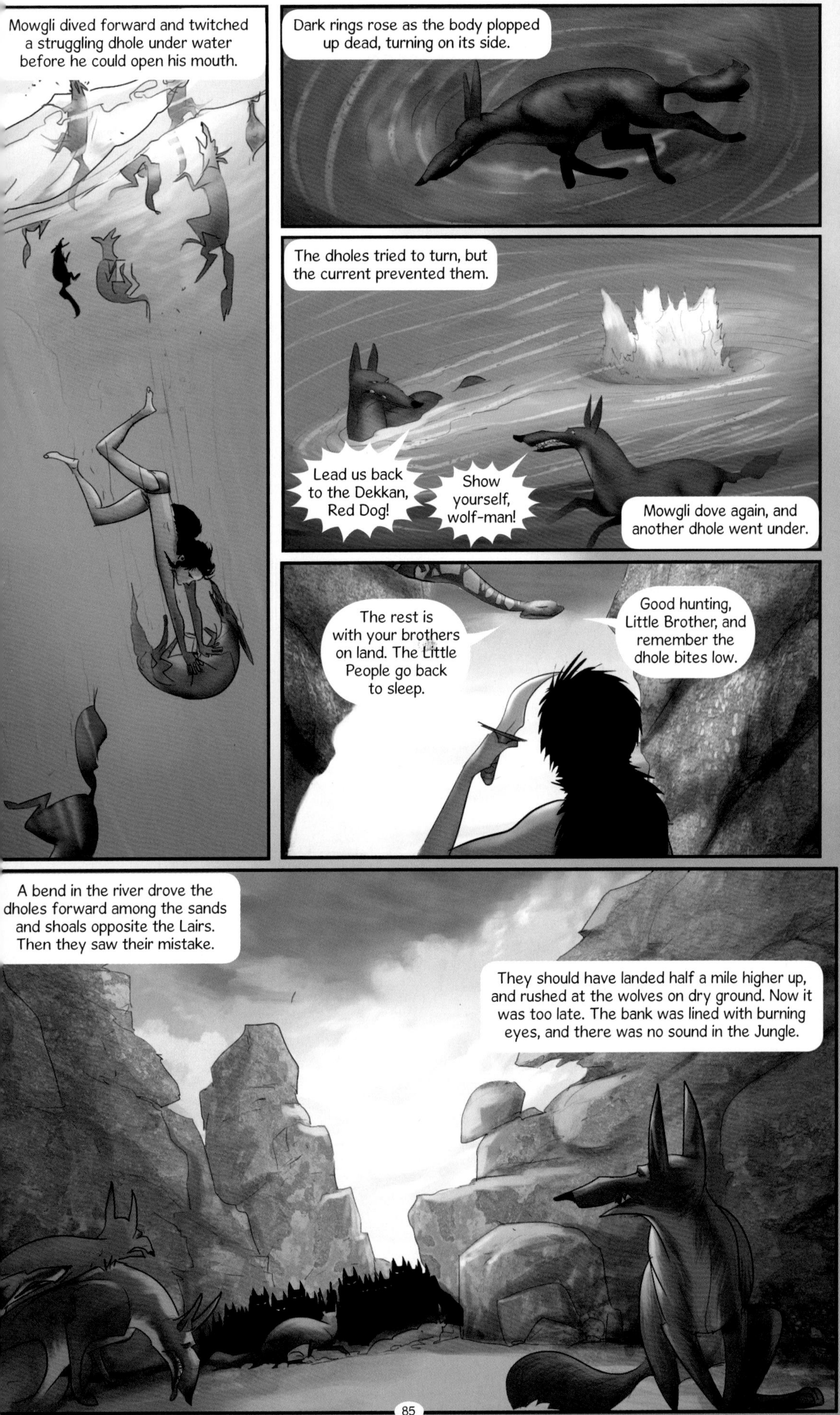

Mowgli dived forward and twitched a struggling dhole under water before he could open his mouth.
Dark rings rose as the body plopped up dead, turning on its side.
The dholes tried to turn, but the current prevented them.
Lead us back to the Dekkan, Red Dog!
Show yourself, wolf-man!
Mowgli dove again, and another dhole went under.
The rest is with your brothers on land. The Little People go back to sleep.
Good hunting, Little Brother, and remember the dhole bites low.
A bend in the river drove the dholes forward among the sands and shoals opposite the Lairs. Then they saw their mistake.
They should have landed half a mile higher up, and rushed at the wolves on dry ground. Now it was too late. The bank was lined with burning eyes, and there was no sound in the Jungle.

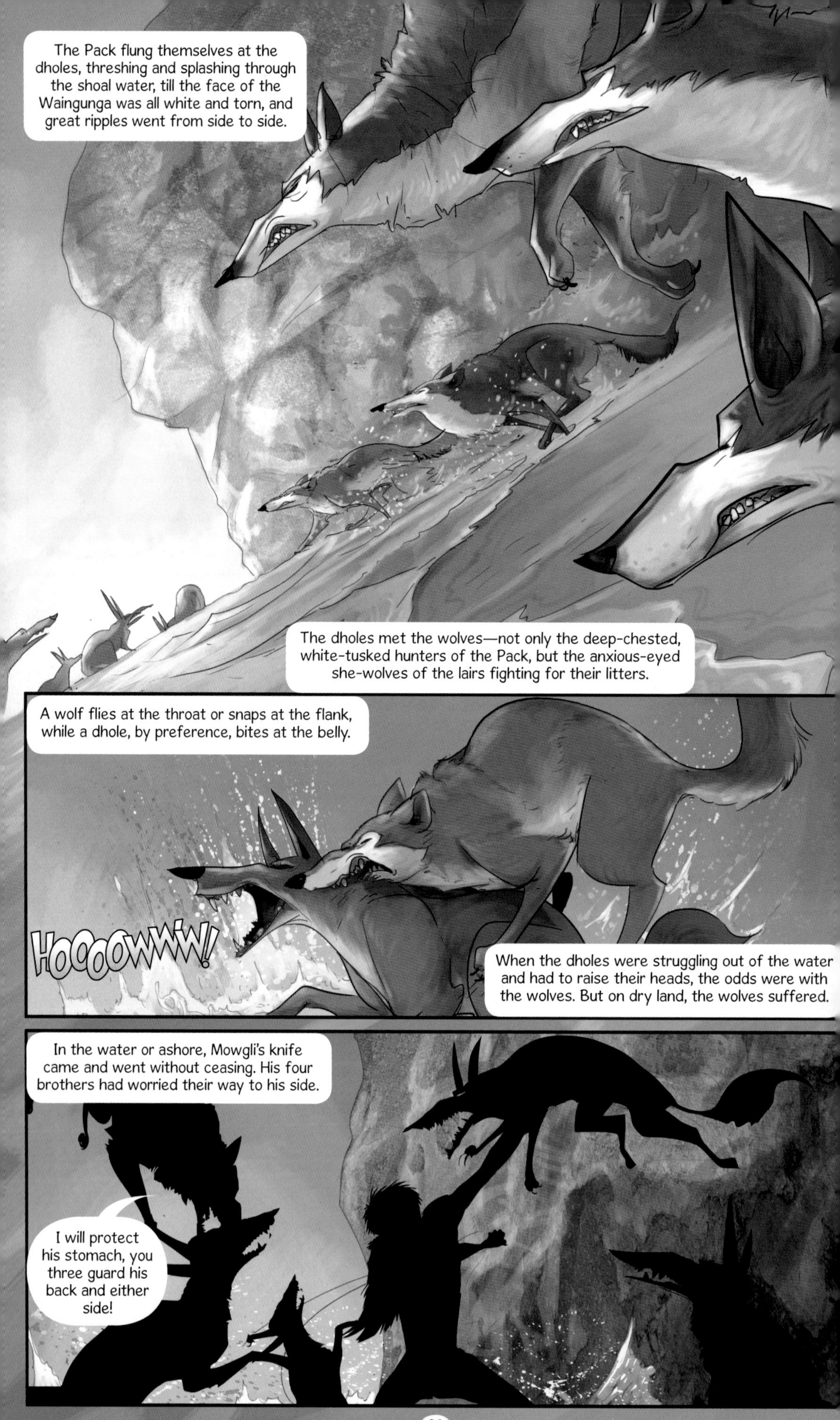
The Pack flung themselves at the dholes, threshing and splashing through the shoal water, till the face of the Waingunga was all white and torn, and great ripples went from side to side.
The dholes met the wolves—not only the deep-chested, white-tusked hunters of the Pack, but the anxious-eyed she-wolves of the lairs fighting for their litters.
A wolf flies at the throat or snaps at the flank, while a dhole, by preference, bites at the belly.
HOOOOWWW!
When the dholes were struggling out of the water and had to raise their heads, the odds were with the wolves. But on dry land, the wolves suffered.
In the water or ashore, Mowgli's knife came and went without ceasing. His four brothers had worried their way to his side.
I will protect his stomach, you three guard his back and either side!

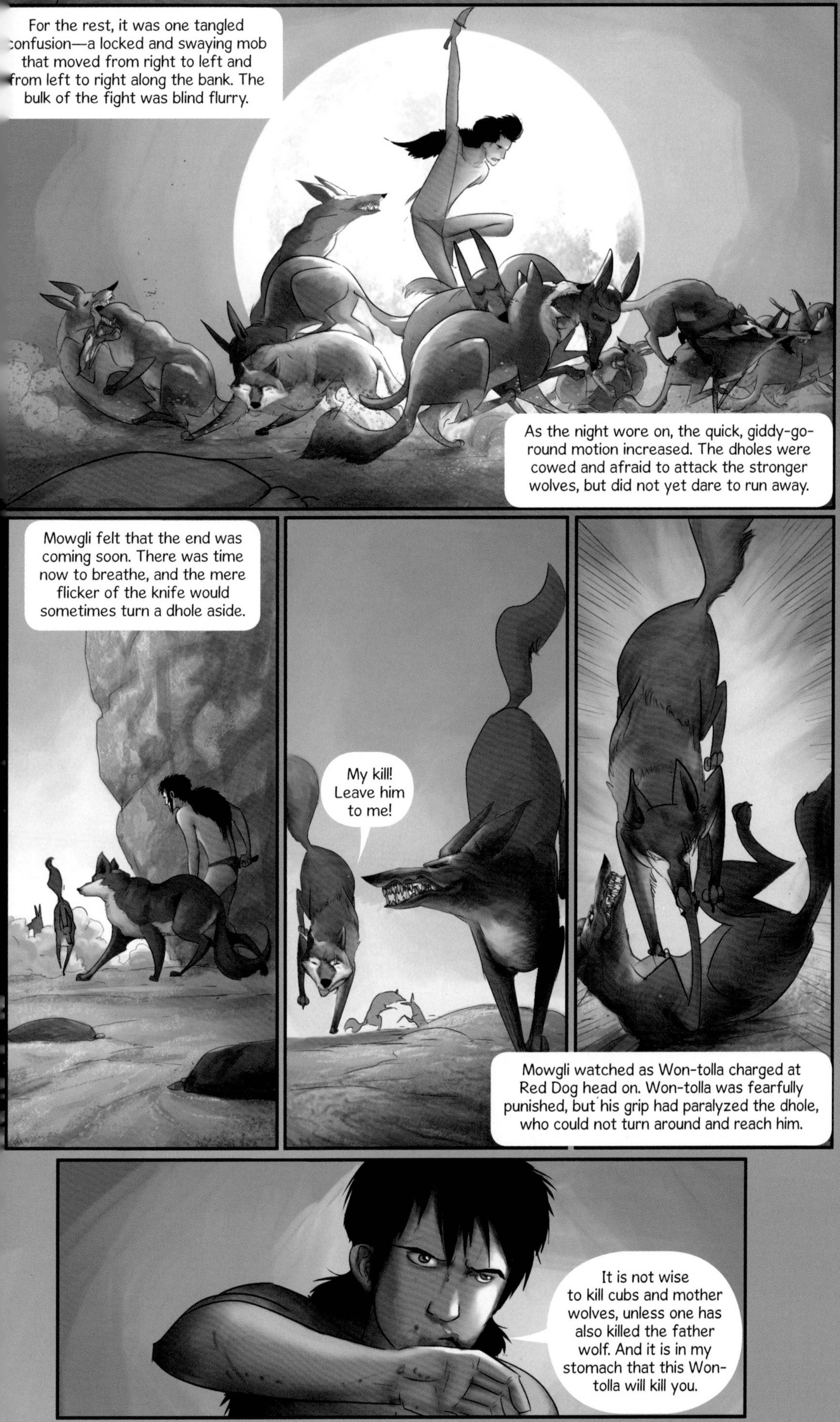
For the rest, it was one tangled confusion—a locked and swaying mob that moved from right to left and from left to right along the bank. The bulk of the fight was blind flurry.
As the night wore on, the quick, giddy-go-round motion increased. The dholes were cowed and afraid to attack the stronger wolves, but did not yet dare to run away.
Mowgli felt that the end was coming soon. There was time now to breathe, and the mere flicker of the knife would sometimes turn a dhole aside.
My kill! Leave him to me!
Mowgli watched as Won-tolla charged at Red Dog head on. Won-tolla was fearfully punished, but his grip had paralyzed the dhole, who could not turn around and reach him.
It is not wise to kill cubs and mother wolves, unless one has also killed the father wolf. And it is in my stomach that this Won-tolla will kill you.

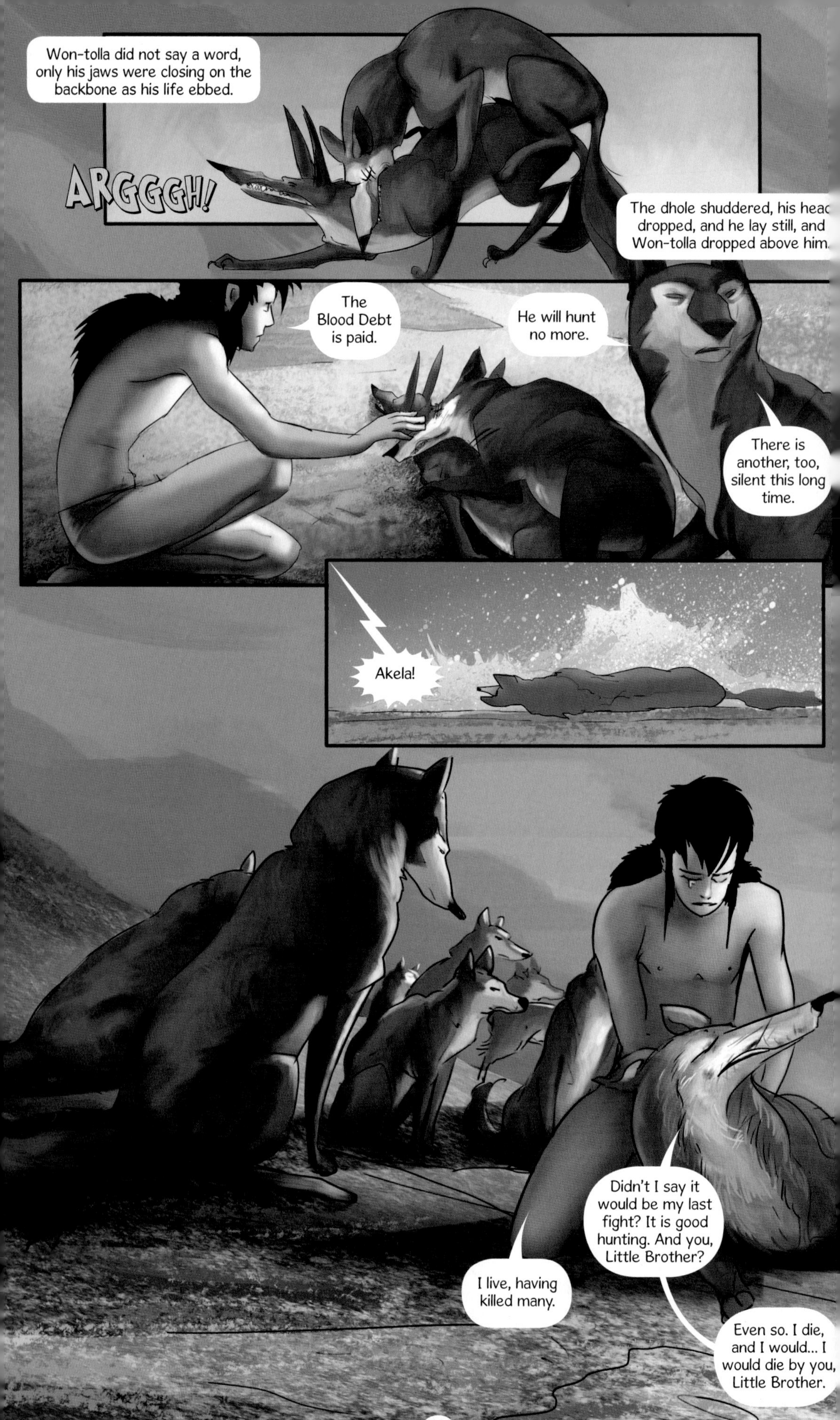
Won-tolla did not say a word, only his jaws were closing on the backbone as his life ebbed.
ARGGGH!
The dhole shuddered, his head dropped, and he lay still, and Won-tolla dropped above him.
The Blood Debt is paid.
He will hunt no more.
There is another, too, silent this long time.
Akela!
Didn't I say it would be my last fight? It is good hunting. And you, Little Brother?
I live, having killed many.
Even so. I die, and I would... I would die by you, Little Brother.

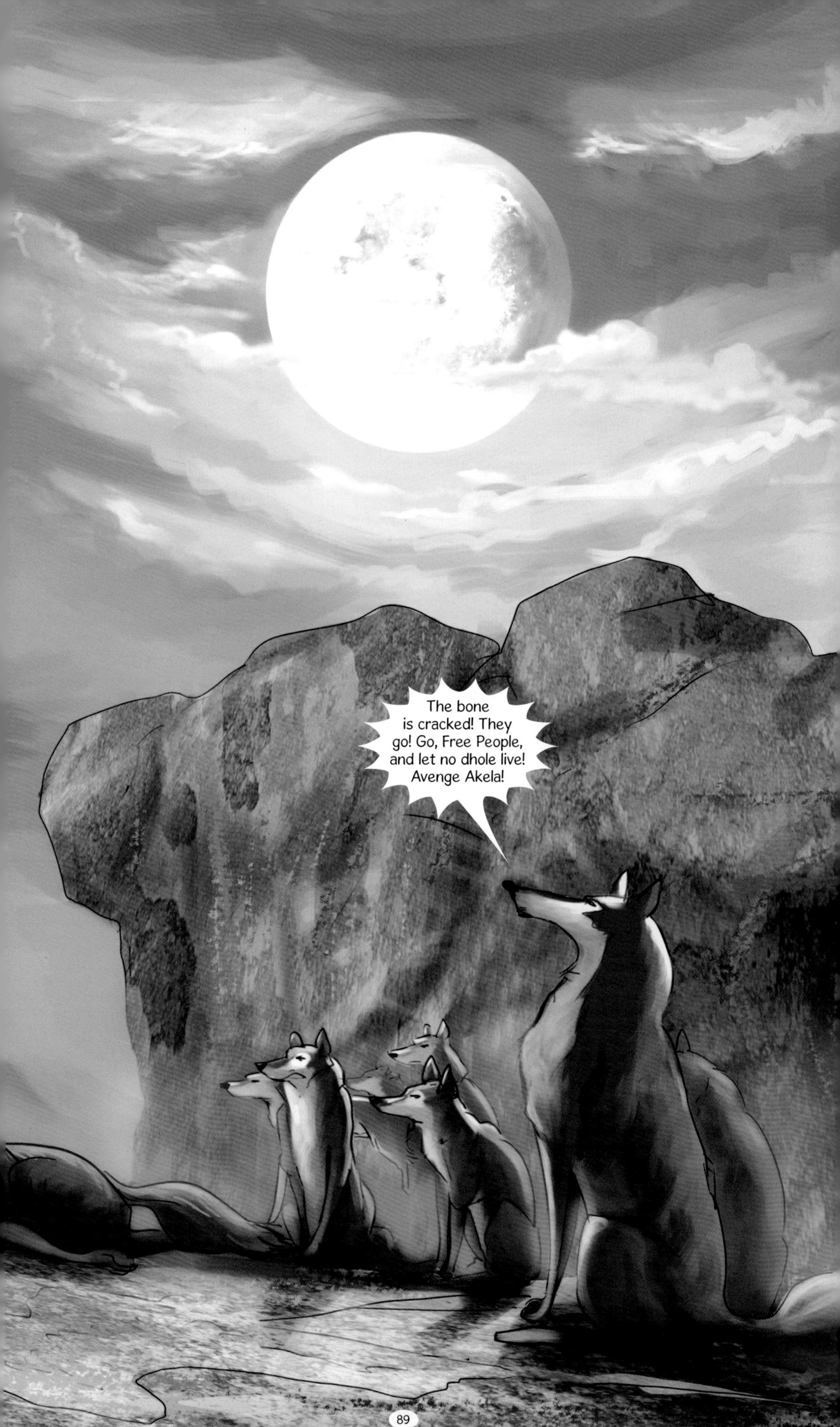
The bone is cracked! They go! Go, Free People, and let no dhole live! Avenge Akela!

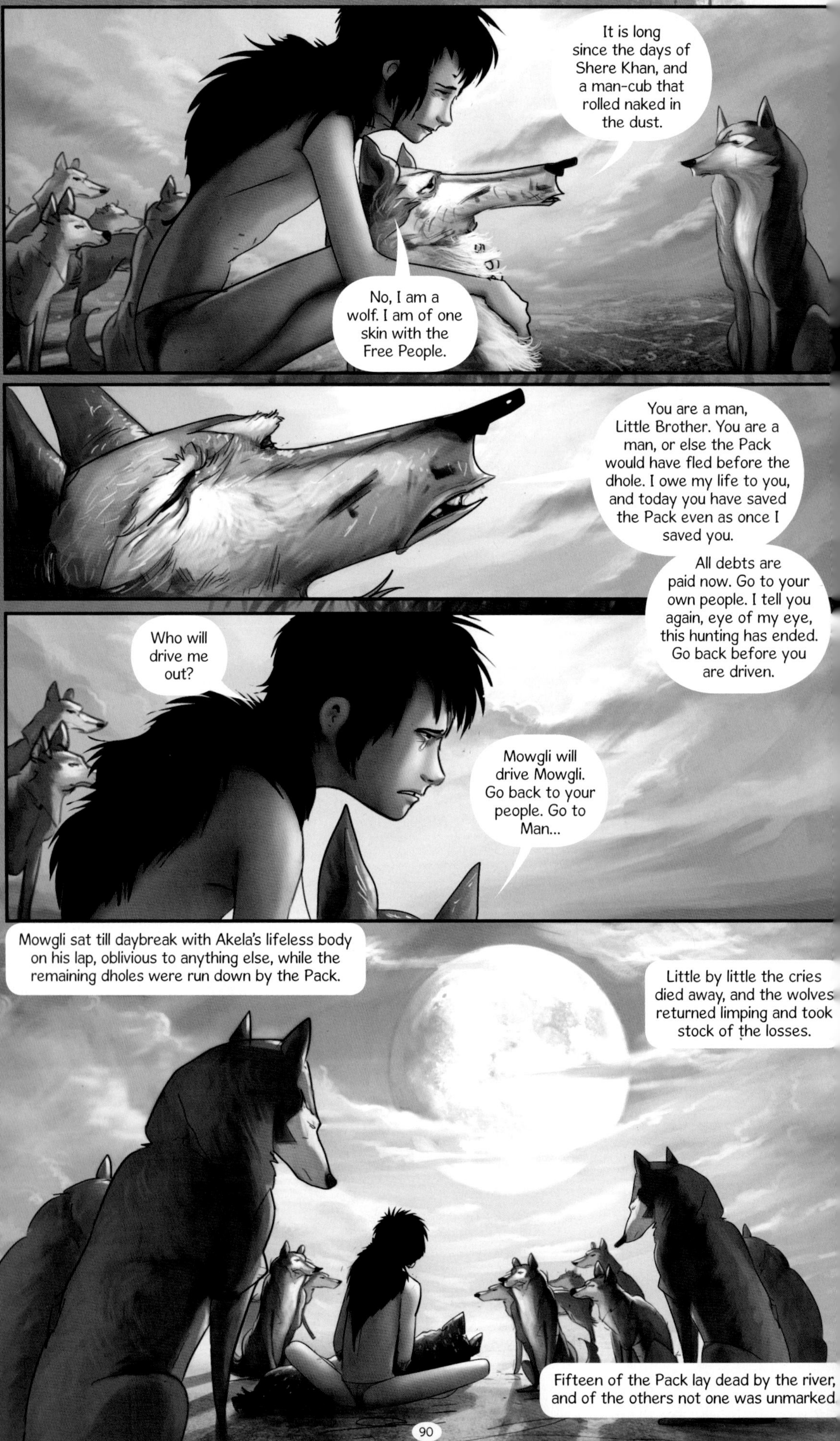

It is long since the days of Shere Khan, and a man-cub that rolled naked in the dust.
No, I am a wolf. I am of one skin with the Free People.
You are a man, Little Brother. You are a man, or else the Pack would have fled before the dhole. I owe my life to you, and today you have saved the Pack even as once I saved you.
All debts are paid now. Go to your own people. I tell you again, eye of my eye, this hunting has ended. Go back before you are driven.
Who will drive me out?
Mowgli will drive Mowgli. Go back to your people. Go to Man...
Mowgli sat till daybreak with Akela's lifeless body on his lap, oblivious to anything else, while the remaining dholes were run down by the Pack.
Little by little the cries died away, and the wolves returned limping and took stock of the losses.
Fifteen of the Pack lay dead by the river, and of the others not one was unmarked

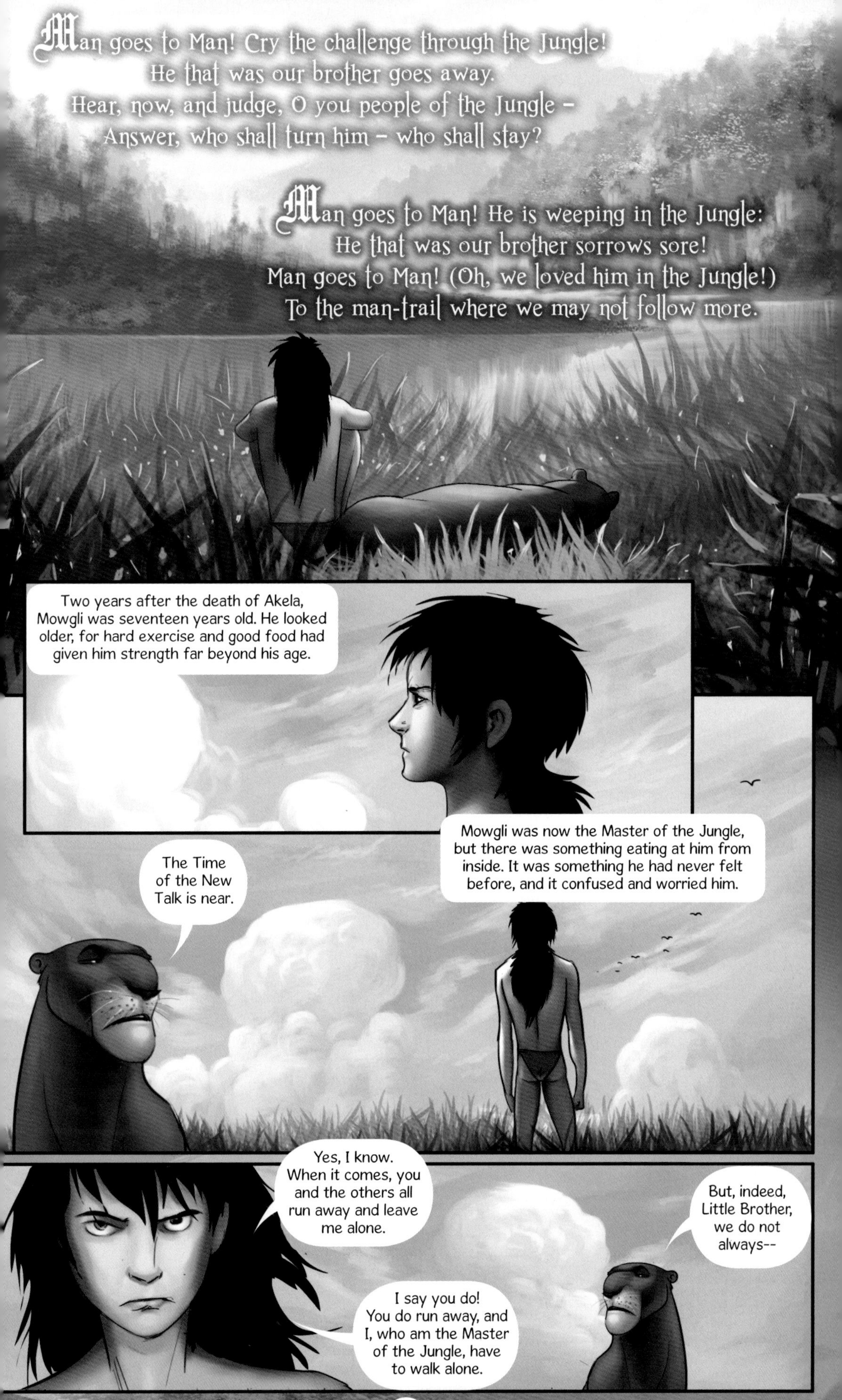
Man goes to Man! Cry the challenge through the Jungle!
He that was our brother goes away.
Hear, now, and judge, O you people of the Jungle –
Answer, who shall turn him – who shall stay?
Man goes to Man! He is weeping in the Jungle:
He that was our brother sorrows sore!
Man goes to Man! (Oh, we loved him in the Jungle!)
To the man-trail where we may not follow more.
Two years after the death of Akela, Mowgli was seventeen years old. He looked older, for hard exercise and good food had given him strength far beyond his age.
The Time of the New Talk is near.
Mowgli was now the Master of the Jungle, but there was something eating at him from inside. It was something he had never felt before, and it confused and worried him.
Yes, I know. When it comes, you and the others all run away and leave me alone.
But, indeed, Little Brother, we do not always--
I say you do! You do run away, and I, who am the Master of the Jungle, have to walk alone.

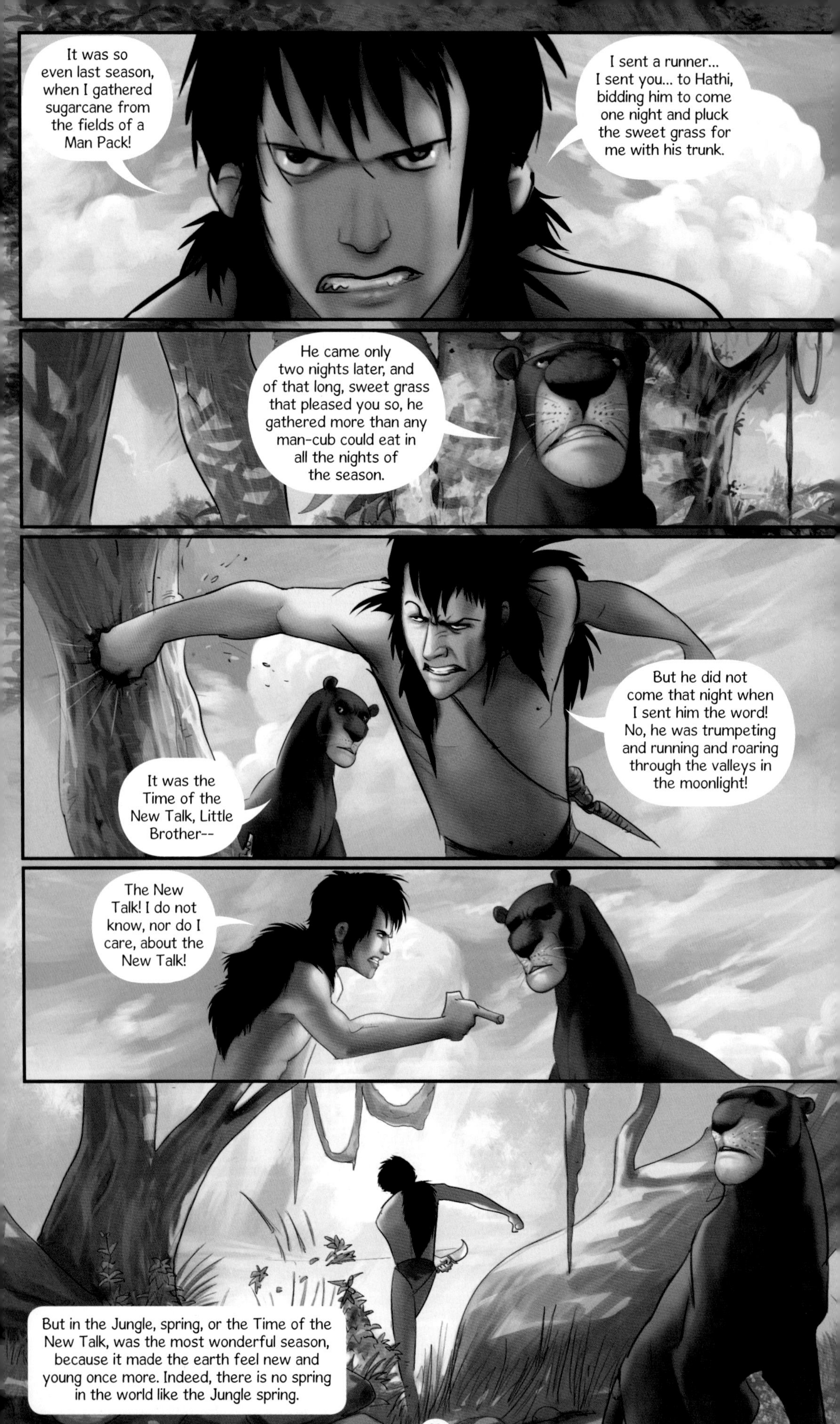
It was so even last season, when I gathered sugarcane from the fields of a Man Pack!
I sent a runner... I sent you... to Hathi, bidding him to come one night and pluck the sweet grass for me with his trunk.
He came only two nights later, and of that long, sweet grass that pleased you so, he gathered more than any man-cub could eat in all the nights of the season.
But he did not come that night when I sent him the word! No, he was trumpeting and running and roaring through the valleys in the moonlight!
It was the Time of the New Talk, Little Brother--
The New Talk! I do not know, nor do I care, about the New Talk!
But in the Jungle, spring, or the Time of the New Talk, was the most wonderful season, because it made the earth feel new and young once more. Indeed, there is no spring in the world like the Jungle spring.

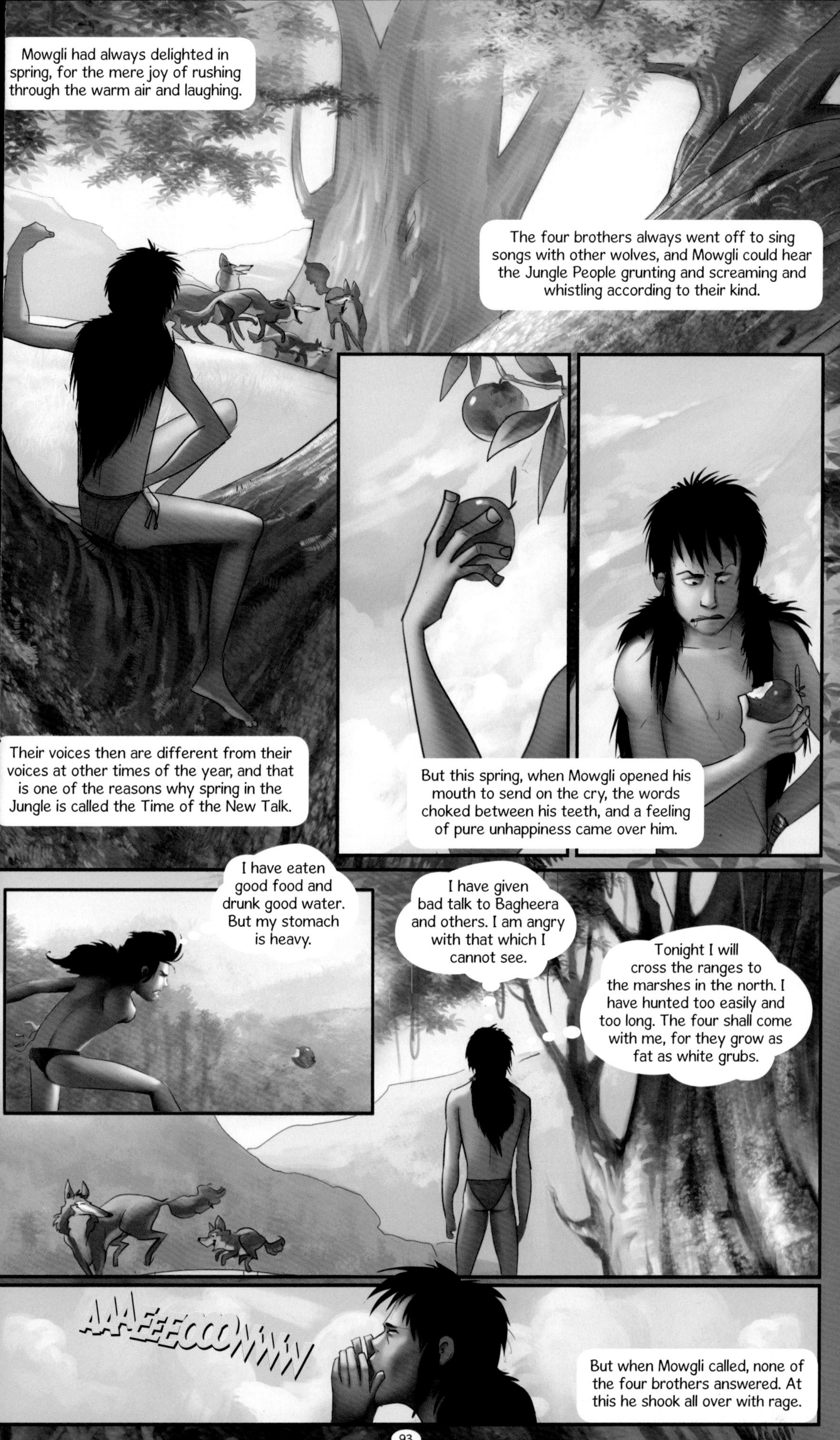
Mowgli had always delighted in spring, for the mere joy of rushing through the warm air and laughing.
The four brothers always went off to sing songs with other wolves, and Mowgli could hear the Jungle People grunting and screaming and whistling according to their kind.
Their voices then are different from their voices at other times of the year, and that is one of the reasons why spring in the Jungle is called the Time of the New Talk.
But this spring, when Mowgli opened his mouth to send on the cry, the words choked between his teeth, and a feeling of pure unhappiness came over him.
I have eaten good food and drunk good water. But my stomach is heavy.
I have given bad talk to Bagheera and others. I am angry with that which I cannot see.
Tonight I will cross the ranges to the marshes in the north. I have hunted too easily and too long. The four shall come with me, for they grow as fat as white grubs.
AAAEEEOOONNNN
But when Mowgli called, none of the four brothers answered. At this he shook all over with rage.

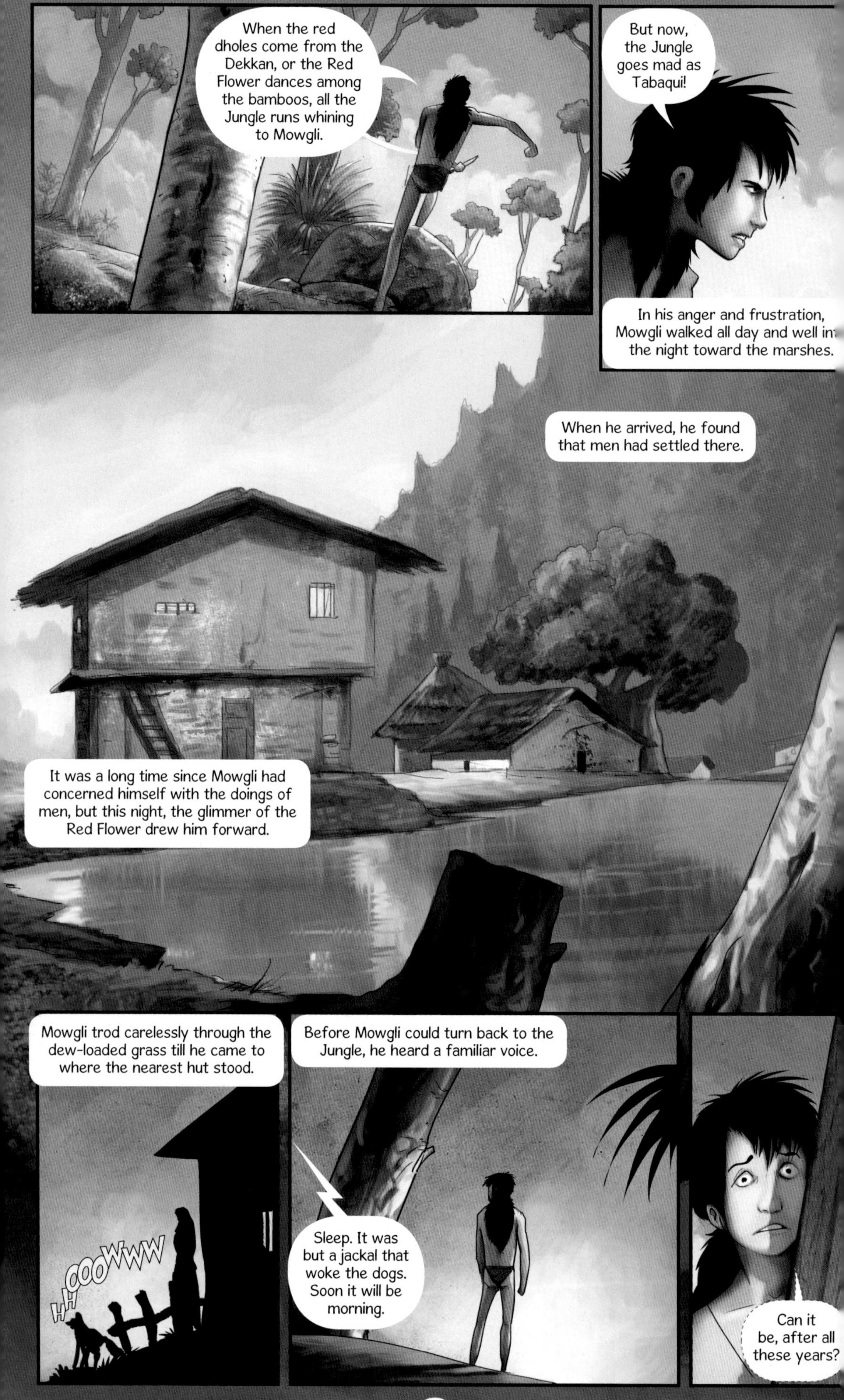
When the red dholes come from the Dekkan, or the Red Flower dances among the bamboos, all the Jungle runs whining to Mowgli.
But now, the Jungle goes mad as Tabaqui!
In his anger and frustration, Mowgli walked all day and well into the night toward the marshes.
When he arrived, he found that men had settled there.
It was a long time since Mowgli had concerned himself with the doings of men, but this night, the glimmer of the Red Flower drew him forward.
Mowgli trod carelessly through the dew-loaded grass till he came to where the nearest hut stood.
HHOOOWWW
Before Mowgli could turn back to the Jungle, he heard a familiar voice.
Sleep. It was but a jackal that woke the dogs. Soon it will be morning.
Can it be, after all these years?

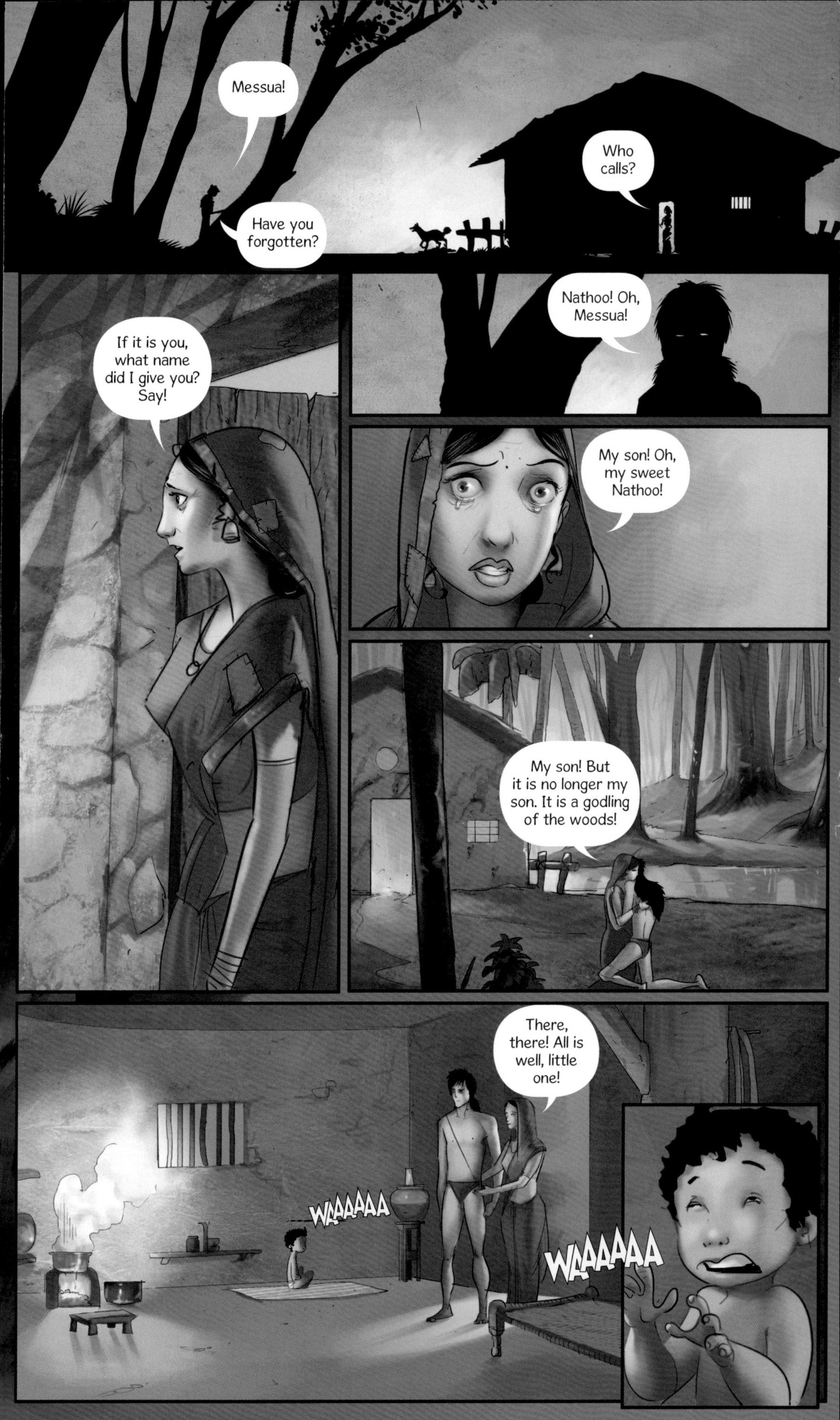

Messua!
Have you forgotten?
Who calls?
If it is you, what name did I give you? Say!
Nathoo! Oh, Messua!
My son! Oh, my sweet Nathoo!
My son! But it is no longer my son. It is a godling of the woods!
WAAAAAA
There, there! All is well, little one!
WAAAAAA

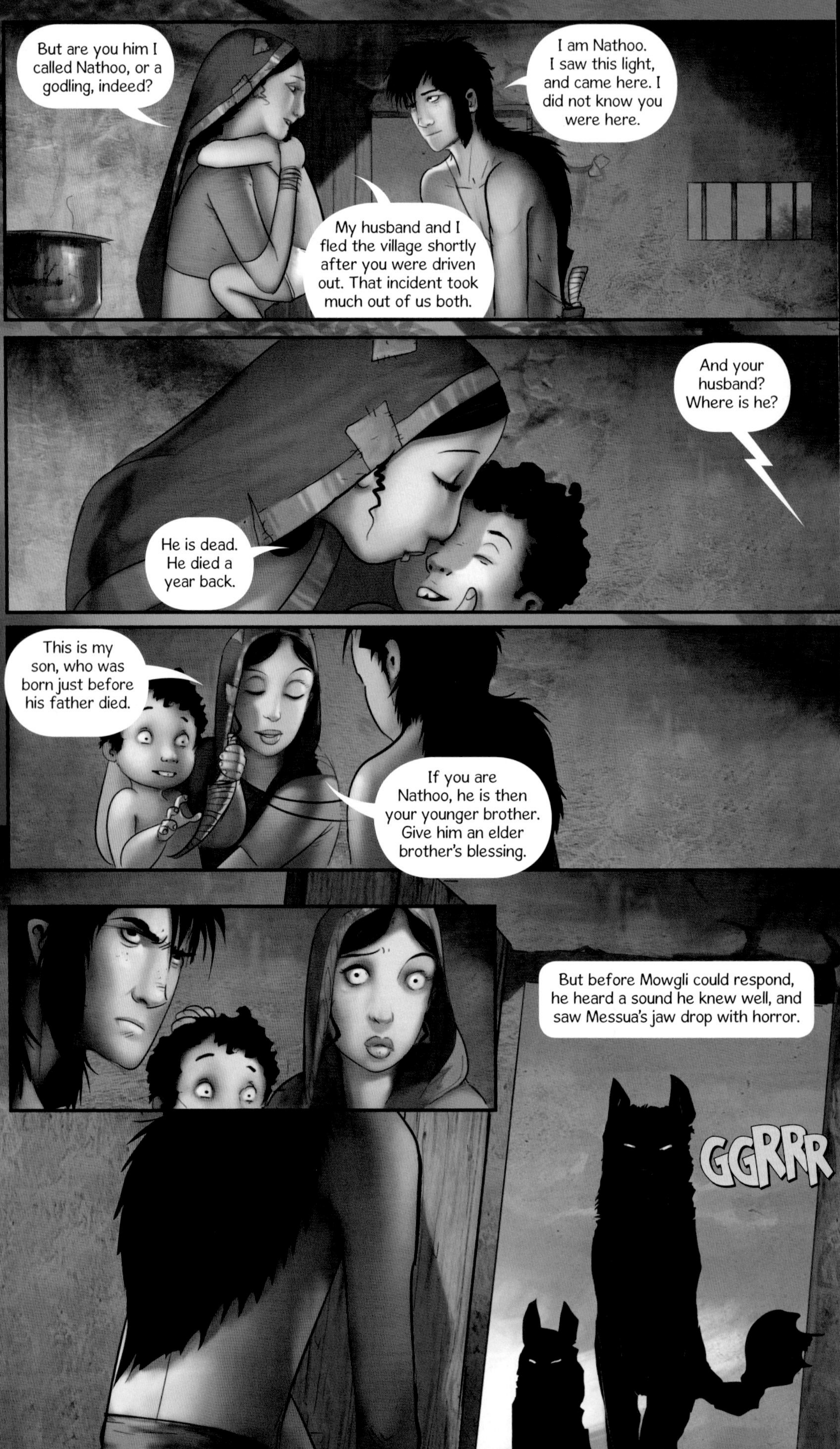
But are you him I called Nathoo, or a godling, indeed?
I am Nathoo. I saw this light, and came here. I did not know you were here.
My husband and I fled the village shortly after you were driven out. That incident took much out of us both.
And your husband? Where is he?
He is dead. He died a year back.
This is my son, who was born just before his father died.
If you are Nathoo, he is then your younger brother. Give him an elder brother's blessing.
But before Mowgli could respond, he heard a sound he knew well, and saw Messua's jaw drop with horror.
GGRRR

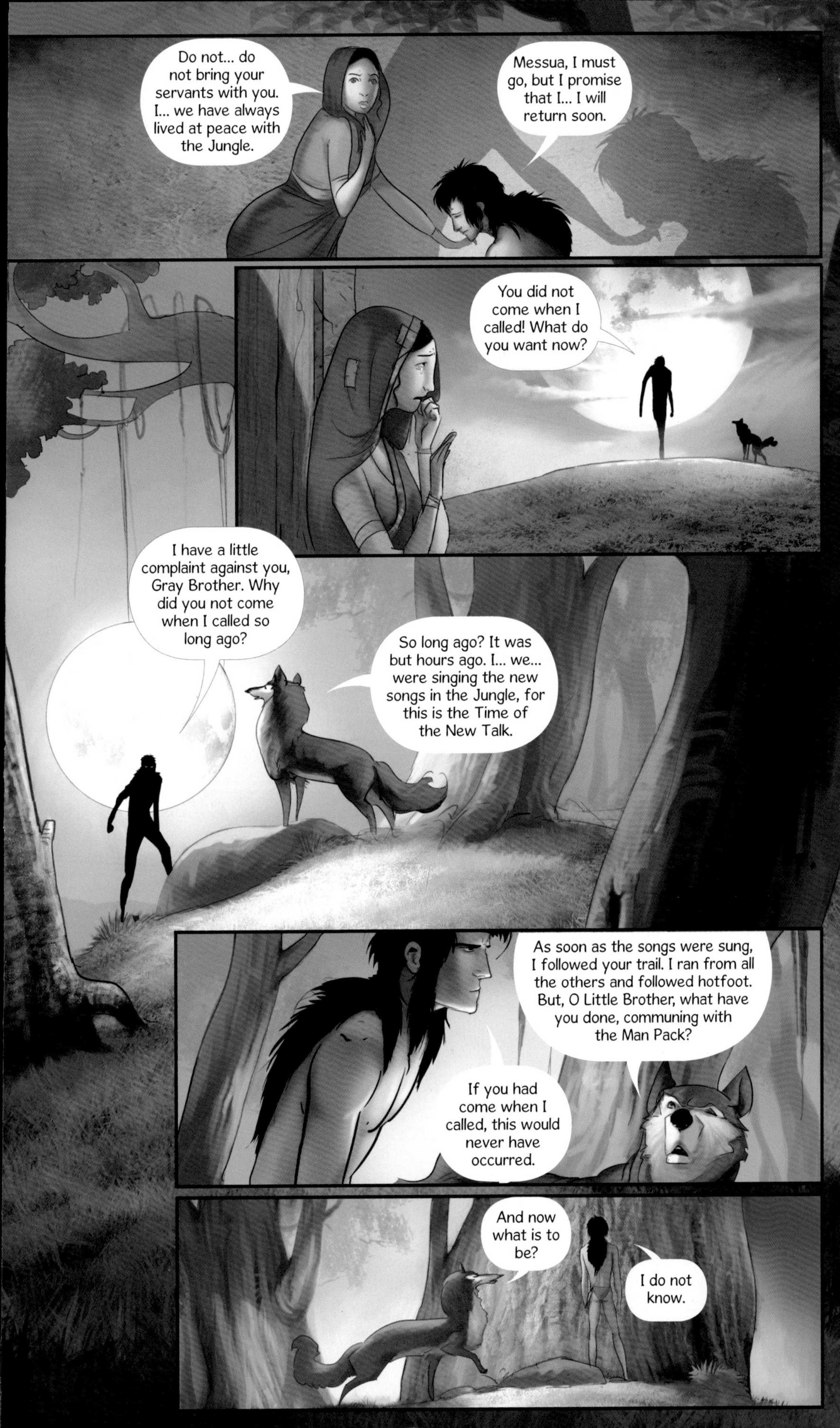
Do not... do not bring your servants with you. I... we have always lived at peace with the Jungle.
Messua, I must go, but I promise that I... I will return soon.
You did not come when I called! What do you want now?
I have a little complaint against you, Gray Brother. Why did you not come when I called so long ago?
So long ago? It was but hours ago. I... we... were singing the new songs in the Jungle, for this is the Time of the New Talk.
As soon as the songs were sung, I followed your trail. I ran from all the others and followed hotfoot. But, O Little Brother, what have you done, communing with the Man Pack?
If you had come when I called, this would never have occurred.
And now what is to be?
I do not know.

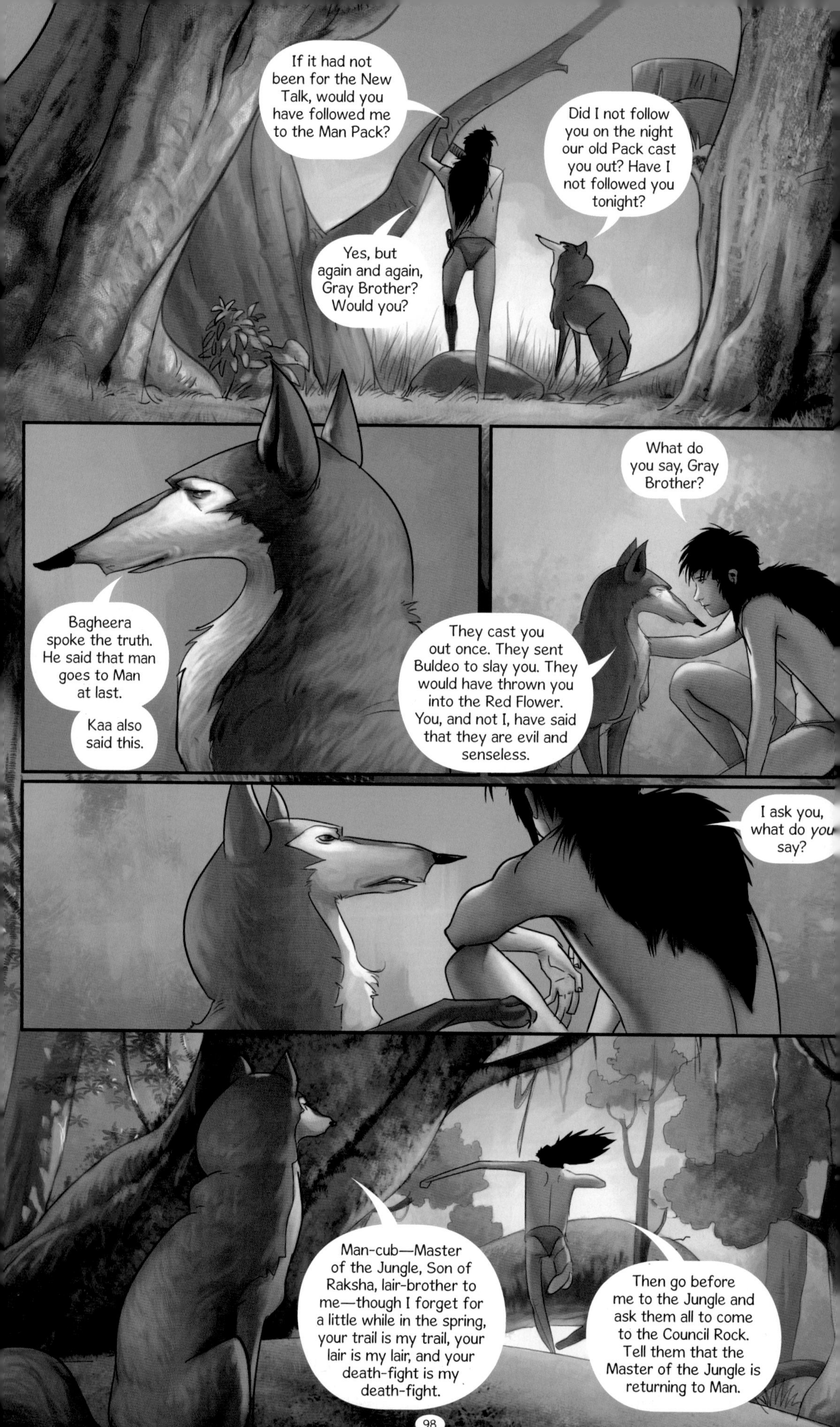
If it had not been for the New Talk, would you have followed me to the Man Pack?
Did I not follow you on the night our old Pack cast you out? Have I not followed you tonight?
Yes, but again and again, Gray Brother? Would you?
Bagheera spoke the truth. He said that man goes to Man at last.
Kaa also said this.
What do you say, Gray Brother?
They cast you out once. They sent Buldeo to slay you. They would have thrown you into the Red Flower. You, and not I, have said that they are evil and senseless.
I ask you, what do *you* say?
Man-cub—Master of the Jungle, Son of Raksha, lair-brother to me—though I forget for a little while in the spring, your trail is my trail, your lair is my lair, and your death-fight is my death-fight.
Then go before me to the Jungle and ask them all to come to the Council Rock. Tell them that the Master of the Jungle is returning to Man.

When Mowgli came to the Council Rock, he found only the four brothers, Baloo, and Kaa around Akela's empty seat.

Your trail ends here then, manling?

By night and by day, I hear a double step upon my trail. When I turn my head, it is as though one has hidden himself from me that instant.

I lie down, but I do not rest. I bathe, but I am not made cool. The Red Flower is in my body, my bones are water... and... I know not what I know.

Akela said it by the river that Mowgli will drive Mowgli back to the Man Pack. I said it too. But who listens to Baloo now?

When we met at the Cold Lairs, manling, I knew it. Man goes to Man at the end, though the Jungle does not cast him out.

The Jungle does not cast me out, then?

So long as we live, none shall dare!

I know not what I know! I would not go, but I am drawn by both feet. How shall I endure these nights?

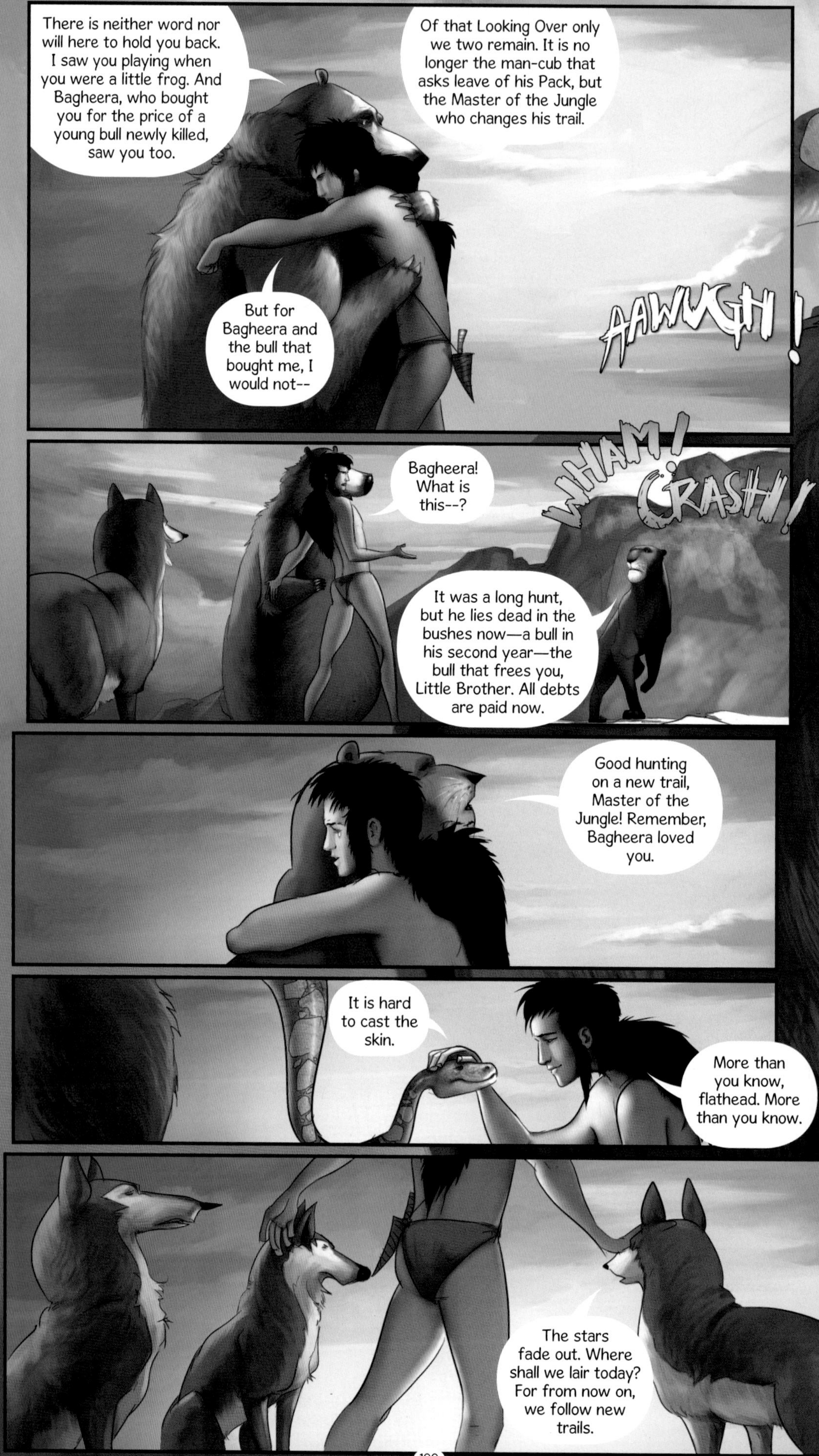

There is neither word nor will here to hold you back. I saw you playing when you were a little frog. And Bagheera, who bought you for the price of a young bull newly killed, saw you too.
Of that Looking Over only we two remain. It is no longer the man-cub that asks leave of his Pack, but the Master of the Jungle who changes his trail.
But for Bagheera and the bull that bought me, I would not--
AAWUGH!
Bagheera! What is this--?
WHAM!
CRASH!
It was a long hunt, but he lies dead in the bushes now—a bull in his second year—the bull that frees you, Little Brother. All debts are paid now.
Good hunting on a new trail, Master of the Jungle! Remember, Bagheera loved you.
It is hard to cast the skin.
More than you know, flathead. More than you know.
The stars fade out. Where shall we lair today? For from now on, we follow new trails.

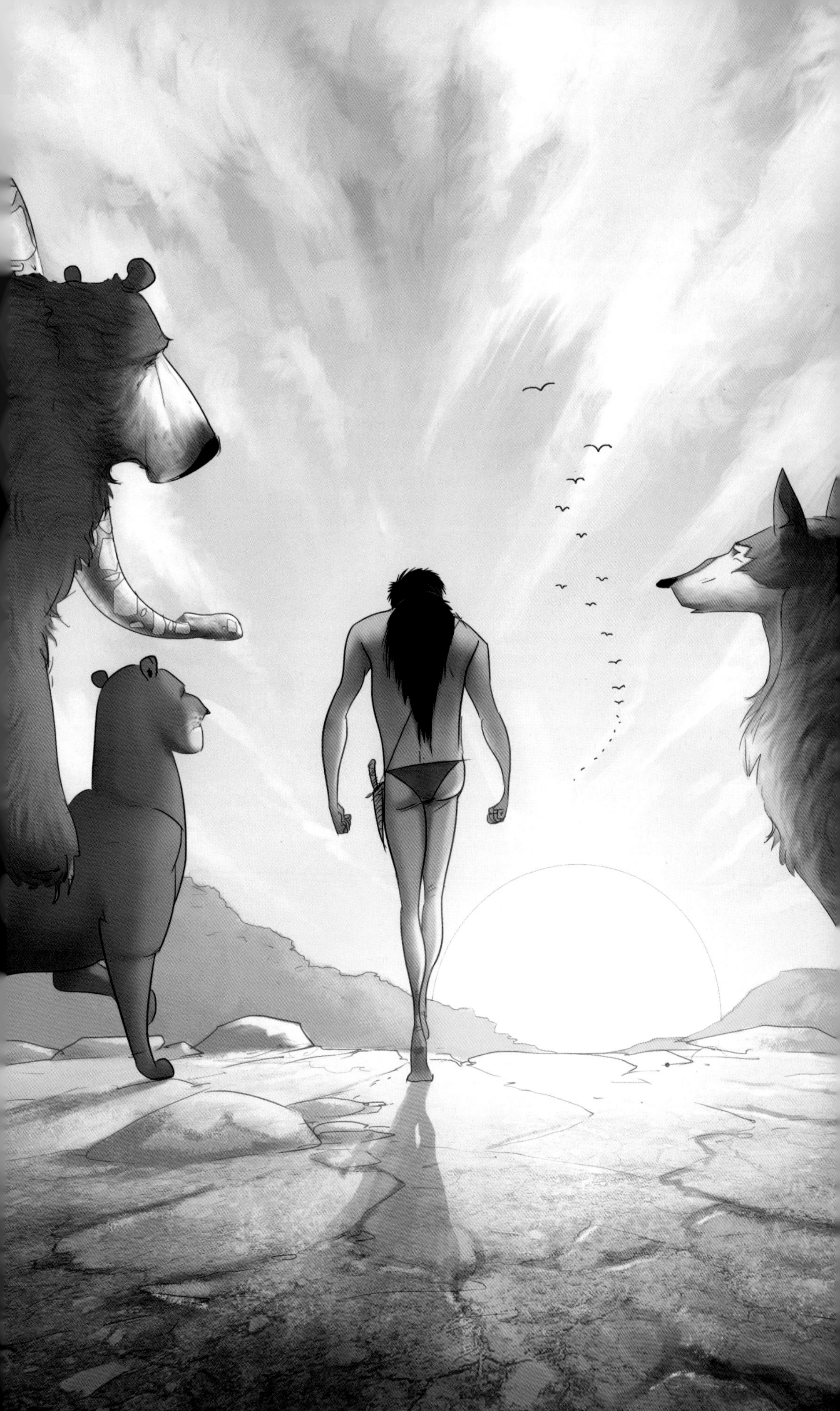

Law of the Jungle

You have come across the expression 'Law of the Jungle' quite a few times in the story. Today it has come to mean 'every man for himself'. But in *The Jungle Book*, Kipling uses it to denote the string of rules that the inhabitants of the jungle must follow in order to survive in the forest. This is what Baloo teaches the wolf-cubs and Mowgli through his maxims. In *The Second Jungle Book*, these rules are laid down in the poem 'The Law of the Jungle', where the wolf-cubs are instructed to 'kill not for pleasure', to share their game with the pack, and not to hunt men—an act that could upset the comfortable set-up of their existence. So, in a way, these laws help maintain the jungle's ecological balance.

Mowgli and the Feral Child

Mowgli is believed to be the forerunner of many feral children in literature, including Edgar Rice Burroughs's Tarzan (*Tarzan*, 1912) and Olaf Baker's Shasta (*Shasta of the Wolves*, 1919). But did you know that there have been real, documented feral children in history? Peter the Wild Boy of Hanover, Germany, discovered in 1725, is a famous example; Marie-Angélique Memmie Le Blanc of Wisconsin, found at the age of nineteen in 1731, is another.

Peter had been surviving on forest flora before he was found. King George I took an interest in him and had him brought to Great Britain. However, Peter remained the wild child he had been, unable to learn how to read or write. The only words he could ever utter were 'Peter' and 'King George'.

Marie-Angélique successfully learned to read and write. Sold off as a slave when her Amerindian tribe was defeated by the French, she was bought by Madame de Courtemanche, who took her to France. In November 1721, she ran off to the woods of Provence, only to be recaptured ten years later at the village of Songy. She is therefore also known as the Wild Child of Songy.